FIRST CRUSH

THE RUSSO SISTERS, BOOK 2

LINDA SEED

GET A LINDA SEED SHORT STORY FREE

Sign up for Linda's no-spam newsletter and get a free copy of the Main Street Merchants short story "Jacks Are Wild" and more exclusive content at no cost.

Claim the story at the following web address:

https://claims.prolificworks.com/free/TFPZoP8q

This is a work of fiction. Any characters, organizations, places, or events portrayed in this novel are either products of the author's imagination or are used fictitiously.

FIRST CRUSH
Copyright © 2019 by Linda Seed

This ebook is licensed for your personal enjoyment only. This ebook may not be resold or given away to other people. If you would like to share this book with another person, please purchase an additional copy for each recipient. If you're reading this book and did not purchase it, or it was not purchased for your use only, then please return to Smashwords.com and purchase your own copy. Thank you for respecting the hard work of this author.

All rights reserved. No part of this book may be reproduced in any form or by any means without the prior written consent of the author, excepting brief quotes used in reviews.

The author is available for book signings, book club discussions, conferences, and other appearances.
Linda Seed may be contacted via e-mail at linda@lindaseed.com or on Facebook at www.facebook.com/LindaSeedAuthor. Learn more about Linda Seed's novels at www.lindaseed.com.

Cover design by Teaberry Creative.

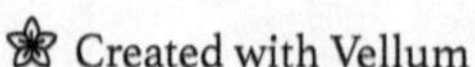 Created with Vellum

BY LINDA SEED

The Main Street Merchants

Moonstone Beach

Like That Endless Cambria Sky

Nearly Wild

Fire and Glass

The Delaneys of Cambria

A Long, Cool Rain

The Promise of Lightning

Loving the Storm

Searching for Sunshine

The Russo Sisters

Saving Sofia

First Crush

1

———

The babies were to blame.

For a long time, Bianca had been okay with the fact that she'd put her career ahead of getting married and having children. Her work as a pediatrician was important, not only to her but to the patients she helped every day.

Medical school, an internship, residency—none of that had been compatible with motherhood or, for that matter, with finding a man to father her hypothetical offspring.

She'd been at peace with that, mostly. But the babies were starting to make her doubt her life decisions.

Bianca performed well-baby exams almost every day—the red-faced, blinking newborns, the nine-month-olds with their toothless smiles and their rolls of thigh fat, the toddlers with their endless, good-natured curiosity, their chubby hands reaching out to grab her stethoscope or a handful of her hair.

Every one of them made her long for motherhood with ferocious yearning.

And that, she reflected, was how she'd ended up in a relationship with Peter—a man she had zero chemistry with but who had looked, at first, like perfect husband and father material.

On their regularly scheduled Friday night date, Bianca tried to be patient as Peter inspected his menu at Neptune, a high-end restaurant on Main Street.

"Do you suppose the seafood risotto has gluten?" He peered at the menu and didn't wait for Bianca to respond. "They'll say it doesn't, but if they use a broth that has hydrolyzed wheat protein ..."

"Maybe try the salmon?" Bianca suggested.

"*Mmm.* Probably farmed."

Bianca had made her entrée selection long ago. So long ago, in fact, the waiter had been sent away twice. Her stomach was growling, so she took a roll from the basket on the table. At least she didn't have to share the bread, with Peter avoiding gluten.

The waiter was walking past their table, and Peter flagged him down. "Are these salad greens organic?" They were. "And what about the butter you use on the scampi? Does it contain rBST?"

They went through this every time they ate out, which was why Bianca had suggested they eat at home. But Peter had something important to talk to her about, and he'd insisted they do it at Neptune, one of the most well-regarded restaurants in Cambria.

Of course, if he couldn't manage to order a meal, it seemed doubtful they would ever get to the topic he'd wanted to discuss.

"Peter?" Bianca couldn't quite get the irritation out of her voice. "Maybe just have the chef's salad?" That was what he would order, in the end. It was what he always ordered. But, for some reason, he seemed compelled to make a production of considering other options before settling on the thing they both knew he would eat.

"*Hmm.* Maybe the bisque ..." He squinted at his menu because he'd left his reading glasses at home.

"I'm getting hungry," she said.

Finally, after ten more minutes of contemplation, they placed their orders: linguine with clams for her, chef's salad—hold the bacon—for him.

Bianca was the daughter of Italian parents, and she'd been raised to love food, especially fresh bread and pasta. Watching Peter reject entire classifications of food was both painful and baffling to her. He didn't have a health condition that required it—if he had, she'd have understood. Instead, it seemed more like an affectation, or perhaps a hobby. Instead of assembling model boats, say, or golfing, Peter obsessed about the origin and ingredients of his food.

Now that he'd ordered and his menu had been taken from him—confiscated, more like—he folded his hands on the table and smiled at Bianca.

"You look pretty tonight," he told her.

And Peter looked … like Peter. Five foot ten, medium brown hair, average frame, eyes a medium blue. He had the bland good looks of a TV anchorman. Not bad genes to pass on to a baby—as long as he didn't pass along his eccentricities as well.

"What was it you wanted to talk about?" Bianca prompted him. The restaurant was half-full, and classical music was playing softly in the background. The candle in the center of their table glowed a gentle orange.

"Well." He cleared his throat. "We've been dating awhile now."

"Six months," Bianca provided.

"Right. And with me living in San Luis Obispo and you living in Cambria …" He picked up his napkin, refolded it, and put it back down. "It's inconvenient, that's all, you coming to me or me coming to you.…"

"It's not that inconvenient," she said. "You're only twenty minutes away from my office."

"Well, okay, I suppose …"

Was he worried about gas mileage? Fuel emissions? Wasted productivity from his time in the car?

"I thought … Maybe it's time we move in together."

Bianca didn't respond at first. She'd known this was coming. He'd been making noises about how San Luis Obispo was superior to Cambria in terms of efficiency and convenience. He'd passed it off as idle conversation at the time, but she'd known where he was heading.

Now that it was out there, she didn't know how to respond. Wasn't she dating him because he'd seemed like a good prospect for marriage and a future? Wasn't this what she'd had in mind when she'd first agreed to go out with him?

And yet, the idea of living with him full-time seemed utterly exhausting.

"Well, that's certainly ... an offer," she said.

"It makes sense financially," he went on. "Combining our expenses, consolidating our belongings. Saving commuting time will reduce our carbon footprint, too."

All of the times Bianca had imagined a man inviting her to live with him, she'd envisioned proclamations of love, of passion, of burning need. Instead, she was hearing about consolidated belongings and carbon emissions.

"I suppose you're right about the carbon footprint," she said. "And you were thinking ... your place?" Bianca and her three sisters lived in a renovated 1920s log cabin their parents had left them. Carmela and Aldo were gone now, but the house made Bianca feel connected to them, as though, in some little way, they were still with her.

"Ah." Peter folded his hands on the table, clearly prepared for this question. "You know I love your house. And your sisters are great. But ..."

"But?"

"But I thought we might want something more ... up to date. And more private. Someplace that's just for the two of us. My condo has solar, which cuts down on the energy expense, and it has water-efficient plumbing fixtures and drought-tolerant landscaping. Plus, the commute to your office from my place is eight minutes shorter."

"Eight minutes?"

"I checked it on Google Maps."

Bianca sat there with a glass of wine in her hand, trying but failing to imagine a less romantic way in which Peter might have presented his case.

"I suppose the heating costs will be reduced if we're sharing a bed," she said dryly. "All of that body warmth."

"Exactly." He seemed pleased with her observation. "I hadn't thought of that, but yes, I imagine you're right."

"Can I think about it?"

"Of course. I've made some notes on the pros and cons. I'll e-mail them to you." He held up his glass of wine for a toast. "To us, Bianca."

She clinked her glass against his without comment.

"You make me so happy," he said.

She supposed he had an analysis of that, too—some kind of happiness vs. unhappiness bar graph. Or maybe it was a pie chart. But despite the lack of romance, he had a lot to offer. He was stable, honest, consistent, and decent. She'd done her own pro-con analysis of her relationship with him, and the pros were ahead.

It was hard to argue with the data.

"Peter wants us to live together," Bianca told her sisters the next morning at breakfast.

They were gathered around their big kitchen island, busy with the usual morning activities related to food and beverages. Sofia was pouring a mug of coffee from the pot; Martina was steeping some kind of herbal tea she'd blended herself; Benny was pouring a bowl of Cap'n Crunch; and Bianca was sitting with a plate of whole wheat toast in front of her.

Bianca's sisters stopped what they were doing and turned, as one, to look at her.

"Here?" Benny broke the silence. Bianca noted the horror in her sister's voice.

"No. At his place."

"What did you say?" Martina asked.

"I said I'd think about it." Bianca picked up her toast, considered it, then put it back down. Her sisters looked at each other, then back at Bianca.

"But—" Sofia said.

"I'll take this one," Benny offered, interrupting. Her dark hair was arranged in two stubby buns on the top of her head, her bangs short and straight. She pointed at Bianca with one finger, its nail polished in black. "You can't possibly be considering it."

"I am."

"But—" Sofia tried again.

"What the hell for?" Benny demanded. "What do you see in that guy? Is he some kind of magical prodigy in bed? Because otherwise …"

"Oh, believe me. He's not." Bianca was probably betraying Peter by admitting that, but if she'd said otherwise, her sisters would have known she was lying. She didn't have the kind of acting skills it would have taken to pretend that Peter made her body sing in ways she'd only dreamed of.

"Then why?" Sofia finally managed to get out a full sentence, albeit one of only two words.

"Because I'm getting old!" Bianca threw her hands into the air in frustration. The idea of breakfast didn't seem appetizing anymore, so she got up and took her plate to the sink.

"You're only thirty-six," Martina pointed out.

"Exactly. I'm thirty-six. Do you know that if I got pregnant right now, today, it would be considered higher risk because of advanced maternal age? Advanced! I need to have babies now, or it's never going to happen."

Benny wrinkled her nose. "You want *Peter's* babies? Ew."

"Peter is …" Bianca grasped for a flattering adjective. "He's responsible. He's intelligent. He's a doctor."

"You're a doctor," Sofia pointed out. "So, the pressure's off. You don't need to marry one."

"Marry? Yikes." Benny shuddered. "You're not thinking of marrying him, are you? Because—"

"We haven't discussed it." Bianca put her plate into the sink. "We've only discussed me moving into his condo. To save natural resources." She couldn't help smirking.

Martina looked thoughtful. "I suppose you'd save gas on the commute, but … Oh, God. Please tell me he didn't propose it to you that way."

"He did." Bianca slumped against the kitchen counter. She hadn't wanted to complain about Peter to her sisters, but she couldn't help it. "He actually did! He talked about his drought-tolerant landscaping."

"That's it," Sofia said. "I'm dumping Patrick, and I'm going to throw myself at Peter. No woman in her right mind can resist drought-tolerant landscaping."

"Very funny." At the mention of Patrick, Bianca felt a fresh surge of despair. What Sofia had with her fiancé was everything Bianca wanted. It was romantic. It was passionate. It was *real*. Bianca had always imagined she would have that with someone, someday—but she'd waited too long, and now what did she have? Aging ovaries and a man who was inordinately concerned with his bowel habits. Of course, he *was* a gastroenterologist, but still …

"It's not funny at all," Martina said. "You can't say yes. You know you can't. It would be a huge mistake."

"I want children, Martina." Bianca felt herself on the verge of tears. "I'm out of time to wait for the perfect guy."

"Does Peter even want kids?" Sofia asked.

"Yes! He does!" The question was, did she want Peter?

2

"C'mon, let's move it," TJ said to his son as the boy poked at his cereal with his spoon. "We've got to be out the door in five, or you're going to be late for school."

"Do I have to go? I'm tired."

It was a complaint TJ had been hearing more and more often from Owen, and it was starting to concern him. Moaning about school was pretty typical for a twelve-year-old in middle school, he figured, but Owen had always liked school—until recently.

"Did you sleep okay last night?" he asked.

"I guess."

TJ seemed to remember that being tired a lot was an adolescent thing—something to do with rapid growth, or hormones, or something like that. Probably nothing to worry about. "Well, finish breakfast so we can get going."

"I'm not hungry."

That, TJ reflected, was not an adolescent boy thing. He seemed to recall eating so much at that age, he'd devoured the family's grocery supply as soon as it was brought into the house.

"You feeling okay?" he asked his son.

"Yeah. Just tired."

The kid's color seemed off, too. TJ would have to call and make him an appointment for a physical. After he got him off to school.

THE THING about the doctor's appointment was that Owen didn't actually have a doctor.

TJ and his son had moved to Cambria just a month earlier, right after TJ's divorce from Owen's mother had been finalized. With everything that had been going on—finding work, moving, getting Owen settled in at his new school—neither of them had gotten established with a local doctor yet.

He had a PPO, so that was good—he could take Owen to anyone he wanted. But choosing someone was another question. He'd have to ask around. In the meantime, he wasn't even sure when Owen had last had a physical or who his previous doctor had been—both pieces of information a new provider would ask about.

He gathered up his manly resolve and called his ex.

"What do you want, TJ?" Penny sounded tired.

"How's your mom, Pen?" TJ had custody of Owen—for the time being, at least—because Penny was nursing her mother through multiple catastrophic health issues, including liver disease. Neither of them had wanted Owen to be subjected to that. Adolescence was hard enough, they'd reasoned, without having to watch your grandmother suffer.

"They're not considering her for a transplant yet," Penny said. "Which is good, in a way, because it means they don't think she's sick enough. But it's also bad, because nothing else seems to be helping her."

"I'm sorry." TJ had never exactly bonded with his mother-in-law, but she and Penny were as close as a mother and daughter could be. He wished there was something he could do, but he supposed he was doing it by taking care of their son so Penny could focus on her mother.

"Yeah. Me too," Penny said. "How's Owen? He was supposed to call me last night, but he didn't."

"That's what I was calling about." TJ gave her the rundown on Owen's tiredness, his lack of appetite, his waning enthusiasm for school. "When was his last physical?"

"He had one over the summer. He needed an immunization before he could start seventh grade."

"Ah. And what was his doctor's name again?"

TJ could feel his ex-wife's judgment in the long stretch of silence.

"What?" he said.

"Are you sure you're up to this?" she said. "Being a full-time single parent? Because I've got to tell you, TJ, the fact that you're asking this, when it's something you should already know ..."

"Yeah, yeah."

TJ brushed her off, but privately, he had to admit she had a point. She'd done everything for Owen before the split. The meals. The school permission slips. Shopping for his clothes when he was shooting up in height at a rate that defied credibility. Getting on him about his chores. And taking him to medical appointments.

TJ had always felt that he was doing his part just by earning a living for his wife and son. It was how he'd been raised—his dad worked hard, brought home a paycheck, and then came home to bask in his family's love.

In retrospect, it was possible that attitude had something to do with his divorce.

"TJ?" Penny said. "If you need to bring him back here ..."

"No. I've got this. We're doing fine, and you need to focus on your mom." As he said it, he began to feel more certain that it was true. "Just tell me the doctor's name."

PENNY and her mother lived in San Jose, three hours from Cambria—close enough that Owen could visit his mom, but far enough away that taking the kid to see his old pediatrician was not practical.

TJ and Penny had both grown up in Cambria, and they'd moved up to the Bay Area together after high school. Penny had gotten accepted at San Jose State, and TJ had tagged along because, at eighteen, his imagination had been too small to accommodate anything more than his all-encompassing teenage love for Penny.

She'd studied business management, and TJ had gone to work on a construction crew, a job his dad had set up for him when his parents had been unable to talk him out of leaving. There'd been an electrician on the crew who'd taken an interest in TJ, and that had led to an apprenticeship, trade school, and, eventually, his own business.

Now, eighteen years and one divorce later, here he was, back where he'd started. Well, not exactly where he'd started. He had a son. He had a hell of a lot of life experience. He had work that had been portable for his move back home. And he had an idea that he was well on his way to righting the capsized ship of his life.

The marriage had been a mistake—both he and Penny knew that. But he'd gotten fatherhood out of it, and that was something he would never regret.

He'd spent enough time enjoying the perks of fatherhood without putting in the work. It was time to step up.

He asked around with some of the other parents at the middle school, checked online reviews, looked at education and qualifications on medical practice websites, and finally decided he would take Owen to Bianca Russo's office for a checkup.

He vaguely remembered someone by that name from high school. Could it be the same one? Likely, he decided. The Central Coast wasn't well-populated enough to have more than one of them.

AFTER TJ HAD CALLED and made an appointment for the following week, the idea of Bianca Russo nagged at him. He sort of remembered her, but not very well, and something about that bothered him. He felt like he was missing something, some piece of memory or understanding that was eluding him.

He did what he always did in such situations. He called his mom.

"Hey. Do you remember a Bianca Russo from when I was in high school?" he asked when she picked up the phone.

"Well, hello to you, too, sweetheart," Lily Davenport said to her son.

"Oh. Uh ... yeah." He scratched his stubble. "I just wondered ..."

"Of course I remember Bianca Russo." Her tone said the question was at least a little bit stupid. "She's a pediatrician in Morro Bay now."

"Right. I was thinking of taking Owen to see her."

"Is he sick?" Lily's voice registered immediate concern.

"No, no. At least, I don't think so. He's just been tired lately, and I thought I'd take him in, just to be safe."

"Well, that's sensible."

"Bianca Russo?" he prompted her. "Did I go to high school with her?"

Lily's silence told him he was being an ass—he just wasn't sure how.

"Mom?"

"Yes, Troy, you went to high school with her." His mother was the only one who still called him Troy. "She had a crush on you."

"She did?" This was news to him—though, from his mother's tone, it shouldn't have been.

"Yes, son, she did. Honestly, men. If somebody's not wearing a neon sign ..."

"What makes you think she had a crush?" TJ asked.

"Intuition," she said dryly.

"Intuition? That's all? Mom, I don't think—"

"Intuition, plus the fact that her mother told me when we were in the PTA together. And the fact that Bianca couldn't take her eyes off you her whole junior and senior years. *And* the fact that you broke her heart."

"I ... Wait, a minute. I never ..." TJ felt as though he were engaged in a conversation in which only one of them was speaking English, and he wasn't entirely sure it was him. "What are you talking about? When did I break her heart?"

"When you went on a date with Bianca then started seeing Penny right after. That's when. Why, Carmela Russo told me the poor thing cried in her room for a week."

Okay, now TJ was sure there had been some kind of mistake and that his mother must have her stories mixed up. Was she thinking about Greg? His older brother was the one who broke women's hearts, not him. "I never went out with Bianca Russo. That must have been Greg."

"It was not Greg. It was you. You went out with her and a bunch of your friends—you went to see that movie with Russell Crowe, the one about ancient Rome, I think it was. I can't remember the name."

Gladiator. It was *Gladiator.* He started to get the uncomfortable feeling that she was right and he was wrong. He'd forgotten Bianca was even there that night.

"That wasn't a date, though. It was just a bunch of us hanging out."

"Are you sure?" His mother's voice carried the weight of judgment.

Increasingly, he wasn't sure about anything having to do with this conversation. "How could it have been a date if I didn't know it was a date?" he asked.

But, the more he thought about it, the more he could see it. Everyone else on that outing had been paired up, hadn't they? Only he and Bianca hadn't been. His friend Ray had invited Bianca along, and TJ strained to remember how that had come about. Was it possible he'd been setting TJ and Bianca up? And was it further possible that TJ had been too dense to realize it?

"Oh, jeez," TJ said as the truth of the situation dawned on him. "I mean, yeah, the others were coupled up, but ... I thought she and I were just there on our own. I thought we were the fifth wheels."

And he hadn't even remembered that it was Bianca until his mother had mentioned it, though it didn't seem wise to point that out now. It wasn't that he hadn't thought highly of Bianca at the time. It was that he hadn't thought about her at all. If she'd had a crush big enough that his mother had known about it ...

He was starting to feel like an ass.

And, yeah, he'd had his first date with Penny the following weekend. Had Bianca Russo been waiting for him to call her and ask for another date the whole time he'd been planning to make his move on Penny?

It was sobering to think how little TJ understood about the events of his own life.

"Maybe I'd better take Owen to someone else," he said after a while.

His mother made a noise—something between *psshhht* and *pffft* —and he knew he was about to get a lecture. "Troy James Davenport, I thought I raised you better than that. If she's the best doctor for Owen, she's the best doctor. Don't make your son pay the price just because you were an oblivious jerk in your younger years."

Well. Talking to his mother always seemed to clarify things. Even if what it clarified was the fact that he was an oblivious jerk.

3

TJ had to pull Owen out of school for the appointment because the medical office didn't have any spots available after school. Predictably, that made the idea of getting poked and prodded much more appealing to Owen.

"It's cool that I get to miss algebra." Owen piled into TJ's truck and buckled himself in. His backpack was so stuffed with books, notebooks, and other belongings that it seemed almost as big as he was.

"What've you got in that thing, a body?" TJ asked.

"No, Dad." Owen scoffed. "Like I'd be dumb enough to carry it around with me instead of getting rid of it. Jeez."

TJ glanced at his son with a goofy half grin. The kid was funny. Before Owen had come to live with him, he'd never realized that. How had he missed it?

Owen had shot up in height over the past year, but he still had a slight build and a baby face—a child among the half men of middle school. He had a spray of freckles across his nose, and his medium-brown hair seemed perpetually mussed.

And, yeah, the kid's color was off. He used to have so much bouncy energy he seemed like he was running on rocket fuel, but now he was slumped in the passenger seat, looking like he needed a nap.

TJ turned onto Highway 1 and headed south toward Morro Bay.

~

BIANCA WAS HAVING A BUSY MORNING, and she'd been keeping her head down and focusing on the work.

Maybe that was why she hadn't seen Troy Davenport and his son in the waiting room. If she had, she wouldn't have been struck senseless by the sight of him when she walked into the exam room.

She was holding Owen's chart in her hand, looking down at it, when she walked in.

"You must be Owen," she said, still scanning the chart. "I'm Dr. Russo. And you're Owen's father? It's nice to—" Her words were cut short when she finally looked up and saw who it was she was talking to.

It was really him—Troy Freaking Davenport.

She hadn't thought much about him in years, but now that he was standing in front of her, the memories came rushing back: the way he'd looked in a letterman's jacket and a snug pair of Levi's. The way his smile had said he was just enough trouble to be hot, but not so much trouble that a person would regret having met him. The way she'd written *Bianca Davenport* repeatedly on her Trapper Keeper notebooks. The dearly held fantasies she'd had about marrying him one day. And the pure, crystalline devastation she'd felt when he'd taken up with Penny DeLuca.

He'd changed some—his dark hair was glossy and cut close to his head, in contrast to the Zac Efron shag he'd sported in school—but in other ways, he hadn't changed at all. He still had those startling blue eyes. He was still deliciously tall. And he still had a way of looking at her as though he knew something she didn't.

She realized that she'd been standing there for some time without saying anything. She'd meant to go forward with her usual routine:

introducing herself, establishing the reason for the visit, putting the parent and the patient at ease, etc.

Instead, all she could get out was, "Troy."

"It's TJ now. And this is my son." He put his hand on the boy's shoulder.

Bianca was struck by the fact that Troy—and, by extension, she— was old enough to have a child on the cusp of adolescence. The next thought that hit her was that Troy must be married. She scanned his fingers, but there was no ring.

Divorced? Widowed? She took a look at the chart and saw that he was listed as Owen's primary caregiver, with an address in Cambria. Under *mother*, he'd written *Penny Davenport*: address, San Jose.

Divorced, then. And, *Penny*? Had he married Penny DeLuca?

She looked at Owen and then at Troy. TJ, she reminded herself. So many thoughts were running through her head that she doubted she could properly diagnose the boy if he'd been attacked by a swarm of bees.

"Could I just ... Would you excuse me for a moment? I'll be right back." She scurried out of the room, went to where her sister Sofia was sitting at her station behind the reception desk, grabbed Sofia by the arm, and dragged her into an empty exam room.

"What?" Sofia looked alarmed. "Did I mix up the charts again? Damn it, I thought I was doing better. You're the one who wanted me to work here. I told you I'm not—"

"Troy Davenport is here." Bianca still had a vise-like grip on Sofia's arm.

Sofia blinked a few times. "The kid I put in Room Three? The father is ..."

"That's him."

Sofia had been a freshman at Coast Union High School when Bianca was a senior. It wasn't surprising that she hadn't recognized TJ, who had been in an entirely different social circle than Sofia. She'd seen him around, though, and now her eyes widened in recognition.

Sofia slapped a hand to her mouth. *"I'm having the wedding you planned for him!"*

When Bianca had been a lovestruck teenager, she'd mapped out her fantasy wedding to Troy, and that wedding was the basis for the ceremony Sofia and Patrick would be having next year.

"He's already been married," Bianca said. "To Penny DeLuca."

"The skank he dumped you for?"

"Yep." Except, Penny hadn't been a skank. She'd been a regular girl, much like Bianca, probably plagued with the same insecurities and uncertainties. Penny had been pretty, likable ... and *nice*, Bianca remembered with irritation. Hating her would be both fun and convenient, but not exactly fair.

"Is she here, too?" Sofia hissed in a stage whisper.

"No, they're divorced."

"Serves him right."

Bianca was tempted to agree.

~

WELL, that had been interesting.

TJ had thought he might not remember Bianca when he saw her, but he did. Dark, glossy hair, Mediterranean skin, eyes the color of dark chocolate. Seeing her gave him a burst of quick images from high school: Bianca at sixteen with frizzy hair and a sprinkling of acne, trying to fit in but uncomfortable in her own skin.

She'd grown up nicely.

The acne was gone, and so was the frizz, replaced by the smooth gloss of hair tucked into a tidy bun. He wondered what that hair would look like out of the bun, then scolded himself. He was here for Owen.

He'd doubted what his mother had said about him breaking Bianca's heart—that wasn't how he remembered it—but now, seeing her reaction to him, he knew it was true. She'd blushed and stammered, and had hauled ass out of the room as quickly as possible.

TJ liked to think that if her heart had been broken, it hadn't been his fault. But who the hell knew? He'd been so clueless at that age, anything was possible. He felt a rush of shame over his probable misdeeds, whatever they might have been.

Waiting in the exam room for her to return, TJ looked at his son, who was smirking at him.

"She called you Troy," Owen said.

"Well ... that's my name."

"Troy," Owen said in a singsongy voice, under his breath. The kid seemed to think *Troy* was one of the most ridiculous names he'd ever heard. Privately, TJ agreed—thus the use of his initials in place of the name. Not that he would ever tell his mother that.

When Bianca came back into the room, she had her game face on. No blushing, no stammering—just the polished persona of a seasoned medical professional.

"I'm sorry for making you wait." She focused her reassuring smile on Owen. "You say you've been tired lately? Let's see if we can find out what's going on."

AT THE END of the appointment, Bianca reassured TJ that Owen's fatigue was probably a normal phase of adolescence. Just to be sure, she'd ordered lab work, but she was confident it would show nothing amiss.

She escorted him and Owen out of the exam room, wished them a nice day ... and then couldn't resist milking him for a little information.

"So, are you back in Cambria permanently?" She tried to make the question sound casual—just friendly chitchat.

"I am. I do electrical work, so if you know anyone who needs any ..." He reached into his pocket, pulled out his wallet, and extracted a business card, which he handed to her.

She took the card and slipped it into the pocket of her lab coat. He'd given her his contact information a couple of times now—once on Owen's medical forms, and again with the card. The first was business, and she told herself the second was only courtesy.

Still, she felt the weight of the card in her pocket long after he'd left. She found herself repeatedly reaching into the pocket to touch the card, then she chided herself for being stupid.

Troy Davenport had rejected her once. She had to be an idiot to think he was interested in her now. And even if he was, a lot had changed since high school.

Thank God.

4

"I asked around," Sofia said a couple of days later when she, Patrick, and her sisters were sitting around the dinner table at their house in Cambria's Happy Hill neighborhood. "TJ Davenport has a place in Pine Knolls. His parents still live in town. He's a good electrician, apparently. At least, he is if his Yelp reviews are any indication."

"Why did you ask around? I didn't ask you to do that," Bianca said.

Bianca, generally considered to be her family's best cook, had made an Italian meal of pasta, braised veal, salad, and garlic bread in an approximate imitation of the meals her mother used to serve on Sunday afternoons. Her parents had both been gone for a few years now, and the food was her way of remembering them.

Martina, a vegetarian, had skipped the veal and the meat sauce and was filling up on salad, garlic bread, and pasta with olive oil and Parmesan cheese. She reached for the bottle of Chianti that was sitting in the middle of the table and refilled her glass. "She asked around because you're too proud to do it. And somebody had to."

"I'm not too proud. I'm just ... not interested." Bianca twirled some pasta onto her fork, looking at her plate instead of at her sisters.

"Cool story, sis, but it's bullshit," Benny said. "Am I the only one who remembers your junior year? You told me he was the love of your life. You planned your wedding, for God's sake."

"It's still okay if we use your wedding plan, isn't it?" Patrick asked tentatively. "I mean, if it's not, we'll manage. But we've put down deposits already, so ..."

"It's all yours," Bianca said. "Mainly because I'm not interested in TJ Davenport, except as the father of one of my patients. I'm not sixteen anymore. I've grown up, and so has he."

"He certainly has." Sofia batted her lashes suggestively.

"Hey," Patrick protested.

"Don't worry, honeybun." Sofia linked her arm through Patrick's. "I like the smart, geeky type."

"Geeky?" Patrick said. "I don't think—"

"Can we get back to Bianca?" Benny suggested. "I've been thinking. We can set up an electrical emergency. Not a big one—nothing will catch on fire—but, you know, something that requires a service call." She wiggled her eyebrows at Bianca.

"Would you all stop?" Bianca put her fork down on her plate with a loud clink. "He's my patient's father. That's all."

"And the man you were obsessed with eighteen years ago. Who's back in town. And available," Martina pointed out.

"He's also the man who ripped my heart out when he tossed me aside," Bianca said. "Can we remember that part?"

"It might be good to heal those old scars," Sofia suggested. "I'm just saying."

Bianca had been toying with those same thoughts, though she wouldn't admit it. The problem was, old scars could be healed, but they could also be reopened.

That was something to think about.

TJ took Owen to get the blood test the next morning before breakfast. The test had to be done on an empty stomach, and TJ had expected his son to complain about being hungry.

When he didn't, it sent off alarm bells in TJ's brain.

Yeah, there was something going on.

He didn't want to obsess over his worries, so he decided to obsess about something else, instead. Bianca Russo seemed like a good choice.

Man, she'd changed—and for the better. She'd been flustered when she'd come into the room and seen TJ, that much had been clear. But she'd gotten it together, and when she was in doctor mode, she was all calm professionalism, competence, and cool elegance.

She likely wasn't attracted to him anymore, but what if she was? He hadn't dated anyone since the divorce. What if he asked her out?

He shrugged off the thought. She was Owen's doctor—going out with her would be awkward as hell.

But that didn't mean he couldn't think about it. And maybe she wouldn't always be Owen's doctor. Maybe she'd fix him up and pronounce him to be in good health. It wouldn't be so awkward then, would it?

TJ looked over at Owen, who was slumped in the molded plastic chair in the waiting room of the lab. The kid was falling asleep. TJ elbowed him gently.

"Wake up, kid."

Owen squinted up at his father. "Did they call me?"

"Not yet. What're you so tired for? It's eight a.m."

Owen shrugged. "I dunno. I just am."

There was that worry in TJ's gut again. He hoped Bianca Russo knew her stuff.

BIANCA WOULDN'T HAVE THOUGHT of TJ in years if it hadn't been for Sofia's wedding.

When Bianca was a teenager in love with Troy Davenport, she and her mother had planned an elaborate wedding, including the dress, the cake, the venue—the whole deal. Neither of them had intended for it to be serious. They'd both known it was just a game, an exercise … a way of bonding.

Now her mother was gone.

When Sofia and Patrick had gotten together, Sofia's grief had made it hard for her to move forward with the relationship—so Bianca had offered her the wedding plan as a way of having their mother present when Sofia linked her life with Patrick's.

It had been impossible to think about the wedding plan without thinking—okay, maybe a bit wistfully—about Troy.

And now here he was. It was as though Bianca had somehow conjured him by bringing out the binders full of dress photos and tux rental brochures.

She thought about that at the office as she went about her routine, seeing patients, updating charts, dealing with insurance companies, submitting prescriptions and referrals.

She was still thinking about it that night when Peter came over for dinner.

Peter had been coming to the house more and more often, partly because he and Bianca had been dating long enough that he'd become a fixture in her and her sisters' lives, and also because cooking for him, with his dietary eccentricities, was just easier than going out.

He preferred his own place, but Bianca found his condo cold and sterile, in contrast to the warmth and coziness of the historic log cabin where the Russos lived. After a certain amount of negotiation, Peter had come up with a schedule: Monday and Friday at his place, Tuesday and Saturday at hers. Wednesday, Thursday, and Sunday had been designated as wild card days, during which they might be at either place or they might not see each other at all, at either party's discretion.

Bianca had, with some effort, refrained from rolling her eyes when he'd presented the plan to her, but today—a Tuesday—she was grateful to be able to cook in her own home without having to negotiate anything.

Because of Peter's determination not to eat gluten, Bianca had, with regret, set aside any form of pasta and instead was preparing chicken breasts, quinoa, and sautéed vegetables. In a small pan, she was also making a tofu dish for Martina, who wouldn't eat anything whose mother might mourn it.

Peter was in the living room reading a book while Bianca cooked, and Benny was poking around in the refrigerator for a sugary beverage. She emerged with a bottle of Coke, twisted off the cap, took a long swig, then looked over Bianca's shoulder at the food sizzling on the stove.

"Jeez. Why so healthy? You couldn't deep fry something?" Benny wrinkled her nose.

"It won't kill you to eat something with actual nutrients." Bianca poked at the chicken with her tongs.

"It might," Benny said. "I'm not sure we want to take that risk."

Bianca shot a glance at Peter over her shoulder and then whispered to Benny, "Stop complaining. Do you know how long it took me to find locally sourced, free-range, antibiotic-free, organic, vegetarian-fed chicken? You'll eat it and shut the hell up about it."

Benny smirked and leaned one hip against the counter next to the stove. "If you'd just source yourself a locally grown free-range electrician instead, your life would be a hell of a lot easier."

Bianca seriously doubted that. She flipped the chicken breasts, then went to the refrigerator, pulled out some romaine lettuce, and pushed it into Benny's free hand. "Here, make a salad. If you're going to be standing here, you might as well make yourself useful."

THE THING ABOUT PETER—OR, one of the things about him—was that he tended to act like the Russo sisters' substitute parent instead of Bianca's boyfriend and the other women's friend.

He was doing it again, Bianca reflected as she watched Peter pick at his chicken, inspecting it as though he worried it might have been poisoned by a hostile foreign government.

"You know, Sofia," he said, still squinting at the chicken, "if you were to apply to Cal Poly, you could get into a solid field in a few years. Something with good benefits, maybe a 401K. I'm not saying that working as Bianca's receptionist isn't a good job...."

"Then what are you saying?" Sofia's voice carried an edge of annoyance.

"Just that you should be thinking in terms of a career rather than, well ... just a job." Deciding that the chicken was edible, he cut a small piece and popped it into his mouth, chewing thoughtfully. He swallowed, then pointed his fork toward the spot across the table from him where Sofia was sitting. "Of course, you're going to be a faculty wife, which isn't a bad lifestyle. You'll have Patrick's benefits."

Patrick, who wasn't there that evening, was an English professor at Cal Poly San Luis Obispo. While Sofia would, technically, be a faculty wife by this time the following year, Bianca doubted she saw it as a full-time occupation, and certainly not as an identity.

"Sofia likes what she does," Bianca said. "She's not just a receptionist. She's a small-business owner."

"Well ... ha, ha. All right." Peter chuckled, presumably at the thought that the kayak tours Sofia ran out of San Simeon could be considered a viable business. "But I'm talking about something more ... stable. More reliable."

"Thanks for the advice, Dad," Sofia said. "Maybe if I go to school and work really hard, I can have an exciting future as an accountant."

"Oh, no." Peter was unfazed. "From what Bianca tells me, you were never that great at math. The taxation courses alone ..." He shook his head mournfully.

Sofia looked at Bianca as Peter focused on his food. She widened her eyes and gestured toward Peter with her chin in a wordless plea for Bianca to do something about her man.

"Peter, I'm sure Sofia would make an excellent accountant." Bianca eyed her sister. "But ... ah ... I think her point was—"

"Her point was that she'd rather jump into a bathtub full of scorpions than do someone's taxes," Benny added helpfully.

"It was?" Peter looked surprised.

"I think she was employing sarcasm," Martina put in.

"Oh. Well. In any event—"

"Can I get you some more salad?" Bianca asked Peter before he could step in it any deeper. "It's pesticide-free."

PETER HAD EXPECTED to stay over, but he left after Bianca claimed to have a headache. Once he was gone, the sisters gathered in the kitchen to put away food, load dishes into the dishwasher, and put things back into order.

"Faculty wife?" Sofia gestured with the dirty plate she was holding. " 'You'll have Patrick's benefits!' " She said the last bit in a remarkably good imitation of Peter's voice. "I'd like to shove a diploma up his ass."

"Leave it in the frame when you do it," Benny added.

"Okay, that was bad," Bianca admitted.

"You think?" Even Martina, usually so mild-tempered, was worked up about it.

"But he didn't mean anything by it. He was trying to be helpful!" Bianca added.

"Helpful? Helpful?" Sofia waved her hands in the air in outrage. "Helpful is ... is doing the dishes! Or folding the laundry! Helpful isn't suggesting to your girlfriend's sister that she's too stupid to be an accountant!"

"You don't even want to be an accountant," Bianca pointed out.

"That's not the point!"

"I know. I know it isn't." Bianca's shoulders fell, and she focused on stacking plates in the dishwasher so she wouldn't have to look at her sisters.

"You're not still thinking about moving in with him, are you?" Martina asked. "I hope you told him no."

"I haven't told him anything yet."

In fact, Bianca had been avoiding having the conversation with Peter. That was part of the reason she'd claimed to have a headache.

She knew he wanted to pin her down on the subject, and he almost certainly would have made his case to her again tonight if she hadn't put him off.

She knew she had to give him an answer soon, but she felt trapped. If she said yes, she'd have to move out of the home she loved —a home her parents had renovated with loving care not long before their deaths—and she'd have to face her sisters' scorn. But if she said no, she'd be cutting off what could be her last chance to have a family before her ovaries dried up and her entire reproductive system shut down for good.

It was a lot to think about.

"You don't love him, do you, Bianca?" Martina spoke softly, in contrast to her sisters and their outrage. "Because I don't think you do."

"I care about him," Bianca said.

"That's not the same thing."

Martina was right—it wasn't the same thing. But it was something, wasn't it? Caring could become love. Peter was reliable. He was honest. He was responsible. He was a doctor. He would make a suitable father for her children.

Bianca just had to decide whether *suitable* was good enough.

$$5$$

TJ and Owen lived in a rented two-bedroom cottage in Pine Knolls, on a hill overlooking Main Street. TJ wanted to buy something of his own, but he'd taken a significant financial hit in the divorce. The house was barely big enough for the two of them—one bathroom, and a living room so small it barely accommodated a sofa, a comfortable chair, and the TV.

Still, they were managing. The place had a lot of character, with Craftsman-style details, archways leading from one room into the next, original hardwood floors, and a setting surrounded by grazing deer and Monterey pines.

For the two of them, it was tight, but okay.

But now Owen wanted to get a dog.

"Dad, please? We couldn't get one in San Jose because it was against the rules in our building. But it's not against the rules here. The guy who owns the house even said pets were okay. I heard him. Please?"

TJ rubbed the back of his neck and looked around the little house. "Where are we going to put a dog? There's no fenced yard. There's no place for him to run around...."

"I could walk him."

"I know how that goes," TJ said. "You promise to walk him, then I'm the one who ends up outside at six a.m. in the rain with an umbrella and a bag full of dog poop."

"No, I really will do it. Even if it's raining. Even if it's really early or really late. You can ground me if I don't. You can take away my allowance or my phone." Owen had started in on him early, before breakfast. The boy was still in the T-shirt and pajama pants he'd slept in, his sandy-colored hair sticking up at odd angles, his eyes wide in earnestness.

"Look. You've gotta get ready for school."

"But you'll think about it?"

TJ scrunched up his face in dismay. "Aw, jeez …"

"Please, Dad? Please?"

The thing was, it was hard to say no to him. It had been hard before, even without the divorce. But now, with everything that was going on …

"I'll think about it. Now get some clothes on and have some breakfast before I change my mind."

THE WHOLE TIME TJ was driving Owen to school—a span of about five minutes, because everything in Cambria was close to everything else —he wondered if he was making a mistake to even consider getting Owen a dog.

Owen's grades were falling, for one thing. He'd always been a good student, but lately, he couldn't seem to focus on anything. TJ supposed that was a typical middle school adjustment thing, but still, it didn't seem like he should be rewarding the kid right now.

On the other hand, Owen had, through no fault of his own and without his input, been uprooted from his home and moved two hundred miles away from his friends, his school, and everything he knew.

Sure, he knew Cambria—his grandparents lived here, and there had been visits and vacations—but it wasn't his home. TJ had to *make* it his home, and a dog might go a long way toward accomplishing that.

"It couldn't be a big dog," he said irritably as they pulled into the school parking lot. "We don't have room for a big dog."

"That's okay," Owen said. "I like small dogs."

"It couldn't be a puppy, either. I don't have time to deal with any puppy stuff. Training and all that. I'm a busy guy."

"Does this mean yes?"

Owen was looking at him with such hope, such tender anticipation, that TJ couldn't say anything but yes.

"I guess so."

"Thanks, Dad! Oh, wow. Thanks! I can't wait to tell everybody."

Owen got out of the car, hefted his huge backpack, and headed toward the school. As TJ watched him go, that uneasiness he'd been feeling about Owen's health returned. As excited as he was about the prospect of a dog, the boy still looked tired as hell. And there was something about his walk that didn't look right.

Something was going on with Owen, and TJ needed to find out what it was.

BIANCA HADN'T EXPECTED to find anything concerning in Owen Davenport's lab tests. The boy had looked normal to her—gangly, awkward, with limbs that looked too long for his body, maybe, but normal.

If he was tired, as TJ had reported, that wasn't anything unusual for a boy in early adolescence. They tended to get too little sleep at a time when their bodies were developing at an astounding rate.

Now, sitting in her office during a break between patients, she scanned his results with concern. His blood counts were off, and so were his glucose levels. It was probably nothing to worry about, but she'd have to call him back in for further evaluation.

Seeing Owen Davenport again would mean seeing his father

again. At the thought of it, Bianca felt a little flutter in her chest. She told the flutter to shut the hell up.

How stupid was it that her teenage crush hadn't waned after all these years? How pathetic was it that she still felt the flutter? She wasn't an awkward sixteen-year-old anymore. She was an accomplished professional woman, a mature adult with meaningful work, and goals, and …

And a distinct flutter.

Her office door opened, and Sofia poked her head in. "Bianca? You've got the Miller twins in Room Two."

"Okay." She didn't look up from her iPad.

Sofia's eyebrows rose. "Something wrong?"

"No, no. Well … maybe. Owen Davenport's labs came back."

"Oh, no. He's not sick, is he?"

"Probably not. But I'll have to call his father to schedule a follow-up."

"I'll do that. It's what you hired me for. You don't have to—"

"No, let me," Bianca said, interrupting her.

"Ooh." Sofia grinned suggestively.

"Shut up."

TJ was on a job when he heard from Bianca. He was in somebody's spare bedroom trying to diagnose a dead outlet when his cell phone rang.

"Hello, TJ? This is Dr. Russo. Bianca. Bianca Russo." She said it as though she wasn't certain of her own name.

"Hi, Bianca." He was torn between enjoying that hit of nostalgia from hearing her voice and worrying about why she might be calling him. "Is this about Owen?"

"It is, yes." She cleared her throat. Was she nervous about talking to him? Jeez, his mother had been right. She'd had a crush. Did she still? The idea was … Wait. Was something wrong with Owen?

He zeroed in and focused. "Okay. What's going on?"

"Probably nothing, but I'd like to follow up." She told him about the lab results and asked him to bring Owen in for another appointment to look into what they might mean.

"I can bring him in next week," TJ said. "Is this something I should be worried about?"

"No, no. I wouldn't. It's probably nothing. But it's better to be safe."

Once he was off the phone, he thought, *I knew it. I knew there was something going on.* And, on the heels of that, *Well, shit.*

He really hadn't wanted to be right.

Bianca had tried to talk herself into moving in with Peter. She really had. But every time she imagined packing up her things and leaving her house—her parents' house—for Peter's clean, tidy, energy-efficient condo, she felt a gaping pit of dread in her chest.

All things considered, it probably was a bad idea to make a romantic commitment to someone who inspired a gaping pit of dread.

"I can't do it," she said to Benny one night as she was looking at her furniture, trying to decide what would and would not fit in Peter's condo. "I just ... I can't."

"Yeah. You've got a lot of stuff," Benny said. "You shouldn't even try to do it yourself. You'll need to hire some movers."

"I meant, I can't move in with Peter."

Benny stared at Bianca for a long moment, then broke into a dance complete with hip swivels and fists rhythmically pumping into the air.

"Thank God," she sang to the beat of her dance. "Thank God, thank God, thank God."

"Really? I'm about to break a man's heart, and that's how you react?" Bianca glared at Benny.

"Sorry." Benny stopped dancing. "You're right. But, Bianca, you're not going to break his heart. He'd need to have one first."

"That's not fair."

"Probably not." Benny shrugged. "He's not a bad guy, I guess. And I'm not saying he doesn't really want to be with you. What I'm saying is that he's not in love the way you and I think of it."

"What the hell are you talking about?"

Benny cocked her head and talked as though she were explaining addition to a toddler. "Peter sees you as a sensible addition to his lifestyle. It's genuine, I guess, as far as it goes. But it isn't love."

That stopped Bianca, because she could see the truth of it. Peter didn't make emotional decisions, he made decisions based on data and analysis. If he wanted her to live with him, it was because he'd done a cost/benefit assessment of the situation—not because his heart burned for her.

Peter's heart didn't burn—it pumped blood for the benefit of his vital organs. Nothing more.

Bianca sank onto her bed. It was late, and she was wearing a pair of yoga pants and an oversized T-shirt, her hair damp from the shower.

"You're right." She felt tears spring into her eyes.

"Oh, wait. Shit. I didn't mean—" Benny looked alarmed.

"I know what you meant. And you're right. But that leaves me at square one again, doesn't it? I'm going to be a crazy spinster cat lady."

"No, you won't." Benny sat down beside her and rubbed Bianca's shoulder. Benny was dressed in a Hello Kitty bathrobe, her hair in a high ponytail that resembled a water fountain springing out of her head. "For one thing, you're allergic to cats."

"Benny—"

"And for another thing, you're the alpha sister. If any of us ends up a crazy cat lady, it's going to be Martina."

Bianca laughed, her eyes still damp. "This sucks," she said.

"Not as much as living with Peter would."

SHE HAD TO TELL HIM—AND sooner, rather than later—so she called him from her office and asked if she could come over after work so they could talk.

He was running late because two appointments had gone long, pushing his entire schedule out of whack, but he suggested that she go to his place, let herself in with the key he'd given her, and wait for him.

She got to his place just after six-thirty. Bianca had dawdled at her office, doing paperwork and killing time so she wouldn't have to sit in Peter's condo for too long. It was a nice building with a view of San Luis Obispo's downtown shopping district, but inside, there were few signs of life.

Clean, modular furniture. Bookshelves sparsely dotted with nonfiction titles: medical textbooks, business how-tos. A coffee table with nothing on it—no magazines, no scented candles, no stacks of bills waiting to be opened. A refrigerator stocked with expensive products from Whole Foods.

The more she looked at the place in the silence of Peter's absence, the more certain she was that she couldn't live like this.

At first, she'd thought maybe she could be a warming influence for him and make his lifeless space into a home. But now, she realized that was wrong. This was who he was. She couldn't change him, and why should she even try? He was happy this way. He liked who he was. And that wasn't wrong. It just wasn't for her.

By the time he got home just before seven, she'd worked herself up into a state of nervous dread, but she also realized the breakup was both right and inevitable.

"Peter." She stood up from the sofa to greet him when he came in the door.

"Hi." He gave her a perfunctory kiss on the cheek, barely looking at her, and headed into the kitchen. He opened the refrigerator door, took out a bottle of white wine, and poured himself a glass.

That was unusual. He rarely drank; the wine was there mainly for her.

"Is everything all right?" she asked.

"*Hmm*?" He looked up as though he'd barely noticed she was in the room. "Oh. Yes. Of course. I had a tough patient today, that's all. Colon cancer. Twenty-two years old."

"Oh, no."

She couldn't tell him what she'd come to tell him—not after a day like that. It could wait. Tomorrow, maybe. Or on the weekend—

"So. What did you want to talk about?" Peter sat down on the sofa looking exhausted. His hands, holding his wineglass, were suspended between his knees.

"Oh. It's nothing. I don't think—"

"If you came to tell me you're ready to move in, I want to hear it. After a day like I've had, I could use some good news."

"Oh. I don't ... It wasn't that."

"Ah." His shoulders slumped. "Okay. What, then?"

Bianca froze, unsure how to proceed. She couldn't break up with him now—not after he'd had a terrible day. He looked so tired, so defeated, she didn't think she could add to his problems.

"It's nothing. It can wait," she said at last.

He shot her a look of pure irritation—something that was rare for him. "Waiting is your thing, isn't it?"

"What do you mean?" She sat on the sofa next to him, but at enough of a distance that they didn't touch.

He shrugged. "When I asked you to move in here, I thought you'd be happy. I thought you'd be excited about it. But, no. You wanted to wait and think about it. Now here we are, waiting for you to say whatever it was you came here wanting to tell me. Seems like you enjoy leaving me hanging, that's all."

She sat up straighter and leveled her shoulders. "You've had a hard day, and I didn't want to make it worse."

He didn't look at her as he took a sip of his wine and put the glass on the coffee table. "So, what you're going to say will make it worse, then."

It was clear to Bianca that with that kind of lead-in, he knew what was coming. There was nothing left to do but say it.

"Peter ... I think we should stop seeing each other. It's just not working. I'm sorry. You're a lovely person...."

"Save it." He rubbed his eyes with one hand. "Save the part about me being a lovely person. I'm not lovely enough for you to want to be with me, so what does it matter?"

"It's not—"

"You know, Bianca, did it ever occur to you that I'm not the problem here?" He stood and towered over her, looking down at her.

"What do you mean?"

"I mean, maybe you don't really want all of the things you say you want. You want marriage and a family, but here you are, still without either one of them, turning away the person who's standing here willing to give you both." He shook his head. "Just a thought, that's all."

She stood, picked up her purse from the coffee table, and slung the strap over her shoulder. "I should go."

"I'd tell you that I'll bring your things to you, but you never left anything here, did you?" He laughed bitterly. "Just go."

Bianca left without saying anything else. As she went, she wondered if he was right. Was she deliberately sabotaging her own goals and desires? What if she only *thought* she wanted a family of her own, but was intentionally putting up roadblocks that would prevent it from ever happening?

On the other hand, maybe she just was smart enough to know that she and Peter weren't a match and never would be.

"I DID IT," she told Martina when she got home that night. Sofia and Benny weren't around, but Martina was sitting on the sofa with her legs tucked under her, reading a book. She was wearing a long, floral-printed dress she'd made herself, her feet encased in warm, wool socks. Her long, auburn-dyed hair was tied into a loose bun.

"You did what?" Martina set the book aside.

"I broke up with Peter." Bianca collapsed onto the sofa, still wearing her jacket and holding her purse.

"Oh."

"Yeah."

They were quiet together for a while, then Martina said, "How did he take it?"

"He was mad. He did this 'I should have known you wouldn't realize what's good for you' kind of thing."

"But you do realize what's good for you," Martina said. "That's why you broke up with him."

"Yeah."

Bianca knew she'd done what was necessary, but knowing it didn't make her feel any less awful.

"For what it's worth, Bianca, you did the right thing." Martina laid a hand on Bianca's arm. "He wouldn't have made you happy. And he'd have known he didn't make you happy, so he wouldn't have been happy, either."

That was a lot of talk about happiness, considering the utter lack of it going around.

Owen's follow-up with Dr. Russo was scheduled for later in the week. In the meantime, the kid was completely preoccupied with the business of getting a dog.

TJ tried to put him off, but it was all Owen could talk about: What kind of dog would they get? What would they name it? Where would it sleep? Would it know how to sit or fetch?

In the evenings after dinner, the two of them perused the San Luis Obispo animal shelter website, scanning the offerings of available dogs. They discussed breeds, disposition, possible health problems—and the ever-urgent question of who would walk the dog and clean up after it.

Owen claimed that he would do it every day without having to be asked, but TJ knew better. Still, as long as Owen would do at least part of the work without too much hassle ...

"I guess we can go down there tomorrow after school," TJ said one evening when he'd been sufficiently worn down by Owen's persistence. "I've got some free time in the afternoon."

"Really? That's awesome." Owen hugged him, which he rarely did anymore since he'd become too self-conscious about that sort of thing. "Thanks, Dad. Thanks. I'm going to go text Austin."

The whole thing left TJ feeling fairly pleased with himself—even if he didn't particularly want a dog.

THE MOST COMMON dogs available at the shelter were Chihuahuas and pit bulls. TJ didn't want a Chihuahua because it just wasn't his style—he could hardly imagine himself maintaining his manly dignity while walking a two-pound dog on a leash—and he didn't want a pit bull because it was prohibited in the rental contract for his house. That left everything else, which included hounds and terriers, shepherds and pointers, Labs and mutts.

TJ and Owen walked among the enclosures as the dogs inside barked for their attention, slept in corners, or glared at them suspiciously.

Amid the racket of a hundred different barks, Owen was taken with a small sandy-colored terrier who was scrabbling at the window of his pen, his tail wagging furiously.

"Look, Dad. He likes us. Look at him." Owen put his hand up against the window, and the dog tried to lick it through the glass.

"Maybe." TJ peered at the information card on the door, trying to get a sense of the dog. At the bottom of the card was a notation that the dog had been adopted and was waiting for his new owners to pick him up. "Uh-oh. He's taken."

Just as well, TJ thought. The dog looked excessively energetic, which might translate into destroyed furniture and pillows stripped of their stuffing.

"What about him?" TJ pointed across the hall to a black Lab, his muzzle dotted in gray, sitting silently in his pen.

Owen went over and looked into the pen. "He looks kinda old."

Old meant sedate, TJ thought. Old meant less trouble, less chasing him around to try to get back your shoe.

"That's why he needs us," he said.

The dog's tail thumped slowly and heavily against the floor. Was that a wag? It had to be. Either that or it was having some kind of seizure.

The card on the dog's pen said his name was Gary, he'd had one owner since he was a puppy, and he'd been surrendered to the shelter two days earlier after the man had died. Under the category of age, the card simply said *five plus*.

"Five plus another ten, probably," TJ muttered under his breath.

"Dad, he's too old," Owen said. "Can he even play?"

That was a fair point. TJ knew they should probably get a young and frisky mutt, something like the terrier across the hall. Still, he looked into Gary's eyes, and the old dog seemed to be pleading with him.

He'd lost the only owner he'd ever known. Tough break. A guy shouldn't have to live his final days alone in a shelter, especially when he was grieving.

"What do you think, Gary?" TJ said to the dog. "You want to try living with us?"

"Dad," Owen moaned.

⁓

THERE WAS PAPERWORK, of course, and the practical matters of procuring a dog bed, food and water bowls, a leash and collar, and all of the other things a self-respecting dog needed. TJ pored over the food choices, the treats.

By late afternoon, TJ had brought Gary into the house, fed him, placed his bed in a corner of the living room, and showed him the toys he and Owen had selected for him.

They put Gary's new squeaky hedgehog into the dog bed to try to make it more alluring, but Gary wasn't interested. Instead, the dog waited until TJ sat down on the sofa, then stood next to him with his head on TJ's thigh.

"Wouldn't you rather have a nap in your new bed?" TJ asked.

Gary let out a sigh and blinked at TJ with mournful attention.

At least he wasn't peeing in the house. That was something.

THAT NIGHT—GARY'S first in his new home—TJ tried to get him to sleep in his dog bed. When that didn't work, he moved the bed from the living room into Owen's bedroom, thinking that might help.

TJ said goodnight to his son and to the dog, then closed Owen's door and went to his room to go to bed.

He was just drifting off to sleep when his door opened. He looked up to see Owen, his hair tousled from bed, standing in the doorway in the moonlight coming through the hall window.

"He won't go to sleep, Dad. He keeps scratching at the door."

TJ rubbed his face and sat up. "Okay. You go back to bed. I'll handle him."

Thinking that maybe the dog had to pee, TJ led him to the front door, opened it, and waited. "Go ahead, then. Do your business."

The dog just looked at him patiently.

"Really? Then what's your issue?"

Gary didn't answer.

TJ sighed and headed back to his room. When Gary didn't follow, TJ looked at him and waved him along. "Come on, then. You can bunk with me."

The dog bed was in Owen's room, and TJ didn't want to disturb him, so he grabbed a blanket from the linen closet and put it on the floor. Then TJ got back under the covers. "Well, good night," he told Gary. "Try not to pee on the rug."

Instead of lying down on the blanket, Gary came to stand by the side of TJ's bed. He put his chin on the mattress next to TJ and stared at him, his dark eyes mournful.

"Go lie down," TJ said.

Gary didn't move from his spot. He blinked at TJ and made a soft whining sound.

"Aw, jeez." TJ couldn't sleep with somebody staring at him. He tried rolling over and facing the other direction, hoping the dog would get bored and lie the hell down.

When that didn't work, he sat up and glared at his new housemate. "You are not sleeping on the bed. For one thing, you smell like dog."

Either Gary didn't understand, or he simply disagreed. He put a paw on the bed and made the soft whine again—a kind of *hhhhhhm-mmmmmmmmmmhhhh.*

It was clear how this was going to go. TJ could either waste his time fighting it, or just give in and get some damned sleep.

"All right. Come on up." He patted the bed beside him.

The problem was, Gary was at least in his mid-eighties in dog years. He put both of his front paws on the mattress and scrabbled a bit with one of his rear legs, but he couldn't get up onto the bed.

TJ sighed, got out of bed, picked the dog up with some difficulty —he was a big sucker—and hefted him onto the mattress.

Gary turned in a couple of circles, lay down with his head on TJ's pillow, and promptly went to sleep with a contented sigh.

TJ went to the linen closet, got another pillow, and settled in on what little space the dog had left him. He'd been thinking for a while now that he was tired of sleeping alone, but this wasn't what he'd had in mind.

8

———

Since the breakup with Peter, Bianca had been both sad and relieved. The relief told her she'd done the right thing, but that didn't make it any easier to think she might have broken his heart.

"I saw Peter at the Whole Foods in SLO this morning," Benny said one evening as she came in from work, dropping her bag and her jacket onto the sofa. "He looked like he'd just seen those twins from *The Shining*. He turned around and hauled ass to the frozen foods section."

"That's awkward." Bianca had just gotten in and was still in her work clothes, her hair in a sedate bun.

"Not for me," Benny said. "I could have made friendly conversation, asked him about his recycling efforts and whatnot. But I guess he wasn't up for being friendly."

"Damn it." Bianca kicked off her shoes, grateful to free her feet after a long day in pumps. "I wish he weren't acting this way."

Benny sank down onto the sofa. "Oh, I don't know. I get it. He thought he was going to live with you, maybe get married, kids—the whole bit. He didn't realize how much of a stiff he is, and he thought it was going to work. The guy needs time to adjust."

If even Benny was sympathizing with Peter, then Bianca probably really had done some damage.

"I didn't mean to hurt him. This sucks."

"Yeah." Benny reflected on that for a moment. "There's no way around it, though, right? You get into a relationship, it's either going to go the distance, or you're going to break up and somebody's going to get their ass chapped. When was the last time you dated a guy then mutually agreed to go your separate ways, with everybody on good terms?"

"Never," Bianca said.

Benny nodded. "Right. Never. The ass-chapping was unavoidable."

"I suppose." Bianca put her feet up on the coffee table and wiggled her sore toes.

"On the plus side, you're available to go out with Troy now." Benny grinned and raised her eyebrows suggestively.

Bianca scowled. "That's ridiculous. Who said I wanted to go out with Troy? TJ, I mean. He hasn't asked. And I haven't asked. And neither of us is going to. I'm treating his son, that's all." She was flustered by the mere suggestion.

"The lady doth protest too much," Benny said.

Bianca might have said that her relationship with TJ was simply professional, but that wasn't entirely true, was it? If it were, then she wouldn't be this nervous leading up to Owen Davenport's follow-up appointment.

Okay, maybe she still found TJ attractive. Just a little. He wasn't bad-looking, if you liked broad shoulders and blue eyes, and that manly thing he had going on.

She supposed some women might find that kind of thing appealing.

On the other hand, she probably was only reacting to the memories of her high school crush and the intense, painful feelings it had created. She'd adored him, and he had barely known she existed. The longing, and the anguish over knowing it would never be fulfilled, had been the defining feature of her junior and senior years.

It was hard to think of Troy—TJ, now—without remembering the giddy anticipation she'd felt in the days leading up to their date. Her friends had set them up, and Bianca had imagined that this would be the time when he'd finally notice her. This would be the time when all of her fond imaginings would be realized.

Instead, on the evening of the date, he'd talked to her a little— he'd been nice enough, if distracted—but he'd been so involved with the friends who'd gone with them that he'd barely engaged with her.

At the time, she'd told herself it was understandable. In a group situation, how could she have expected to have his undivided attention? When he asked her out for a second date, she thought, it would be just the two of them, and then they would connect. Then they would get to know each other, and he would realize they belonged together.

Only, there hadn't been a second date. Instead, TJ had started going out with Penny DeLuca.

Within a couple of weeks, he and Penny had been inseparable, Penny wearing TJ's letter jacket, the two of them walking together with their hands tucked into each other's back pockets.

Bianca had attempted to accept this new development with stoicism. When her sisters had mentioned it, she'd acted as though it were no big deal. But, of course, she hadn't fooled anyone. Especially not her mother.

If anything positive had come from the disaster of her failed date with Troy, it had been Carmela's response. Bianca's mother had taken her out to lunch, then they'd gone down to Pismo Beach for shopping and manicures, leaving Bianca's sisters at home.

Carmela hadn't lectured her about the realities of love, but instead had let Bianca talk, or not talk, as she wished. Bianca had started the outing silent and sullen, but little by little she'd opened up until, by midafternoon, she'd cried on her mother's shoulder about Troy, about Penny, about feelings that seemed too big to be contained, and about her own fears that she would never find love.

By the time they got home that evening, Bianca felt a little better.

She hadn't felt *good*—it seemed to her that *good* was an unattainable dream—but she'd felt better, and that was something.

Bianca had put away the binders she and her mother had assembled of plans for Bianca's someday wedding. For Carmela, the plans had been an exercise—a fun way to dream about the future—but to Bianca, they'd been specifically for her and Troy. She hadn't looked at them again until Sofia had expressed a need to have her mother's fingerprint on her own wedding to Patrick.

All of that was in Bianca's head as she went through her morning office routine, knowing that she'd be seeing TJ later that day when he brought Owen in for his appointment.

Patricia, Bianca's nurse, noticed right off that something was amiss.

"Dr. Russo? Do you want me to put in the prescription for Mark Donaldson?" Patricia was looking expectantly at Bianca, who was staring off into space, lost in her thoughts.

"Dr. Russo?" Patricia tried again when Bianca didn't respond.

Bianca tried to focus. "What?"

"Mark Donaldson. The prescription? Do you want me to put it into the computer?"

"Oh. Yes. Thanks, Patricia." Bianca took a deep breath and let it out slowly, trying to center herself.

"Are you okay, Dr. Russo?"

"She's fine," Sofia said from the reception desk, where she'd been eavesdropping. "She's just smitten."

"Really?" Patricia's pale blond eyebrows shot up. "With whom?"

"Sofia." Bianca fired a glare of warning at her sister. The last thing she wanted was to appear unprofessional in front of her staff.

"Oh ... just some guy she met at Jitters yesterday," Sofia lied. "Their eyes met over a soy latte."

"Stop," Bianca said to her sister. Then, to Patricia: "She's joking. There was no guy. There was no soy latte."

"There could be a soy latte," Sofia said, "if you could just get up the nerve to order one."

Owen Davenport's appointment was at two p.m. After what seemed like an eternity of uneasy anticipation, Patricia let Bianca know the patient was in Room One, his chart waiting in a rack beside the door.

Bianca picked up the chart, straightened her white coat, and put a hand to her hair to smooth it. Then, having given herself a silent pep talk about professionalism and focus, she opened the door and went into the room.

Owen was sitting on the exam table, his gangly legs dangling. TJ was in one of the molded plastic chairs Bianca kept for her patients' parents and siblings. He stood up when she came in.

"Hi, Owen," she said. "TJ." She held the chart to her chest like a shield.

During the initial greetings—the hellos, the polite inquiries into everyone's well-being—Bianca was preoccupied with the fact of Troy Davenport standing in front of her and what that might mean after all these years.

But then, when she noticed how Owen looked, she stopped being a woman reminiscing about teenage heartbreak and went back to being a focused, competent physician.

"How are you feeling?" she asked the boy.

Owen responded that he was feeling "fine," which didn't mean anything—a teenage boy, in Bianca's experience, would say he was feeling fine even if he had several broken bones and the flu.

"Still feeling tired?"

"I guess."

Bianca had him lie back on the exam table and pressed his abdomen through his T-shirt.

"That feel tender?"

She pressed, and Owen winced. "Yeah."

"How's his appetite been?" She looked over her shoulder at TJ.

"Okay," TJ responded. "But it's off a little."

"I eat," Owen protested.

"Yeah," TJ said, "but not as much as you used to. He used to go through so many groceries I thought I'd have to get a second job," he told Bianca.

"And now?" she asked.

"Now ... not so much." TJ was starting to look worried. "What's going on?"

"I'm not sure yet." Bianca lifted Owen's pant leg and lowered his sock to look at his ankle, which appeared to be a little swollen. She also noticed some bruising on his leg. "Where'd you get these bruises?" she asked.

"Huh? I didn't even know those were there," Owen said.

"Wait a minute. Bruises?" TJ was becoming alarmed. "I don't know anything about bruises. Owen?"

"I don't know, Dad. I must have walked into something."

"Well ... he is a little clumsy," TJ said. "So was I when I was his age."

"Sure. It's probably nothing." But Bianca didn't really believe it was nothing. She told Owen he could sit up on the exam table, and she looked at his chart. Flipping through the forms, she saw a notation about Owen's family health history.

His maternal grandmother was suffering from liver failure.

"Okay." She kept her voice upbeat. "Owen, I'm going to send you to have another lab test—this one for liver function. Then we'll go from there."

"Liver function?" A note of panic rose in TJ's voice. "Is there something wrong with his liver?"

Bianca turned to Owen. "Owen? Why don't you go on out into the waiting room while I talk to your dad for a bit?"

When he was gone, Bianca sat down on a rolling stool, Owen's chart held tightly in her hands. "Owen has some signs of liver failure. He's a little jaundiced, which was the first thing I noticed. And his abdomen is tender. That, along with the tiredness, the lack of appetite, the swelling in his ankles ..."

"And the family history," TJ concluded for her.

"Yes. The family history."

"So, what does that mean?"

"Maybe nothing," she said. "If the blood test I'm ordering comes back normal, then we'll have to look at other things to see what's going on."

"And if it doesn't come back normal?" TJ asked.

Bianca let out a long breath. "Then I'll refer you to a specialist. A pediatric gastroenterologist. But let's not get ahead of ourselves. Let's start with the blood test."

9

———

Bianca went home that night feeling heartsick. She'd said it might be something else, but it wasn't. Owen had liver damage, and whatever had caused it wasn't something you wanted when you were twelve years old and just trying to navigate middle school and your parents' divorce.

She came in the door tired and beaten. This was part of the job, she told herself. Sometimes kids had serious health issues, and you had to be the bearer of bad news. It wasn't all about pink, bouncing babies and well-child exams.

Bianca sat on the sofa, her purse still on her shoulder, and thought about what might be wrong with Owen Davenport.

The most common genetic cause of liver disease in children was alpha-1 antitrypsin deficiency. It wasn't rare—about one in 2,500. It also wasn't good. If Owen had it, he'd be looking at chronic liver disease, potential lung disease, and a decreased life expectancy.

"Uh-oh. Bad day?" Martina came in with a mug of tea in her hand and froze when she saw the look on Bianca's face.

"One of my patients might have a serious condition."

"*Aww*. That's hard." Martina sat on the sofa next to Bianca and rubbed her sister's shoulder.

"It is." She wanted to tell Martina who it was—that this wasn't just any patient, but TJ Davenport's son—but doctor-patient confidentiality prevented it. She'd lectured Sofia on that, too, before they'd left the office. Bianca had thoroughly schooled Sofia on patient privacy when she'd come to work at the practice, but she'd reinforced it that afternoon, just in case.

This was one of the things that sucked about Bianca's work. She told her sisters everything that was bothering her, but when the thing that was bothering her was a patient's suffering—particularly a patient they all knew—she had to keep quiet no matter how hard it was.

"Is there anything I can do?" Martina asked.

"Thanks, but no."

"Okay. If you change your mind ..."

"As a matter of fact, there is something. Call JJ's and order a large pepperoni and sausage, would you? And a small veggie special for you. You can put it on my debit card."

Nothing she could do tonight would help Owen Davenport. But a little comfort food might help Bianca bury her feelings about it.

TJ PUT on a brave show for Owen. He acted like the information they'd gotten at Bianca's office was no big deal. A little liver failure? So what? They'd find out what had to be done to treat it, and they'd do that. It was just another of life's problems, one that they would tackle the way they did any other issue that came up.

Privately, though, he was trying not to lose his shit. He'd tried to convince himself that Owen's symptoms were normal adolescent stuff, but they weren't.

And the thing about the liver issue being genetic? Penny's mother was in bad shape. Was that what Owen had to look forward to? He was just a kid. He should be worrying about girls and sports and his grades, and whatever nasty thing some asshole at school had said on social media.

He shouldn't be worrying about his own survival.

TJ was quiet as they went about their evening routine: homework, making dinner, walking and feeding Gary, tidying up the house.

Gary seemed to know something was wrong. He usually stuck himself to TJ's side like he was glued there, but tonight, he followed Owen around with sad eyes, whining softly until the boy patted his head and stroked his fur.

TJ held it together the best he could, acting like everything was fine until after Owen had gone to bed. Then, on Bianca Russo's orders, he called his ex to talk about her mother's health.

Penny sounded irritated that he'd called her after ten p.m., but maybe that was him imagining things; maybe she was just exhausted from all she'd been going through.

"I was just about to go to bed," she told TJ, her voice flat. "Is Owen okay?"

"That's what I wanted to talk about." He told her about his symptoms, about the tests that had been ordered, and about the fact that his doctor suspected there was something going on with his liver.

"His liver?" Penny's voice rose. "But he's only twelve."

He explained the main reason he was calling: Owen's doctor had wanted to know more about Beverly DeLuca's diagnosis, in case her disorder was genetic and might be the same thing afflicting Owen.

"They're saying it's alcohol-related," Penny said. "That's what we all thought. She used to have a drinking problem, but she's been sober for years."

Her voice grew thick, and she stopped talking. TJ imagined her trying to gather her emotions.

"Did you tell them she's sober?" he said.

"Of course I did. They said it doesn't matter, that the damage was already done. Which is just what I need, you know? It's all I can do to keep it together without them telling me it's her fault." She started to cry.

"Ah, Pen." He wished he could be there to give her a hug. They hadn't been good together as husband and wife, but he still cared about her. He still thought of her as a friend. He listened quietly while she pulled herself together.

"Who's Owen's doctor?" she asked when she'd composed herself. "I want to call and hear about everything myself."

"Bianca Russo. I'll give you the phone number. Do you have a pen?"

"Bianca Russo?"

"Yeah. The office is in Morro Bay."

"Not the same Bianca Russo we went to high school with, though. Right?"

He cleared his throat. "Actually, it is the same one. She still lives in Cambria. She's a pediatrician now."

Penny was silent. That didn't bode well.

"Pen?"

"You're telling me that when our son needed a doctor, you chose someone who was mooney-eyed over you all through high school? Someone who looked like she wanted to strangle me with her bare hands when we started dating?"

"What? She did not."

"She did."

Had she? And why was TJ the only one who hadn't realized all of this at the time?

"Well ... she's got the highest ratings on Yelp of any pediatrician in the area. So, yeah. That's where I took him."

"Give me the number."

He did.

When they were getting ready to hang up, he said, "Penny? If they're wrong about your mom and the drinking, and if Owen really does have something genetic ... well. Maybe if we figure out what's wrong with him, we'll figure out what's wrong with your mom."

"He has to be okay," she said in a small voice. "He just has to be."

TJ was going to do everything in his power to make it so.

TJ's MIND was all over the place the next day at work. He'd taken Owen to get the latest blood work first thing, as soon as the place opened. Then he'd dropped his son off at school and had gotten to his first appointment of the day ten minutes late.

The homeowner didn't seem to mind—time was a casual concept in Cambria, a fact he'd forgotten but was now being reminded about—and TJ had set to work adding a new outlet to the guy's bathroom.

It was neither a big job nor a hard one, so it gave his mind room to wander—which wasn't exactly a good thing when you were worried about your kid's health.

What if Owen got sick the way Penny's mother was sick? What if his life was at risk?

TJ wouldn't even contemplate the next logical question: *what if he dies?* There were places he wouldn't let his mind go, and that question was first on the list.

Thinking about Owen's health made him feel sick, like a gaping, festering hole was opening in the center of his chest, so he forced himself to think about something else.

Bianca Russo was a nice distraction when he separated the idea of her from the thought of Owen's liver function.

Why hadn't he noticed that she'd been stuck on him in high school? She'd been pretty, she'd been nice to him—and to everyone, as he recalled. She'd been smart as hell.

Maybe that was why he hadn't noticed her. She was one of the smart kids, the college-bound kids, the kids preoccupied with AP classes and SAT prep and extracurricular activities chosen to look good on a college application.

TJ had never been interested in college. He'd had little patience for sitting in a classroom listening to a teacher drone on and on about whatever it was he was supposed to care about but didn't. He liked to work with his hands, and he'd known even then that he wanted to work right out of high school, doing something useful. Something that would bring a paycheck that would make him self-sufficient now, not in four years or longer.

Back then, kids like Bianca didn't hang around with kids like him. She wasn't in his orbit.

Except she was, now that he thought about it, because she'd put herself there. She had been around him, if not in his immediate circle, then adjacent to it. Thinking back on that night of the date-that-wasn't-a-date, he realized there had been no earthly reason for Bianca Russo to be in the group that had gone out together that night.

No reason except him.

He must have known, on some level, that she was attracted to him. And if some part of him had known, why had he decided not to go there?

Probably because she was out of my league.

Even as the thought popped into his head, he knew it was right. TJ hadn't been a guy who liked to lose, and as a result, he hadn't taken a lot of chances. If he'd thought Bianca was too smart for him, too promising, well ... he'd have set his sights elsewhere.

On someone like Penny DeLuca.

Penny had been like him: working-class family, mediocre grades, smart enough to make a life for herself but not smart enough for that life to include more study, more classrooms, more books.

Yeah, maybe he'd settled for Penny. Which seemed harsh and possibly a little cruel, but true. He'd settled for her because she'd seemed attainable, and marrying her had seemed like the logical thing to do.

Penny deserved better than someone who had been settling. And Owen deserved better than to live in a house with parents who knew they didn't belong together.

So, the divorce had been the right thing. It sucked for Owen, though. When you were twelve, you didn't see the bigger picture. You only knew your life had been run through a blender and had spilled out looking like something completely unrecognizable to you.

And then this—the thing with his liver.

TJ felt like his mind was spinning around in circles, always coming back to Owen's health. Because that was the only thing that really mattered, wasn't it? If Owen was okay, then TJ was okay.

He really needed Owen to be okay.

The homeowner peeked around the corner into the room where TJ was down on his knees installing the outlet. The job was taking longer than it should, mostly because TJ's mind was wandering.

"Almost done?" the guy asked. He was retired, in his sixties, with a balding head and a paunch spilling over his beltline.

"Yeah, almost. Sorry it's taking so long. I guess I'm a little distracted."

"Oh." The man's forehead wrinkled even more than usual. "Is that safe? I mean, with electricity and all ..."

TJ paused with his tools in his hand and looked at the guy. "The breaker's off. The only way anybody's getting electrocuted is if lightning strikes us."

"Oh. Well. Ha, ha." The guy rocked back and forth on his loafers.

"Five minutes," TJ told him. "Can you hand me that wall plate?"

10

———

A couple of days went by, and TJ still hadn't heard from Bianca.

She'd said the test results could take a week to come in, but that was bullshit. When you had a kid's health to worry about, who wanted to wait a week?

He told himself not to call her office and ask if, by some unforeseen miracle, the results had come earlier than expected. They were just going to say no, and on top of that, they'd be annoyed. It wasn't going to do anyone any good.

And yet, during a break between jobs around midafternoon, he found himself picking up the phone and calling anyway.

SOFIA WAS the one who took the call. After checking to see if the results were in—they weren't—she held her hand over the big black office phone and caught Bianca as she was passing by behind the reception desk.

"*Psst!*"

Bianca didn't seem to hear her, so she did it louder.

"*PSST!*"

Bianca stopped and blinked a few times. "Sofia, have you sprung a leak?"

"It's TJ Davenport," she mouthed, pointing at the phone in her hand.

"Oh." Bianca forgot what she'd been doing.

Sofia hit the HOLD button and said, "He wants to know if Owen's test results are in yet. They're not, but ... I thought maybe you wanted to tell him yourself." She grinned and bounced a little on her toes.

"I've got patients. I'm already behind schedule."

Sofia's shoulders sagged. "Oh. Okay. I'll tell him to call back in a couple of days and check again." She moved to hit a button on the phone, but Bianca stopped her.

"No, no. Um ... I'll tell him."

"Line two," Sofia said.

"TJ," Bianca said as she picked up the call. "It's Dr. Russo. Bianca."

"Oh. Oh, crap. They only have the doctor talk to you when it's bad, right? Is it bad? Shit."

"No. I mean ... We don't have the results yet."

He exhaled audibly, either in frustration or relief. "Ah. I figured you didn't, but ... I'm kinda driving myself crazy worrying about it, so I thought I'd try."

"I understand." She tucked her hair behind one ear, then recognized that as a flirting gesture—which was stupid, since he couldn't even see her. She put the hair back where it had been. "Look—TJ. I know you're worried, but there's no reason to panic. We don't know what this is yet."

"That's why I'm panicking. If I knew what it was, I could make some kind of plan. I could figure out what to do. But this? This not knowing?" He let out a puff of air.

"As soon as we have some answers, we will make a plan. We will figure out what to do. We'll do whatever's best for Owen," she said. "I promise."

"Yeah."

She heard the skepticism in his voice.

"TJ? What?"

"Well ... doctors always say that, don't they? They say they're there for you. They say they're going to help you, but when it comes down to it, you're just a name on a chart. And I can deal with that when it's me. But when it's my son ..." His voice had grown thick.

"I'm not like other doctors," Bianca said.

AFTER BIANCA GOT off the phone, she thought about what she'd just said to TJ. She'd told him she wasn't like other doctors.

But, was that true?

She thought about her average day: the crush of appointments, the pressure not to let herself get behind schedule, the red tape she and her staff had to wade through to appease the insurance companies.

She knew she didn't give all of her young patients the attention and time they deserved. She did her best, yes. And she did genuinely care. But if she'd been accused of getting her patients in and out quickly, dispensing prescriptions and doing the minimum in order to keep things moving, could she really deny it?

Every doctor she knew was on the edge of burnout because of the demands of the job—not to mention the emotional toll it took when the worst-case scenario happened with a patient.

Was Bianca really any different?

TJ was right to worry that Owen would fall through the cracks. Every parent—and every patient—was right to worry.

But Bianca vowed that she wasn't going to let it happen—not this time.

TJ KNEW it was probably bullshit when Bianca had said she wasn't like other doctors. Yeah, okay, so TJ knew her a little. That didn't mean Owen was any different to her than any of the other kids who came in and out of her office every day.

He sure as hell was different to TJ, though.

As he went about the rest of his day—picking up Owen from school, figuring out what to cook for dinner, putting a load of laundry into the washing machine—TJ nursed a thought that was nagging at him.

He wanted Bianca to get to know Owen as a person, to see how sweet and goofy and smart he was. He wanted her to be personally invested in Owen's care. He wanted her to see Owen as an individual, not as a name on a chart.

As he considered it, there was more going on in his head than that. He was also feeling guilty about breaking her heart back in school. True, he hadn't known that was what he'd done. But he'd done it, nonetheless, and knowing that made him feel like an ass.

He didn't like feeling that way, and he couldn't help thinking that talking to her about it would help. He could tell her that he hadn't known about her feelings for him. He could tell her that he hadn't realized their outing had been a date.

He could plead that he'd been a clueless male—because, hell, it was the truth.

TJ could kill two birds with one stone if he invited her over for dinner. That was something people did, wasn't it? People had other people over for civilized evenings of food and conversation.

She could get to know Owen a little, and TJ could explain that he hadn't intended to hurt her when she was an impressionable teenager and he was a big lunk of a guy just trying to get through each day until graduation.

He knew she was a professional, but he couldn't help worrying that her feelings about him—whatever lingering resentment she might hold toward him—would color her treatment of his son.

Plus, he'd forgotten to tell her what he'd learned about Penny's mom's condition.

There were a lot of reasons to invite her, and very few not to.

That settled it. He resolved to call her—just as soon as he could get up the nerve.

THE NEXT DAY WAS A SATURDAY, and Bianca was home cleaning out the refrigerator when TJ called.

She had taken everything out of the refrigerator and was cleaning the shelves and surfaces with hot, soapy water. Her head was in the refrigerator, her butt sticking out the door, yellow rubber gloves on her hands, when her cell phone buzzed with an incoming call.

"Can somebody get that for me?" she called into the room. The phone was all the way across the living room, and anyway, it was the least the others could do for her, considering that she was possibly saving their lives by discarding any questionable food.

Benny, who was sitting on the sofa typing something into her laptop, snatched up Bianca's phone from the coffee table. "Bianca's phone," she said to the caller. "She can't take your call right now because she's removing biohazards from the refrigerator. May I help you?"

After a moment, she said, "Oh. Hi, TJ. It's Bianca's sister Benny. I was Benedetta in high school. I doubt you remember me, though, because I was a couple of years behind you, and I hung out with the kids who played D&D in the library."

Another pause.

"I'll see if she's available."

Benny lowered the phone from her ear and looked at Bianca, who was staring at her, frozen, the big rubber gloves still on her hands.

"He doesn't remember me," Benny said. "Shocker, right? The guys he hung out with didn't know my crowd existed unless they needed to shake somebody down for lunch money."

Bianca whipped the gloves off her hands and rushed across the room to take the phone.

"TJ?"

"I heard that," he said. "I never shook down anyone for their lunch money. Although some of my dipshit friends might have. I wasn't very discriminating when it came to friends."

Bianca couldn't help grinning.

"He says he never shook anyone down for their lunch money," she said to Benny.

Then, to TJ: "I was just doing some cleaning. But I checked on Owen's test results before I left the office yesterday, and they're not in yet. I'm really sorry, but I'm afraid the lab—"

"That's not why I called."

That stopped her. "It's not?"

She heard him exhale in either nervousness or frustration. "I called because I wondered ... I wanted to ask you to have dinner with me and Owen one night next week. At our house."

"Oh." Was he asking her out? On a date? Because one thing Bianca had learned in life was that a date with Troy Davenport could only lead to heartbreak. "That's very nice of you, but—"

He pressed on before she could get the *no* out of her mouth.

"I just thought ... Well. My mother tells me you had a crush on me in high school, and I was an insensitive jerk about it, and I felt bad. Thought maybe we could clear the air, since you're Owen's doctor and all."

He didn't want a date—he wanted to offer her a pity dinner. As much as she generally enjoyed being humiliated, the idea was less than appealing.

"I'm sorry," she told him. "I'm busy."

THAT NIGHT AT TED'S—A dive bar a block off Main Street where the locals gathered to get away from the constant flow of tourists—Benny brought up the issue of the pity dinner. And the conversation wasn't going in Bianca's favor.

"I say you should go." Benny popped a handful of bar peanuts into her mouth. "So what if it's a pity dinner? It's still a dinner you don't have to cook, with a hot guy to look at. It's a win-win."

Ted's was half-full that night, with groups of people around a few of the round wooden tables and a couple more playing pool. The dark bar smelled like spilled beer and old grease, and the sound system was playing a selection of hits from the eighties. Bianca and her sisters were sitting near the back of the room with a glass of Chardonnay for her, mugs of beer for Benny and Sofia, and a club soda with a wedge of lime for Martina, who was the designated driver.

"No," Martina corrected her. "It's not a win-win. Especially if you still have all of those Troy feelings you had in high school."

"I do not have Troy feelings," Bianca insisted.

"Because if you still have Troy feelings," Martina went on as though Bianca hadn't spoken, "and it isn't really a date, then you're going to get hurt again. And I really don't think any of us is up for a repeat of you crying in your room and blasting Sheryl Crow."

"I don't know," Sofia said thoughtfully. "Maybe he doesn't intend it as a date, but he's single, you're single.... Even if it doesn't start out as a thing, it could become a thing."

"I don't want a *thing* right now," Bianca said. "I just broke up with Peter. I need to regroup."

"That's *why* you need to have a thing." Sofia leaned forward in her seat for emphasis. "You need something to help you put the whole Peter mess behind you."

"A palate cleanser," Benny suggested.

"Exactly." Sofia pointed one finger at Benny.

"Or," Bianca said, "I could behave like an adult, let some time pass between Peter and whoever I date next, and make sure I'm emotionally ready for something new when that next date comes along."

Benny grimaced. "The emotional equivalent of eating kale salad."

"I like kale salad," Martina said.

"Ugh." Bianca scrubbed at her face with her hands. "The problem is, I *do* still have Troy feelings. Maybe. That's why having dinner with him is a really bad idea."

"Aha! I knew it," Benny said, triumphant.

"They're not real feelings," Bianca went on. "Obviously. I haven't seen him in, what, eighteen years? It's just ... there's a flutter." She pressed her hand to her middle. "I don't want to feel a flutter, but it's there."

"It could be the peanuts." Martina picked up the bowl from the center of the table. "God knows where these things have been."

"It's not the peanuts," Sofia said. "And maybe they are real feelings. You could have dinner with him and find out."

The whole conversation was making Bianca uncomfortable. Crying and blasting Sheryl Crow had been the least of it back in high school. Bianca hadn't just felt sad when Troy had started dating Penny DeLuca—she'd felt *crushed*. She'd felt as though every good, buoyant thing within her had been scooped out, leaving nothing but a hollow shell of misery and regret.

She didn't want to go through that again. And yet ... there was the flutter.

"His son will be there," she said. "So, how risky could it be?"

"You're thinking about it," Sofia said. "Aren't you?"

"I mean ... he's back in town, he's being friendly ... his kid is sick," Bianca went on. "I don't want to be *rude*...."

"Oh, boy." Martina shook her head sadly. "Here we go again. And I don't even like Sheryl Crow."

Bianca called him on Sunday morning and said she'd changed her mind—she would love to have dinner with him and his son.

After that, she spent the rest of the day second-guessing her decision. She couldn't seem to decide whether having a meal with TJ Davenport would be neighborly or stupid, casual or momentous, harmless or foolhardy.

Well, she'd agreed to it now. There was nothing to do but wait and find out.

11

TJ had been relieved when Bianca had turned down his invitation. He was man enough to admit that to himself. He'd asked, and then she'd said no, and that was that. When she'd called and told him she'd changed her mind, he'd had to rearrange his thoughts on the matter, reminding himself this was a good thing.

It was just dinner with an old high school friend, that was all. Not even a friend—an acquaintance. There was no reason it should have him all tied up in knots.

Except, there were a lot of reasons, when you thought about it.

He started out thinking about Owen—about how it was important for Bianca to see Owen as a person and not just as a patient. But as he pushed his cart up and down the aisles of the Morro Bay Albertson's, shopping for the dinner, his thoughts expanded to include so much more.

For instance, Bianca had liked him in high school. More than liked him, according to pretty much everyone who remembered the two of them back then. Was it possible that she still liked him now?

She'd blossomed nicely since high school. She'd been somewhat awkward then—as they all had been—but now she was a poised, mature woman with a hell of a lot of appeal.

It was the eyes, he thought. She had those deep brown doe eyes. And that olive-toned skin.

"Excuse me? Excuse me!"

He looked up to realize he was blocking access to the canned tomatoes. A middle-aged woman with dyed blond hair and blue eye shadow right out of the seventies was waiting impatiently for him to move.

"Oh. Sorry." He pushed his cart out of the way and tried to focus on what he was doing.

Would it be so bad if Bianca still had feelings for him? He hadn't dated anyone since the divorce, and sometimes he got lonely. Having his son and his dog to keep him company was nice, sure, but it wasn't the same as being in a relationship.

He missed having someone in his life. Things had been bad with Penny for a while, but he remembered when they weren't, and he missed it. He didn't miss Penny—not exactly—but he missed the feeling of being wanted by someone. Of belonging to someone.

It probably wasn't ideal for him to start something with Owen's doctor, but, hell, if things didn't work out between them, there were other pediatricians in San Luis Obispo County. He was sure Bianca would be professional enough to refer them to someone else should things go awry.

Nothing's going awry, because nothing's going to happen.

TJ reminded himself that he was jumping the gun by a good three seconds. He didn't know if Bianca still liked him that way. He didn't know if he liked *her* that way. He was spinning a fantasy in his head about something that might never come to pass.

But still, there were those deep brown, doe eyes.

Just shop, Davenport. For God's sake, buy a chicken. You can do that without planning the next five years, can't you?

So he bought a chicken. No matter what might go wrong during the dinner, at least he knew how to roast a damned chicken.

MONDAY AFTER WORK, Bianca fussed with her clothes. When you didn't know whether what you were doing was a date, it was difficult to know how to dress.

Sexy was out, because A) TJ's son would be there, and B) that would assume things that were better left unassumed. Professional was an option, but that would send *back off* vibes if he really was open to something more.

Something more? Shut up.

Bianca chided herself for even thinking it. She'd been so humiliated junior year when she'd gotten her hopes up about TJ and he'd started parading around school with someone else.

She had no desire to get her hopes up again, only to have them dashed.

Entire lifetimes, epic tragedies, romances, and fantasies were being played out in her mind, and they hadn't even eaten together yet.

Clothing, right.

She opted for casual—a soft sweater, jeans, a pair of boots, with gold hoop earrings dangling from her lobes. She brushed out her hair until it was soft and shiny, then she carefully applied makeup, the eyes just a little smokier than she would have made them for work, the lips just a little redder.

When she was done, she looked at herself in the mirror.

"Why am I doing this?" she said aloud to her reflection.

"Because you need to get laid!" Benny called to her from the next room.

WHEN BIANCA GOT to TJ's place, the dog answered the door.

She'd noticed that the door wasn't latched all the way, so she'd knocked on the doorjamb when she noticed there wasn't a bell. The door had opened slowly, with a creak, and Bianca thought at first that no one was there—until she looked down and saw an old Lab looking up at her, its muzzle sprinkled with gray.

"Oh. Hello." Bianca bent down to scratch the dog behind its ears, and the animal leaned against her thigh with a heavy sigh of contentment.

"TJ?" she called into the house.

A moment later, he came to the door with an apron—a manly one—tied around his waist. "Oh, hey. I didn't hear you. I see you've met Gary."

Bianca looked down at the dog, who was still pressed against her. "Hi, Gary." She gave his ears another rub. "How are you, boy?"

"Ancient," TJ answered for the dog. "But he's hanging in there."

He ushered her into the house, a small Craftsman-style bungalow with a stone fireplace and built-in, dark wood bookshelves. It was a cold February day, and a fire was burning in the hearth.

One of the nice things about Cambria was the lack of cookie-cutter tract housing. The town was made up of a charming mishmash of historic Victorians, log cabins, modern beach houses, immense estates, tiny cottages in dire need of repair, A-frames with steeply pitched roofs, and other styles too numerous to mention. No two houses were exactly alike.

TJ's house had been built with love and with a keen eye for detail. Crown moldings, arched doorways, and detailed woodwork made the space both welcoming and charming.

"This is lovely."

"It's a rental." He scratched the back of his neck as though the topic made him uncomfortable. "I wanted to buy a house, but ... there was the divorce, and the alimony, and the upheaval of the move. I'm hoping to make a deal to buy this place once things are more settled."

Bianca would have thought the subject of divorce, alimony, and money troubles would have been off limits so early on; it seemed to her that most men would have attempted to put up a good front. His candor was disarming.

"Is Owen home?" Bianca asked.

TJ nodded. "Yeah, he's in his room, probably texting his friends in San Jose."

"Oh. I imagine the move was hard on him."

"Yes and no. He misses his friends and his mom, but he likes Cambria. He wants to learn to surf. Owen!" TJ raised his voice so his son could hear him through the closed door. "Dr. Russo's here! Come out and say hello."

It was clear from the look on Owen's face when he came out of his room that the idea of having his doctor over for dinner was just slightly less embarrassing than parading down Main Street in a chicken suit. He had that scrawny look some boys had when they hadn't filled out yet, his limbs not up to the challenge of giving shape to his jeans and T-shirt. His sandy hair had fallen into his eyes, and he swiped it away with one hand.

"Hey," he said.

His skin and eyes looked a little yellow to her, as they had at his office visit. That wasn't good, and she worried about what the blood tests would show when the results finally came back.

But this evening was social; she was here as a friend, not as a doctor. She smiled and tried a conversational gambit that she thought might put him at ease.

"Is Gary your dog?" she asked him.

He relaxed visibly, and when he smiled, she could see the resemblance to TJ for the first time.

"He was supposed to be my dog. But he likes Dad better. Don'tcha, Gary?" Gary had wandered over to Owen when he came into the room, and the boy laid his hand on the dog's back. Gary wagged his tail in a slow, languorous arc.

"He does not," TJ protested.

"Dad, you know he does." And then, to Bianca: "He didn't even want a dog, but now Gary sleeps in his bed with him." Owen made a sound that was either a scoff or a snicker. Maybe both.

Bianca raised an eyebrow. "He does?"

TJ shrugged, embarrassed. "Yeah, well ... the poor guy's traumatized from being in the pound. What else could I do?"

A delicious smell was wafting into the living room from the kitchen. "What are you cooking?" Bianca asked. "It smells great."

"Oh, crap, the chicken." TJ headed for the small kitchen, waving for her to follow. "Come on in, it should be about done."

BIANCA WAS IMPRESSED with the meal when it was spread out over the kitchen table: roast chicken with lemon and rosemary; roast fingerling potatoes; warm rolls; and a salad of fresh greens and colorful vegetables.

They had just sat down, and TJ was pouring Bianca a glass of Chardonnay.

"You're quite a cook," she told him.

Owen made the scoffing sound again. "It's the only meal he knows how to make. Every time we have anybody over, he makes the exact same thing."

Unperturbed, TJ said, "Why mess with a winner? If it's good, it's good."

Bianca buttered a roll still hot from the oven. "What will you do if you have me over again?"

"Then you'll get to see my skills microwaving frozen entrees," TJ said.

The idea that there might be a second time—that TJ might invite her into his home for another visit, another meal—made Bianca feel warm and nearly giddy. Clearly, her teen crush hadn't subsided.

But the feeling of attraction she still had for him was one thing. She'd expected that. What she hadn't expected was to feel so comfortable here with him and his son, so at ease.

They ate and chatted as Gary snored in his dog bed by the fireplace. Bianca could feel the easy affection between TJ and Owen as the two teased each other and bantered back and forth. TJ ribbed Owen about a girl he'd hung out with at a recent school dance; Owen made a joke about how TJ, who'd chaperoned, danced like he was being electrocuted.

"I'd like to see that," Bianca said, laughing.

TJ raised his eyebrows at her. "We should go out sometime, and maybe you will."

Owen blushed.

Bianca didn't, but the birds that had been fluttering inside her began beating their wings.

TJ HADN'T PLANNED to ask Bianca out. Certainly not like that, in front of Owen. But the words had come so naturally and easily that he'd barely noticed them until they were out of his mouth.

He didn't particularly want to take them back.

The offer of a date hadn't been intentional, but still, a lot had gone into it. His loneliness since the divorce—and, hell, since a long time before it. The way it felt to be sitting at his dinner table with a woman again. The effortless way she'd put Owen at ease as soon as she'd arrived. Those dark brown eyes. And something about her spirit—her *aura*, he might have said, if he believed in that kind of thing. She gave off a feeling of warmth and confidence that appealed to him and made him want more of it.

So, yeah, he might have asked her differently if he'd thought about it. He might have waited longer, until they knew each other better. But he'd have asked eventually. The more he considered it, the more he knew that was true.

The way Bianca was looking at him now, he knew she was still attracted to him. He knew that whatever she'd felt for him back in high school was still there in some form.

He might not have recognized it then, but he did now. So he relaxed and smiled at her and turned on whatever TJ charm he possessed while she absorbed what he'd just said.

He'd been led to believe—by his mother, at least—that his TJ charm was considerable. Which was why it surprised him when she hesitated, fidgeted with her napkin, and said, "Oh. Well ... we'll see."

TJ had spent enough time around women to know that *we'll see* didn't mean *yes* or even *maybe. We'll see* meant *we'll do it when hell freezes over, and maybe not even then.*

Had he misread her attraction to him? No. He was sure he hadn't. So what did that leave? Professional concerns? Resentment over what happened in high school? Was she involved with someone else?

Now wasn't the time to get to the bottom of it, not with Owen sitting there picking at his chicken and trying to pretend he wasn't listening.

TJ changed the subject to Owen's extracurricular activities—band and chess—and they finished their meal making companionable small talk.

~

WHEN THEY'D FINISHED EATING, Owen went to his room to start his homework, and Bianca helped TJ clean up. He'd tried to shoo her away, saying that guests shouldn't have to wash dishes, but she insisted.

As they worked side by side, TJ putting leftovers in plastic containers and Bianca rinsing plates and stacking them in the dishwasher, he told her what he'd found out about his former mother-in-law.

"They're saying it's alcohol." He snapped a lid on a container and slid it into the refrigerator. "Which is fair enough, I guess, since Beverly used to drink pretty hard. But she's been sober for years. Liver disease wouldn't show up now, would it?"

Bianca put a dish in the dishwasher, dried her hands on a towel, and put a fist on her hip. "That's hard to say. It's possible she's had alcoholic hepatitis for years without showing symptoms."

"Yeah. Okay." He rubbed his temples as though the idea of it hurt him.

"My other thought is, they might have misdiagnosed her."

He closed the refrigerator and faced her. "Okay. Tell me more about that."

"Well. If Owen has liver damage—and I'm not saying he does,

without the test results—then that's unusual. I mean, it could be viral hepatitis, but ..."

"Go on," he prompted her.

"I'm just thinking it would be more likely to be something genetic, especially considering his grandmother's health history."

He crossed his arms and leaned his butt against the counter, considering it. "You're saying Beverly might have a genetic condition that's been passed down to Owen."

"I can't say that without evidence."

"Right. Sure. But you're thinking it."

"I'm thinking it's worth looking into."

TJ WALKED Bianca to the door feeling encouraged about Owen's health. If the kid had a genetic disorder, that could be bad news. But at least Bianca had some idea what to look for. At least she wasn't brushing them off, telling them it was all in their heads. Because TJ knew it wasn't.

Now that he'd talked it over with her, he was free to think about other things for a while. Like why she didn't want to go out with him on a real date—just the two of them.

He waited until they were standing next to Bianca's car, a fat moon above them, before he said, "So. *We'll see*, huh?"

She smiled a little—the faintest tug of her lips. "I didn't want to turn you down in front of your son. I thought it might hurt your ego."

"Considerate." He nodded. "But why say no at all?"

She cocked her head slightly as though she was considering giving him an answer. Then she put out her hand for him to shake instead.

"Good night, TJ. Thank you for dinner. I enjoyed it."

He took her hand in his, but instead of shaking it, he held it. "It was my pleasure."

12

Bianca drove home still feeling a tingling in her hand where they'd touched. Okay, there wasn't a real tingle—it was a construct of her imagination—but it felt real. It felt as though he'd sent an electric current from her fingers, through her hands, down to her belly, and then lower.

How could she still be this attracted after so many years? How was it that she hadn't left her Troy Davenport fixation behind with her butterfly hair clips and her frosted lip gloss?

She'd imagined this, she was embarrassed to admit to herself. She'd imagined Troy Davenport coming back into her life one day, recognizing his mistake, and declaring his need for her.

When he'd held her hand and looked at her the way he had, it felt like all of those fantasies of her redeeming herself in his eyes might finally come true.

And then she'd said goodnight.

Bianca was a fundamentally practical person, and she knew better than to put the crazy product of her imaginings above what was real. Her career was real, as was her responsibility to TJ's son. Her heartbreak had been real. And her relationship with Peter had been real, too, even if it hadn't been sustainable.

She was certain that when she finally found her lifetime match—if she did, indeed, find him—he wouldn't be some insanely attractive figure from her past. He'd be like Peter: stable, sensible. Ordinary.

Her sisters would have told her not to settle for ordinary—they'd said it about Peter so many times she could recite their arguments verbatim. But the thing about *ordinary* was that it wouldn't leave you sobbing on your bed under a poster of Justin Timberlake.

And she'd turned him down for another reason, too. Because there was another part to her fantasy about what might have been with Troy Davenport. In that part, Bianca was the one being pursued, and he was the one being rejected.

She wasn't the kind of person who would turn someone down just for the fun of hurting them. But she had to admit that it had felt good to be the one with the power, the one making the decisions instead of being helpless with desire.

But she was second-guessing herself now. She'd never actually said no—not as such. She could call him and say she would love to go out with him.

She was still considering her options when she got home. Sofia was at Patrick's place, but Benny and Martina were sprawled on the sofa in their pajamas watching TV with a bowl of popcorn between them.

When Bianca came in, Benny grabbed the remote and paused whatever they were watching.

"You don't have to turn it off," Bianca told her. "I didn't mean to interrupt."

"I did have to turn it off," Benny said. "If I didn't, how could I grill you about how things went with TJ?"

"You could just not grill me." Bianca hung her coat and purse on a hook by the door.

"That's not an option," Benny said.

"No, it's really not," Martina put in.

Bianca sat on the sofa next to Martina. She reached past her sister to grab a few pieces of popcorn from the bowl and began munching on them. "It went fine. It was fine."

"One *fine* sounds like it was okay but boring. Two *fines* sounds like you're bullshitting us," Benny observed.

Bianca's shoulders slumped. "He asked me out."

"No shit," Benny said. "That's where you just were. You were out."

"No." Bianca brushed the popcorn dust off her hands. "This wasn't a date. His son was there. It was ... friendly. But definitely not a date."

"But he asked you out on an actual date," Martina clarified.

"He did."

"God, that must have been sweet after all these years. So, when are you going?" Benny did a little dance with her feet, which were encased in fuzzy slippers.

"I'm not."

"You're not?" Martina sat up straighter and stared at her. "Why not?"

"Because I said no. Well, I didn't actually say no. I said 'we'll see,' and then I shook his hand."

"You shook his hand," Benny said.

"I ... yes."

"Is that code for some perverse sex act? Because otherwise, this doesn't compute," Benny said.

"Stop," Martina told Benny. "She's making him work for it a little. There's nothing wrong with that. Why shouldn't he work?"

"I'm not making him work, and it's not code for anything," Bianca insisted. "I didn't want to go out with him!"

"Well, now you're just lying," Benny said.

Bianca didn't want to explain herself, didn't want to painstakingly dissect the conflicting emotions that were rushing through her. So she got up, took the remote from where it sat on the coffee table, and restarted the movie.

"I'm not lying," she lied. "I'm going to bed."

THE HAND-SHAKING thing should have annoyed TJ. Instead, he was intrigued. Unless he'd completely lost his ability to read women, he knew she still had a thing for him. So why hadn't she said yes when he'd asked her out? Why the handshake?

Earlier, when she'd hit him with the *we'll see,* he'd wondered if maybe she was seeing someone. That was possible. But if so, wouldn't she have mentioned it when he'd invited her for dinner? Wasn't that something that would have come up?

He wouldn't have said he was the kind of man who would pursue a woman just because she turned him down—just to prove he could do it—but here he was, thinking about her and wondering how he might change her mind.

And, hell, it wasn't just because he had something to prove. He wanted her to like him. Was that so wrong?

Once she was gone, TJ checked Owen's homework, then they watched some TV together, with Gary sitting between them on the sofa. The dog had needed TJ to haul him up there, because he was too old to jump up. TJ's back wasn't what it used to be; he was going to have to build some dog stairs or a ramp or something.

After the show ended, TJ sent Owen off to bed, dealing with the usual delays and excuses, the usual indignant speech: *I'm not a baby anymore, why do I have to have a bedtime?* The truth was, Owen had to go to bed at ten p.m. because that was when TJ got tired. Though TJ wasn't about to admit such a frailty to his son.

This time of the evening—the time after Owen was in bed, when TJ had only himself for company—was when he really felt the loss of his marriage. It wasn't the sex he missed, though he did miss that. It was the companionship. It would have been nice to have someone to talk to about his day, someone to sympathize about the little struggles of both of their lives, someone to listen to his stupid jokes or offer opinions about random things.

Penny had been good at that at first. Early in their marriage, they'd sat in bed late at night and talked about so many things: their fears, their memories, their plans. But the longer they were together, the less they'd talked to each other. It was as though they'd only had a finite number of words for each other, and as the supply neared its end, they'd had to ration them to keep from running out entirely.

Talking with Bianca at dinner had been fun and easy. He wanted that with someone again. And he wouldn't mind at all if that someone was Bianca.

He turned out the lights, stripped down to his boxers, and got into bed, but sleep didn't come. He picked up his phone from the bedside table and scrolled through his social media for a while, waiting for his eyelids to get heavy.

Then, against his better judgment, he brought up his texting app and composed a message for Bianca. She was probably asleep, as he should be, but if so, she'd get it in the morning. He liked the thought that his message would be waiting for her when she woke up.

I enjoyed tonight. Thanks for coming. Then, with a grin, he typed: *You really should consider going out with me sometime, without Owen.*

He sent the text and put the phone down, not expecting an answer.

A moment later, his phone pinged with a response.

We'll see.

He couldn't help laughing.

13

———

The next day, a Tuesday, Bianca was going about her day in a cloud of contentment, thinking about TJ and his text, when Owen's test results came in and ruined everything.

"It's here," Sofia said as Bianca passed behind the reception desk on her way to an exam room.

"What's here?"

"Owen Davenport's lab results. You said you wanted to know right away, so …"

"Oh. Right. Yes. Okay." Melissa Starkey could wait in Room Three for a little longer. Bianca went into her office, sat down at her desk, and pulled up the results on her desktop computer.

Shit.

His viral serology tests were negative for hepatitis, but his liver function panel was all over the place. There was something going on, and it was serious. She'd known that just from talking to the boy, just from looking at him, but she hadn't wanted it to be true.

She couldn't call TJ now; it was flu season. If she got behind schedule, before she knew it she'd have angry parents and restless kids stacking up in her waiting room and spilling out into the hall.

She'd call as soon as she got a break, or, if there wasn't a break, she'd call as soon as her last patient left. She was never eager to break bad news, anyway. Her least favorite part of the job was making those calls that ruined a parent's day.

She left her office and headed toward the exam room where Melissa Starkey was waiting for her. On her way, Sofia caught the look on her face and knew.

"Oh, no," she said.

Bianca hesitated at her sister's look of sympathy. Then she fixed a pleasant, businesslike expression on her own face and went to examine Melissa Starkey.

WHEN THE LAST patients had gone and Bianca's nurse had left for the day, Sofia tidied up the reception desk and asked, "Do you want me to stay?"

Sometimes they drove in together, but today, Bianca had come in early to catch up on some paperwork, so they'd arrived separately.

"No," Bianca said. "You go ahead. Thank you, though."

"Are you sure?"

"I'm fine. It's fine." And it was, Bianca reassured herself. She gave parents bad news all the time, and after all, this wasn't the *worst* news; no one had cancer, to her knowledge. No one had a terminal diagnosis. Still, something was going on, and it wasn't minor.

When Sofia had gone and Bianca was alone in the office, she settled in at her desk and called TJ. The fact that she was calling from her office phone rather than her cell might have tipped him off that this was official, because he already sounded tense and guarded when he answered the phone.

"Bianca. What's up?"

"Hi, TJ. Do you have a moment to talk?" And when had that sentence ever led to anything good?

She told him about Owen's test results. She told him what they did and did not mean. She explained how much was still unknown, and she laid out the possibilities for the most likely things that could be going on.

"I'm going to refer Owen to a pediatric gastroenterologist," she said. "You'll want to get him in as soon as you can."

"As soon as I can? That sounds ominous."

"Well." She wanted to reassure him that it could be nothing, but there was no scenario in which this was nothing. "It's just not something you want to take lightly." Not that he was. She could hear the tension in his voice. She could hear the fear.

"My office will get this approved through your insurance company in the next day or two, but I'm going to give you the specialist's name and number now, and I want you to call tomorrow. Make the appointment, and you can give them the paperwork later."

Her urgency was going to alarm him, she knew, but there was no way around it. She needed him to be alarmed.

When she'd given him the information and he'd taken it down, she offered what reassuring words she could. "Dr. Temple is very good. Whatever this is, she'll deal with it."

"Right," he said. "Right." She could tell that he was trying to keep himself calm and matter-of-fact.

As a woman who'd never had kids, Bianca couldn't quite imagine the fear of knowing your child was seriously ill. She tried to imagine it so she would be empathetic with her patients' parents. But imagining it was one thing. Living it was something else.

"TJ? Call me anytime, if you have questions or if you need help. Just ... call me." It was all she had to offer.

TJ HELD HIS SHIT TOGETHER, because what choice did he have? He didn't even know what they were dealing with yet. There might come a time when he'd lose his shit, but for now, it would be a waste of effort. Especially when he had to save his strength to deal with his ex-wife.

He gave Owen his dinner, then waited until the kid was in his room with his headphones on, blasting God knew what kind of music, before he called Penny.

"Pen. How's your mom?" He led with that, because no matter what he might be dealing with, he never wanted to forget that Penny was going through something hellish of her own.

"Oh ... the medication they're giving her doesn't seem to be helping anymore. They're finally going to evaluate her for a transplant. But what if they put her on the list and she doesn't get a liver?"

"She'll get one," he said, because he needed to say something that didn't sound utterly useless. He wasn't sure he succeeded.

"Sure."

"Listen, Pen ... I'm calling because Owen got his test results from his doctor."

"You mean Bianca. Dr. Russo."

"Yeah." He told her what Bianca had said, then explained about the specialist—and about the need for them not to waste time.

"Oh, God."

He wished he hadn't had to tell her. He wished he could let her deal with one emergency at a time, because he'd loved her once and because she was still the mother of his child.

"They said it was her drinking," Penny said, interrupting his thoughts.

"What?"

"My mother. They said it was the alcohol. But if Owen's sick, and it's his liver ... I mean, that can't be a coincidence, can it?"

Bianca had suggested the same thing.

"How do you know she even knows what she's talking about?" Penny said before he could answer her. "Bianca Russo, I mean ... What if she's wrong? I don't know why you couldn't take him to a *real* doctor, TJ. One who doesn't have a thing for you. Is that why you took him there? So you could get into her pants? Because that's a shitty way to treat your son's health, TJ. For God's sake ..."

"She is a real doctor." He could have taken the rest point by point, but he knew Penny was just lashing out at him because she was scared. Hell, so was he.

"Yeah, just because she's got some paper on the wall doesn't mean—"

"We'll handle it, Penny." He said it in his most soothing voice. "We'll get him the help he needs, and we'll handle it."

Penny started to cry.

"Penny? Trust me. I'm on this."

"Tell me everything you find out. Tell me every goddamned thing." He could see Penny's face in his mind, the way she was struggling for her composure, her lips compressed, her eyes hard and determined.

"I will."

"Promise me."

"I promise."

He wished he could promise her that Owen would be okay. But that was a promise nobody could make.

14

———

T J tried to make an appointment with the specialist the next day, but the earliest spot they could offer him was more than a month away—which was bullshit.

"My son's doctor said he needs to be seen right away," he told the woman who'd answered the phone. "She said not to wait. So I don't—"

"I understand, sir." Her tone suggested she said the same thing to worried parents dozens of times per day. "But that's the earliest appointment the doctor has available. Would you like me to put your son on our waiting list in case someone cancels?"

TJ hung up without answering her.

When he called Bianca, he didn't bother with the office phone, because he'd have to go through Sofia at the front desk, and he didn't want to go through anyone, or leave a message, or wait for a return call. He wanted to talk to her directly, and he wanted it to happen right damned now.

The call went to her voice mail, so he bit off an obscenity and left a message as calmly as he could manage. He was about to get into his truck and drive over there when she called him back.

"TJ? Is everything okay?"

"Hell no, it's not okay."

"Is it Owen? What's going on?" She sounded alarmed, which immediately made him feel guilty.

"It's just ..." He rubbed at his forehead with his hand. "The specialist you referred us to. She can't see us for a month."

"What?"

"Four weeks."

"Did you tell them I said he needs to be seen sooner? Did you—"

"I told them." To his own ears, he already sounded defeated, and he knew that whatever was happening to Owen, this was likely only the beginning. He couldn't afford to be defeated. Screw defeat.

"All right. I'll call them and see what I can do."

He was so grateful for that—for her willingness to intervene—that he sagged in relief. "Thank you. I appreciate it, Bianca." He wondered if he should be calling her Dr. Russo—if it was somehow disrespectful to use her first name in this context—but he went with it. The more she felt connected to the situation, and to Owen in particular, the better this was going to go.

THE PROBLEM with referring kids to specialists on the Central Coast was that there weren't very many to choose from. Bianca could refer Owen to a different pediatric gastroenterologist, but it would mean he and TJ would have to go all the way to Santa Barbara—a drive of more than two hours.

That would be fine for a single consultation, but if Owen had a serious condition—and Bianca was certain that he did—then it was going to be more than one visit, and probably more than several.

She called the office of the specialist who'd put them off, but she didn't get anywhere. The availability was what it was, she was told. Could Bianca add more hours to the day? Could she, perhaps, suggest which sick kid they should bump in order to get Owen Davenport in earlier?

She hung up discouraged.

Bianca did have a resource, and one that was close by. Though she might be attempting to cross a bridge that had been burned to ashes.

With only slight hesitation, she called Peter.

~

"Owen has an appointment with a gastroenterologist tomorrow at ten," she told TJ on the phone later that morning.

"He does? That's ... Thank you. But why did they tell me there wasn't anything available if they had a spot open at ten? Did somebody cancel? Because—"

"It's not the same doctor."

"Oh. Okay. But it's a pediatric gastroenterologist?"

"Not pediatric. But he's excellent, and he's local. Owen will be in good hands."

"That's great. That's just ... great. Thanks, Bianca."

She squirmed a little and wondered whether to tell him. Then she decided that there was no benefit in not telling him.

"There's just one thing."

"Oh?"

"Peter ... Dr. DeVries ... is ..."

"He's what?" TJ asked.

"He's my ex." When TJ didn't say anything immediately, Bianca pressed on. "We dated. For a while. And then we broke up. Recently. Really recently. Not that it should affect anything. He's an excellent doctor. And it's not like he's going to know that there's ... anything between us."

"I wasn't aware that there *was* anything between us," TJ said.

At first, Bianca felt like she'd been slapped. Here it was again, the same rejection she'd experienced in high school. The same hot shame, the same—

"Of course," he went on, "if you *want* there to be something between us, we could make that happen."

She blushed. She was actually blushing. When was she going to outgrow this childish crush on TJ Davenport?

Probably never.

"I'll text you Peter's information. Let me know how the appointment goes," she said, then hung up.

TJ SPENT the rest of that day thinking about the next day's appointment—and about Bianca. He'd flirted with her during a phone conversation about his sick kid. What kind of father did that?

The kind who needs to think about something other than what might happen to his son.

That was the truth of it. TJ needed to take care of business for Owen, and he was doing that. But he also needed an escape from his worries. Flirting with Bianca had seemed like a harmless way to achieve that.

He was working for a general contractor today. A new house was going up in the Marine Terrace neighborhood, and TJ and a small team of guys he'd hired were handling the wiring.

Tomorrow was supposed to be a full day of work on the project, but now TJ had to beg off for an hour or two to take Owen to his appointment. One of the nice things about marriage, he reflected, was being able to trade off with your spouse on stuff like this.

Now there was no spouse, so it was all up to TJ. He'd promised Penny he would be on top of this, and he would be. Both she and Owen were counting on him.

He just hoped he wouldn't get any shit for taking the time off. He'd happily tell the general contractor to shove his house project up his ass if it came to that, but TJ's guys needed their paychecks as much as he did.

Well, if he could get ahead of schedule today, that would help his case for tomorrow.

He skipped lunch and dug in, focusing on the job now so he could focus on his son tomorrow.

"You okay?" Jason, a guy on his crew, peered at TJ when he came back from his lunch break and saw that TJ had never left. "Did something happen with the inspection?"

"Nah." TJ had just come out of the crawlspace under the house, and he straightened up and dusted himself off. "Just trying to get a jump on things, that's all."

〜

THAT NIGHT, TJ told himself that he was Googling Peter DeVries to find out whether the guy was a good doctor. And that was mostly true. But as hard as he tried, it was difficult to separate the man's professional information—education, credentials, Yelp reviews—from the fact that he was Bianca's ex.

Looking at DeVries's picture, TJ wasn't especially impressed. If someone had created an image labeled Average White Male, it would probably look something like this. Medium brown hair, cut conservatively. Medium complexion. Medium build. It was impossible to know the guy's height based on a head shot, but TJ would have bet it was medium.

The Yelp reviews, though—they were outstanding. People with one horrific gastrointestinal ailment after another thanked him for either saving their lives or improving their quality of life to such an extent that it was practically the same thing.

Moving beyond Yelp, TJ discovered that DeVries had published papers on irritable bowel syndrome, esophageal ulcers—and hepatitis. The guy knew something about the liver, so that was good.

Reading through all of it, the first thing TJ felt was relief. The man was obviously good at his job, and he was going to be on Owen's case in the morning. The second thing he felt was reassurance. Surely, whatever Owen had, this guy would know what to do about it.

The third thing he felt was intimidation.

This was the kind of guy Bianca dated? Of course it was. She was a doctor—it made sense she would date other doctors. TJ was a good electrician, but he was just an electrician. He hadn't gone to college. He hadn't earned an advanced degree—or any degree at all. He played with wiring and made the lights go on. An honorable trade, sure, but how could he hope to impress a woman like Bianca?

Because he did want to impress her. The more he knew about her, the more he was certain of that. The *we'll see* had been a challenge, and he was never one to shy away from a challenge.

I Googled DeVries, he told her via text message that night after dinner, when Owen was at the kitchen table hunched over his math book. *Looks like he knows his stuff. Thanks for setting us up with him.*

A few minutes later, the reply came in: *You're welcome. Call me after the appointment.*

I will.

TJ put down his phone and tried to go back to his business—in this case, watching a basketball game on TV. But he kept thinking of Bianca, and thinking of her made it hard to concentrate on the game.

He got his phone from the side table and typed in another message: *"We'll see" doesn't mean no. Have you decided whether you're going to go out with me?*

When he didn't get an answer right away, he figured he was probably screwed.

"WHY ARE you staring at that phone?"

Bianca and Martina were at the Cookie Crock, their cart parked in the cereal aisle. Martina was perusing the muesli and granola while Bianca, distracted, frowned at the screen on her iPhone.

"Bianca?"

"*Hmm?*" Bianca didn't look up.

"I've decided we should all go gluten free and vegan," Martina said. "I'm going to buy a box of tree bark, and we're all going to have to eat it."

"That's good," Bianca murmured, still looking at the phone.

"Give me that." Martina snatched the phone out of Bianca's hand,

and Bianca blinked as though she were awakening from a particularly deep nap.

"What? What are you … Give me that." Bianca reached for the phone, but Martina held it out of her reach.

Martina looked at the screen, and her eyes widened. "Ooh."

"May I have my phone?" Bianca held her hand out expectantly.

Martina handed it back. "So, why haven't you answered him?"

"Because I don't know the answer. Let's just … buy cereal."

"How can you not know the answer?" Martina wanted to know. "Either you're still interested in him or you're not."

"It's not that simple."

An elderly woman maneuvered her cart down the aisle, and Martina pushed her own cart aside to make room.

"Dear, can I just get to the shredded wheat?" The woman pointed to the cereal in question with a wrinkled hand.

"Oh. Of course," Martina said as she and Bianca moved fifteen feet down the aisle and continued their conversation.

"Yes, it is that simple," Martina said once they were settled in their new location. "You had a nice time at his place for dinner, right?"

"Yes, but—"

"But what?"

"But I don't think that was a date."

"So what? He wants to have a date. He said so right here." She reached out and tapped the screen of Bianca's phone with her fingernail.

"I know. But I don't think it's a good idea. I'm on the rebound," Bianca said.

"Well, God forbid you should have a good time with a hot guy to help you get over Peter." Martina began ticking points off on her fingers: "TJ is wildly attractive. He's a good father. He's got his own company, and people will always need electricians, so he's got a stable career. And he grew up, Bianca. He's not the teenager who broke your heart anymore."

The shredded wheat woman, who'd been trying to look like she wasn't listening in, turned to them, the box of cereal in her hand.

"You don't want to let go of a reliable electrician on the Central Coast. Trust me. You should marry him."

While Bianca was distracted by that, Martina grabbed the phone out of her hand again. She typed in a text and pressed SEND.

"Oh, my God. What did you say? Martina, I swear ..."

"I said what you should have said days ago." Martina had an annoying smirk on her face, and her loose bun was listing to one side on the top of her head.

Bianca looked at the text her sister had sent: *Name the time and place.*

"Oh, God," Bianca said.

"You're welcome," Martina told her. "Now pick out some cereal so we can get out of here."

THE TIME he named was the next night. The place was The Sandpiper, a restaurant on Moonstone Beach.

Bianca thought about explaining that Martina had sent the text agreeing to the date, not her. But the truth was that she wanted to go. She knew it wasn't wise, but she wanted it.

What would it hurt to be unwise, just this once?

TJ's son was sick, and Bianca could imagine that he needed the chance to think about something else for a while. Something happy. She liked the idea that she could be that happy thing.

This is stupid. You're being stupid.

He hadn't meant to hurt her in high school—she could see that—but regardless of his intention, she'd been crushed into dust by his disregard. She didn't want to be crushed into dust again. And he could do it, if he wanted to. She told herself she was beyond it, that she was grown now and no longer subject to that kind of soul-destroying angst. But the feelings were still there—the flutter in her belly, the warm, syrupy feeling that ran through her when she saw him.

He still had power over her.

Going out with him was risky, and she wasn't sure she wanted that kind of risk, especially so soon after her breakup with Peter. Logic said you needed to take a break from men after ending a long-term relationship. Logic said you needed to take a step back and reassess in order to move forward in a smart, sensible way.

There was nothing logical about throwing yourself at your teenage crush.

Except that I'm not going to throw myself at him. It's just dinner.

What she wanted and what she knew was smart were warring inside her. Usually when that happened, the smart won. Among her sisters, Bianca was the one who could be counted on to do what was sensible and reasonable.

Right now, sensible and reasonable sucked.

15

___

Bianca had thought she might cancel right up until the moment TJ rang the doorbell to pick her up. She could have canceled even then, she supposed, by pleading a sudden stomach virus.

Because her stomach did do funny things when she saw him.

He was wearing nice slacks and a sport jacket over a dress shirt that was open at the throat. He was freshly shaved, his hair combed and possibly newly cut. She'd never seen him dressed up before, and it might have short-circuited her brain. There was a humming in her head that made it hard to think.

"TJ. Hi. You look … nice." *Nice,* because it would have been unwise to say what she really thought—that he looked so good she wanted to strip him naked right there in the doorway.

"You too." She could tell he meant it; the mischievous half-smile on his face suggested that he might be having thoughts that weren't suitable for polite conversation.

Bianca silently sent her thanks to Benny, who'd helped her choose an outfit: black skinny jeans, a loose, silky top with a deep neckline, chunky silver necklace, high-heeled boots.

The jeans were hers, but everything else was Sofia's. Most of what

Bianca owned leaned toward practical instead of sexy. In retrospect, it was an apt metaphor for her relationship with Peter. It had been all practicality and no excitement.

If this thing with TJ went anywhere, she was pretty sure lack of excitement would not be an issue.

THE RESTAURANT WAS ONLY HALF-FULL, which wasn't surprising for an evening in February in the middle of the week. Cambria got tourists year round, but there was a distinct lull during the first few months of the year, when the cold wind blowing in off the ocean made walking on the Moonstone Beach boardwalk an exercise in endurance.

The inside of the restaurant was warm and dim, with subtle lighting and candles in chunky glass jars on the tabletops.

The hostess seated them at a table by the window, but the sun had already set, and where there would have been a stunning view of the ocean, they could now see only their own reflections in the darkened glass.

Once their wine had been served—Chardonnay for her, merlot for him—Bianca asked about Owen's appointment that morning with Dr. DeVries. TJ was so worried that it made his head hurt, and he didn't want to feel that way right now. He wanted to get his mind off it. Still, he knew he had to tell her so they could move past it and he could get to the escape part, if only for one evening.

"He said something about alpha ... Shit, I can't remember. I wrote it down, but I don't have my notes with me."

"Alpha-1-antitrypsin deficiency," she finished for him. "After viral hepatitis, it's the first place I'd look, too."

"Okay." He nodded. "He wants to do a biopsy."

She looked at him with such compassion that it made his chest ache. "I know that's frightening, but it's a safe procedure. It's outpatient, and the risks—"

"Yeah. I'm not worried about the biopsy itself so much as what it might show, you know?"

"I know. But if he does have AAT, that doesn't mean—"

"Bianca?" He rubbed his forehead with his fingers, trying to ease the tension just behind his eyes. "I'd really like to not talk about it anymore right now, if that's okay. The reason I asked you out—besides the fact that I like you—was that I really need to think about something else for a while."

"Oh. Of course."

"Owen's spending the night at a friend's house, so he's having a good time, and I ... I just need to have a good time, too."

She smiled, and the smile made her look like that girl he'd sort of known in high school. Why hadn't he noticed then how great her smile was?

"Let's order." He picked up his menu. "I'm starving."

THEY DIDN'T TALK any further about Owen's illness. They did talk about Owen, though—about what he liked to do, and who his friends were, and how he was doing in school. They talked about Bianca's sisters, and how they'd all started living together in the log cabin after their parents had died and left the house to them. They talked about their jobs: how Bianca had decided to go into medicine, and how TJ had thwarted his parents' desire for him to go to law school by skipping college entirely and becoming a tradesman.

They didn't talk about Penny, and they didn't talk about Peter, except in the context of Owen's health. They'd made a silent agreement that the subject of exes could wait for another day.

Bianca ate seafood pasta, and TJ had a steak, medium rare. The food was good, and the restaurant was full of the low murmur of the other diners, and before either of them realized it, they'd been talking and eating and drinking wine for more than two hours.

There was so much more he wanted to know. He wanted to know how her parents had died, but he didn't want to think about death. He wanted to know how she managed the demands and the stresses of her job, but he didn't want to think about children with serious illnesses. So instead, they talked about the books he liked and the movies she enjoyed; his plans for his business and her interest in traveling to Italy to meet the relatives she'd never known.

By the time he'd paid the check and they were walking out of the restaurant, his hand resting lightly on the small of her back, he felt good for the first time since he'd realized Owen was sick.

He felt light and happy. Since the divorce, he'd almost forgotten what it was like to feel light and happy.

ABOUT HALFWAY THROUGH the main course, Bianca forgot that TJ was the boy who'd thwarted her tender hopes in high school. He stopped being the symbol of her awkward, painful adolescence and started being a real person.

That would have allowed her to relax, finally, and have a good time—if not for the fact that the real person he had become was someone she was desperately attracted to.

She knew she shouldn't compare him to Peter, but when had she ever had this much fun with Peter? When had Peter made her feel so interested, so intrigued?

He paid the bill and walked her out to his truck, then opened the passenger door for her. He was standing so close to her that she could smell the clean scent of soap and warm skin.

A swift breeze had kicked in off the ocean, and it ruffled her hair and gave her a chill as she stood next to him.

"You cold?" His deep voice made something stir at the base of her spine.

"A little." She wanted so much to walk into his arms and let him warm her with his body, but she knew she should get into the truck instead. She hesitated, waiting to see what would happen.

HE KNEW she wanted him to kiss her. Why else was she standing there looking at him that way instead of getting into the truck?

And what the hell was he waiting for?

Tentatively, he reached out and touched her face with the palm of his hand. She leaned into it, and her eyes slipped closed.

It was all the permission he needed. He touched his lips to hers gently, and she let out a soft sigh. The sigh was almost enough to break a man's self-control. But he tried to be a better man than most, so he pulled back a little, waiting.

"Bianca?" He stroked his thumb against the softness of her lower lip.

If he'd had any doubts that she wanted this, they fled as she put her arms around him and kissed him deeply, taking control, taking initiative in a way that was hot as hell.

It only lasted a moment, but it left him stunned, dazzled.

For a long minute after she'd pulled away from him and had gotten into his truck, he stood there reliving the kiss with the breeze chilling his skin, the ocean waves roaring in his ears.

Then he got into the truck, started the engine, and tried to pretend that he hadn't just had his knees knocked out from under him by a woman.

OF COURSE BIANCA'S sisters grilled her about the date when she got home, and she considered trying to put them off. But, really, what was the point? She would deny that anything special had happened, and they would accuse her—correctly—of lying, and she would eventually break down and spill the whole thing.

It just seemed more efficient to eliminate a few steps.

"Yes, he kissed me, and yes, it was incredible," she announced from the doorway before she'd even taken off her coat. "Any questions?"

Sofia, Benny, Martina, and Patrick all froze amid their various activities and stared at her. Benny had been watching something on

TV, and she reached for the remote and turned it off, so the only sound in the room was the echo of Bianca's pronouncement.

"Hell, yes, I've got questions." Benny rubbed her hands together in glee. "I thought I was going to have to pry it out of you. Sit your ass down and let's get started."

~

TEN MINUTES LATER, Bianca had filled them in on the details. By now, she'd shed her coat and put away her purse, and she was sitting on the sofa with a glass of wine, her shoes kicked off under the coffee table.

"It was nice. Really nice. Just sitting and talking to him, and eating a good meal. And he didn't take twenty minutes with the menu! Let me tell you, that alone ..."

"Yeah, yeah." Sofia made a rolling *move along* motion with her hand. "Let's get to the kiss."

"Ah ... should I leave for this part?" Patrick was just coming into the living room from the kitchen with a mug of tea.

"No, you're fine," Bianca told him. "You're about to be family. You might as well practice dealing with our issues."

"Still. I think I have some ... socks to fold." He vanished down the hallway toward Sofia's room before anyone could object.

"Wimp!" Benny called after him.

"I don't think I've ever dated a man who actually folded socks," Martina mused.

"Let's get back to the point," Sofia said. "The kiss."

Bianca sighed and looked at the wineglass in her hands. "I'd pretty much convinced myself that the real TJ could never match up to the Troy fantasy. You know? I thought that when and if we actually kissed, it wouldn't be anything like what I imagined."

"And?" Benny leaned forward in her seat.

"And ... my bones melted. That's what it felt like—like my bones actually melted. Like everything in my body went all hot and liquid, and there were cartoon birds flying around tweeting the theme from *Dr. Zhivago*. This is bad. This is really bad."

"Yeah. That's freaking tragic," Benny quipped dryly. "You should join a support group."

"You don't get it!" Bianca said. "Part of me thought that if I just got to know him ... or, yes, maybe if I kissed him ... the spell would be broken. I'd see that he's just a regular guy with—I don't know—with bad breath or annoying habits, or that he was a really bad kisser. But he's not a bad kisser, Benny. He's not!"

"So, he's a better kisser than Peter?" Martina asked.

It was tempting to say that Peter's kisses and TJ's were only related insofar as they both could be classified as the same basic act. That Peter's kisses were fine—they were competent—but that comparing them to TJ's would be like comparing steamed broccoli to warm chocolate ganache.

But Bianca didn't want to bad-mouth Peter. He hadn't done anything wrong, and he didn't deserve it. Instead, she fumbled the question.

"Peter's not ... He's just ... This isn't ..."

"Yes, TJ's a better kisser than Peter," Sofia cut in. "I'm not sure Peter has ever rendered her incoherent."

Bianca didn't argue the point. Instead, she tried to get them all to focus on the real issue. "Can we please discuss the fact that the birds and the theme song are going to turn my brain to jelly and make me do stupid things I'll regret for the rest of my life? Can we just address that for a moment?"

Sofia cocked her head to the side, considering the question. "I seem to recall that when I was afraid to commit to Patrick, you were one of the people telling me to get my head out of my butt and take a chance on him."

"I never told you to get your head out of your butt," Bianca said.

"Yeah, that was me," Benny added.

"In any case," Sofia went on, "it was good advice. What if he's worth it? What if it turns out to be real? Do you really want to turn your back on that just because it compromises your all-important need to control things?"

Bianca blinked a few times. "I don't have an all-important need to control things."

Martina let out a rude scoffing noise.

Benny coughed loudly into her hand, and the cough sounded suspiciously like the word *bullshit*.

"Do I?" Bianca asked doubtfully.

"It's something to think about," Sofia said.

16

———————

TJ knew he had to get his mind off the kiss and focus on his son. The biopsy was scheduled for the day after tomorrow, and Owen had to be scared. TJ needed to show up for his son; he needed to be a good, attentive father. It would be hard to do that if he was busy wondering how Bianca looked naked.

"It's going to be a piece of cake," TJ said to Owen as he drove him home from school the afternoon after the date. "They won't even need to put you under. And you won't have to stay at the hospital overnight—it's just like a doctor's appointment."

"I know, Dad. You told me. Three times." Owen was looking out the window and not at TJ.

"Okay, well ... I just want you to know it's going to be okay. You don't have to be worried." TJ glanced at Owen as he drove through town toward Pine Knolls. Owen was slumped in his seat, a sullen look on his face. Teenagers were supposed to be sullen, weren't they? TJ told himself not to make too much of it.

Still, not all teenagers were about to have a piece of their liver extracted.

"You know it's not going to hurt that much, right?" TJ tried.

"Yeah."

"You just seem kinda …"

"I'm not worried that it's gonna *hurt*, Dad." Owen looked at him as though TJ were being unbearably dense—which, maybe he was. "I'm worried about what the test is gonna *say*. I'm not an idiot. I know that a biopsy means they think I have cancer."

Was that what he thought? Even the word *cancer* in relation to his son was like a gut punch.

"Owen, where did you get that? Nobody's saying it's cancer."

"But they're not saying it *isn't*, are they? They don't know what it is. And they're doing a biopsy, so you do the math."

In that moment, TJ realized that he'd been handling this all wrong. He'd thought the smart move was to tell Owen only what he needed to know, when he needed to know it. But Owen wasn't a kindergartner anymore. He wasn't a toddler.

He had Google, and he knew how to use it.

When they got home, Owen lugged his backpack into the house and TJ let Gary out to pee on the trunk of an oak tree in the front yard. When that was done, TJ decided to make another attempt to talk to his son about his condition—this time without bungling it.

Owen was already in his room with the door closed.

"Owen?" TJ knocked softly on the bedroom door.

No answer.

"Owen?" He knocked louder.

When he still didn't get a response, TJ opened the door and peeked inside. Owen was lying on his belly on the bed, a pair of noise-canceling earphones on his head. TJ went to the bed and sat down on the edge next to his son. Owen looked up at him and took off the earphones.

"What?" he said.

"I'm sorry I let you think it was cancer," TJ said. "For the record, nobody—not Dr. Russo, and not Dr. DeVries—has said the word *cancer* to me, even once."

Owen shrugged. But there was fear in his face that he was trying to hide under a mask of irritated indifference.

TJ had tried saying little in an effort to shield Owen. That hadn't worked. It was time to tell him what he knew, and what he didn't.

"Look. We know something's wrong with your liver, but we don't know what it is. Liver cancer in kids your age is super rare. It's much more likely to be something else. The biopsy is going to help them figure it out, that's all."

"Something else, like what?" Owen had dropped his defensive tone and was looking at TJ with earnestness and fear.

"Well ... there are a few hereditary diseases they're looking at. With what's going on with your grandmother, it seems likely that something might have gotten passed down to you."

"But Mom's worried that Grandma's going to die. That's what she said."

TJ's heart hurt as he looked at his son. The one thing he was supposed to do as a parent—the only thing—was to protect his boy. But he couldn't protect him from this, and that made TJ feel like a profound failure. It made him feel helpless.

"Whatever your grandmother has, it wasn't caught until she was pretty sick. With you, we're hoping that we're catching it early, so it can be treated."

Please, God, let it be treatable.

"So, if they'd caught it early, Grandma would be okay?" Owen looked hopeful for the first time, and it was tempting to lie to him. But TJ knew he couldn't do that.

"I don't know. They're still not even sure what's causing her illness, so ... I don't know."

Owen rolled onto his back and looked at the ceiling. "I'm scared."

TJ reached out and brushed a lock of hair from Owen's forehead. "Me too. But we're going to do whatever has to be done, okay? Whatever we have to do to diagnose this and treat it, that's what we're going to do."

"Okay." He looked at TJ. "Dad?"

"*Hmm?*"

"I want Mom."

"Do you want to call her?"

"I just really want to see her."

TJ nodded. "She's coming for the biopsy." He ruffled Owen's hair with his hand. "She'll be there holding your hand."

Owen grimaced. "I don't need her to *hold my hand*, Dad. I'm not a little kid. I just wouldn't mind seeing her, that's all."

TJ knew his divorce had been the right thing. He knew it had been inevitable. And he knew that both he and Penny were likely better off as a result. But none of that lifted the weight of guilt he felt for putting Owen into a broken home.

It hadn't been Owen's fault that his parents had married too early, or that they'd been unable to keep their shit together for the long haul. But now he was the one feeling the worst consequences of it.

Of course the kid needed his mom.

Right now, TJ needed his own mom pretty badly.

TJ HAD a break in his schedule the next day, after a homeowner with outdated wiring forgot about their appointment, leaving TJ standing on the guy's doorstep to find that no one was home.

The place just happened to be two blocks from TJ's parents' house, so he made a detour over there on his way to his next job.

He'd brought Gary to work with him, because the dog had been growing more and more attached to TJ and had taken to whimpering pitifully whenever TJ left the house.

At his parents' house, he helped Gary out of the truck and the two of them went up the front walkway and onto the porch. TJ could hear his mother inside, talking to someone on the phone.

"Well, no, Loretta. I hosted last year, so it's somebody else's turn. Why can't Jean do it?"

TJ went in the front door without knocking, Gary following timidly behind.

When Lily saw him, she smiled in a way that transformed her. And that made TJ feel like an ass for not coming by more often.

"Oh, hi, sweetie," she said. Then, into the phone: "Loretta? I've got to call you back. Troy's here."

"I really wish you wouldn't call me Troy," he said when she'd disconnected the call.

"Well, it's your name, son."

"One I haven't used in more than ten years."

"I don't know why not. It's a perfectly good name." Lily, who didn't have a dog herself but who'd fallen in love with Gary the moment they'd met, went to her kitchen cupboard, found a box of Milk-Bones she kept just for him, and offered him two biscuits.

Gary took the biscuits gingerly into his mouth, went to the living room rug, deposited the biscuits on top of the floral-patterned wool, and lay down to eat them.

"What, he gets a snack and not me?" TJ teased.

"You can get your own snack," Lily said. "And Troy's a fine name. Why, I can't help it if I was in love with Troy Donahue. You should have seen him back in his prime. That wavy blond hair. And those eyes!"

"Yeah, yeah." But TJ couldn't help smiling at the story. The thought of his mother as a young woman, fresh and full of girlish dreams about a handsome movie star, made him wish he could have known her then. She'd been a beauty, he knew from the photo albums she brought out from time to time, and she still had the fine, almost regal features that had surely enraptured his father when they'd met.

"Where's Dad?"

"Oh, he's with his club." She waved a hand airily. "You know how he is. They're getting ready for the wildflower show this weekend."

TJ's father had been a member of a local naturalist group for the past several years—ever since retirement had left him with not enough to do. TJ imagined him in his sun hat and hiking boots, happily snipping specimens.

Lily waited until TJ was settled at the kitchen table with a bottle of Coke from the refrigerator and a couple of cookies from the jar on the counter. Then, with a line of worry set deep between her eyebrows, she asked about her grandson.

"So ... how is he?"

TJ shrugged, his eyes on the table so he wouldn't have to look at his mother. "I don't know. The biopsy's tomorrow. That'll tell us more, I guess."

"Is he scared? He must be scared."

"He is, but he's trying to keep it together. We both are."

"I can come to the surgery center to be with the two of you, if you think he'd like that. I can hold his hand, or—"

"Thanks, Mom. But Penny's going to be there, so it's going to be a crowd already. Plus, I don't want to freak Owen out any more than he already is. If everybody shows up, he's going to think he's dying."

He'd delivered the line casually enough, but that last word felt thick in his throat. He blinked a few times to clear the heat that was building up in his eyes, then did his best to change the tone.

"Anyway, you'd probably try to counsel me and Penny if all of us were in the same room, so ..."

"Would that be so wrong?"

TJ was at peace with his divorce. His mother, though, saw it differently. To her, the breakup was baffling, unfathomable. She saw the split as a foolish and impulsive move that could, and would, be corrected when everyone came to their senses.

"It would be pointless, that's all. And, anyway, I don't want you pressuring Penny. She's got a lot going on right now, with her mother."

"How is Beverly?" Lily asked. Before the divorce, Lily had gotten along well with Penny's mother. TJ thought it was too bad they hadn't been able to maintain their friendship after the split, but it made sense, given the fact that the women were on opposite teams: Team Penny vs. Team TJ.

"Not good." TJ took a swig of his Coke and shook his head. "It's not encouraging."

"Oh, honey." Lily looked close to tears.

"You could go see her, you know."

For a moment, she looked hopeful—as though she'd been wanting just that but hadn't dared to imagine it might happen. Then her face hardened. "I don't think so."

Beverly had supported Penny's decision to leave the marriage, and that, to Lily, had been unforgivable. Lily sincerely hoped for Beverly's recovery—TJ knew that—but the tension between the two women was thick and stifling.

"You know, Mom … you don't have to be mad at Beverly, or at Penny, for that matter. I've moved on. It would be nice if you could, too."

"*Hmm.*" The sound didn't indicate that Lily was seriously considering what TJ had said—only that she was acknowledging that he'd said it. "Speaking of moving on … how is Bianca Russo?"

TJ hadn't told her that he'd gone out with Bianca. He certainly hadn't told her they'd kissed. And he hadn't told her that whenever he wasn't thinking about Owen, he was thinking about Bianca.

So how did she know?

"She's fine, I guess." He tried to sound casual.

"You guess?"

"Well … yeah."

"So you didn't go out to dinner with her?" Lily looked at TJ with scorn. "Carolyn Parker's daughter is the hostess at The Sandpiper. She told me the two of you were there together. Are you going to tell me that was a meeting to discuss Owen's care?"

"Ah, jeez," TJ muttered. "Remind me why I moved back to Cambria again?" In San Jose, he could have dated anyone he wanted and remained anonymous. Here, if he blew his nose on Main Street his mother would call to ask if he was sick.

"TJ, honey, how do you expect to get back together with Penny if you're going around with other women like … like Bianca Russo?" She said the name as though it had a bad taste.

"I don't expect to get back together with Penny, Mom. That's what I've been telling you."

"Well. It could happen if you wanted it enough."

What he wanted, at the moment, was to stop talking about it. He changed the subject. "So, Mom, how are things with Friends of the Library?"

17

Bianca hadn't planned to go to the biopsy. TJ hadn't asked her to—in fact, they hadn't discussed such a thing at all. But the procedure was scheduled for a Friday afternoon, which just happened to be a time when Bianca's office was closed. And she was worried about Owen. And the more she thought about it, the more it seemed to her that TJ might need the support.

Plus, her sisters had been right that she was controlling. She knew it was irrational—Peter was an excellent doctor—but she couldn't help feeling that things would go more smoothly if she were there to keep an eye on the proceedings.

When she walked into the surgical center, TJ and Owen were still sitting in the waiting room, both of them looking nervous. Owen was fidgeting with his cell phone, and TJ was staring at the wall, his left knee jiggling with nervous energy.

As she always tried to do with her patients, she greeted Owen first.

"Owen, hi. How are you feeling?" She sat down in a vacant chair next to him.

"Okay, I guess." But he didn't look okay. He looked jaundiced, and he looked frightened.

TJ looked at her with surprise. "Bianca. What are you doing here? I didn't expect—"

"If me being here is overstepping, I'll go. But I wanted to make sure everything went well, and I thought … Well, I thought you might like to see a friendly face."

"Yeah." TJ rubbed at the stubble on his chin. He looked like he hadn't slept much the night before. "Yeah, it's good to see you. You want some water? I could use some water."

TJ got up and went down a short hallway to a water cooler with a stack of paper cups on top of it. Bianca followed him.

He filled a cup with water, drank, and then threw the cup into the trash. He sighed deeply and ran a hand through his hair.

"Are you okay?" she asked.

"I'm … jeez. I'm holding it together, but just barely."

She put a hand on his face, went up onto her toes, and kissed him. Just once, and just for a moment, to reassure him. To comfort him.

When they turned to go back to the sitting area, TJ froze. Bianca looked up at him to see what was wrong, then she followed his gaze to the waiting room, where a woman she vaguely recognized was standing with her arms crossed, glaring at him.

"Oh. Hi, Penny," he said.

Bianca hadn't known that Penny was coming. Hell, she hadn't known *she* was coming until she'd made the decision at the last minute. Now, her own presence seemed like a spectacularly bad idea.

"TJ, I'd better go. I didn't mean … I'll just say goodbye to Owen. I'll call you later, okay?"

If she'd thought she could get past Penny without a conversation, she was mistaken.

"Bianca Russo, isn't it?" Penny put out a hand, limp-fish style, for Bianca to shake. "I'd say it's good to see you again, but under the circumstances, awkward is more like it."

"Hi, Penny." Bianca shook the boneless hand. "I just came to make sure Owen was in good hands. Which he is. So I'll just ..." She pointed to the front door to indicate her intention to get the hell out of there as fast as her low-heeled pumps would carry her.

"TJ, can I talk to you?" Penny grabbed his arm and hauled him into the hallway where the water cooler was.

Bianca looked at the two of them, at the angry set of Penny's jaw and the defensive way TJ was standing with his arms crossed over his chest. Then she looked at Owen, who had been scared before but who now was both scared and apprehensive about whether his parents were about to have a fight.

It didn't seem right to just leave him there.

She sat beside him and tried to engage him in small talk about school, movies—anything she could think of.

"So, Owen, does Mr. Davies still teach at the middle school? Because when I was there—"

"When your son needs a doctor, this is what you do? You take him to see your *girlfriend*?" Penny's voice carried to where Bianca was sitting.

Bianca couldn't hear TJ's entire response, as he said it under his breath, but she did hear the phrase, "not my girlfriend." It was true, considering that they'd just started seeing each other. Still, it hurt to hear.

Owen, gamely trying to hold up his end of the conversation, said something about how he didn't know a Mr. Davies, but he had a Mr. Davis. They were not the same person.

Penny was pointing a finger at TJ's chest, and she poked him with it to emphasize key words she was saying to him. "You are *not* going to *compromise* our son's *care* just because you're *sleeping* with his *doctor*." Poke, poke, poke, poke, poke.

"I am not sleeping with her," TJ hissed. Again, true enough. But the vehemence with which he said it suggested that he wasn't even considering such a thing. Bianca sure as hell had been considering it.

"Oh, boy." Owen looked miserably at his parents and then at Bianca. "Are you? Sleeping with my dad, I mean?"

"No. No, we're just … we're friends," Bianca said. Part true, part lie. The scorecard was getting confusing.

"I'm taking him home. I'm taking him home right now," Penny said.

"No, you're not," TJ countered. "He needs the biopsy. You're not going to keep him from getting it just because you're pissed, Pen. And there's nothing going on—not really. You're pissed about *nothing*."

The receptionist, who'd been watching it all with first concern and then alarm, slipped into a back room. Moments later, Peter emerged dressed in blue scrubs, looking bewildered.

"Mr. Davenport, hello." He turned to Penny and extended his hand. "I'm Dr. DeVries."

"I'm Penny Davenport. Well, DeLuca now. Owen's mother. I was just telling TJ that Owen and I are leaving." She left Peter's hand just hanging there, partnerless.

"Is there a problem?" Peter said.

"The problem is that my ex is thinking with his dick," Penny announced.

That was when Peter noticed Bianca in the waiting room. "Bianca? What are you doing here?"

"I just … I thought …" Bianca stammered.

"She's here because she's sleeping with Owen's father," Penny supplied.

"I told you, she's not," TJ said.

"What?" Peter looked stunned. "Bianca? Are you?"

"What do you care what she does?" Penny wanted to know.

Peter looked at Penny, his face now studiously blank. "I suppose I care because she just broke up with me." He turned to Bianca. "Is he the reason? Were you already seeing him?"

AFTER THAT, everyone started talking at once. The receptionist herded them all into a conference room—except for Owen. She led him away, patting his shoulder and speaking softly to him.

Peter told them that he didn't have a lot of time to sort out everyone's personal lives because he had patients lined up back-to-back. There was some yelling, some accusations, and some pleading, and amid it all, the two doctors agreed on one thing: Owen needed the biopsy, and it would be both reckless and stupid to delay it because of the various parties' relationships to one another.

Owen's parents finally conceded the point—TJ gratefully, Penny grudgingly. Peter shot Bianca a glare, then went into professional mode with TJ and Penny, reassuring them that regardless of any feelings he might have about all that had happened, he would give Owen the best of care.

Bianca left just as Owen was being prepped for the procedure.

As she was heading to her car, stinging tears threatening to spill from her eyes, she heard TJ running up behind her.

"Bianca? Bianca, wait."

She took a deep, steadying breath, and turned to face him. "TJ, I'm sorry about this. All of this. I shouldn't have come. You and Penny need to focus on Owen."

"It was nice that you came. It was sweet that you wanted to see if we were okay. I appreciate it. It's just …"

It's just that you and Penny and Owen are a family, Bianca mentally concluded for him.

"I get it," she said. "Just go back in there and take care of your son."

BIANCA KNEW PETER WOULD CALL, but she'd thought he would at least wait until the end of the work day. Instead, he barely waited until she'd gotten home.

"What the hell was that, Bianca?" he asked as soon as she picked up the call.

"How did Owen's biopsy go?" Because that was all that was important, in her mind. That was the thing that mattered.

"Are you going to answer my question?" he said.

"Yes. After you answer mine."

He let out a tired sigh, and she could picture him doing that thing he did—pinching the bridge of his nose as though all of his troubles and anxieties lived there.

"All right. The biopsy went fine. It was routine. It'll take a couple of days for the pathology report, but ..."

"Okay. Thank you." The results of the biopsy might not turn out to be what they wanted, but at least the procedure itself hadn't caused any problems—which sometimes happened. That, at least, was a relief.

"Now tell me what's going on. Are you dating Owen Davenport's father?"

"I ... we ... sort of." When she'd awakened this morning, that question would have seemed like a simple one. Yes, they were dating. But after she'd heard him downplay things between them to Penny, nothing seemed straightforward anymore.

"Right. Okay. Is that why you broke up with me? Were you already seeing him?" The hurt and indignation in Peter's voice made a guilt headache start at the back of her head, even though she hadn't done what he was accusing her of.

"No. I didn't go out with him until later."

"Not much later, though," he shot back. "I mean, you got right on it, Bianca. So I can only assume that he was around before then, even if you hadn't actually started dating yet."

She couldn't deny that, so she didn't say anything.

"That's what I thought," he said, in answer to her silence.

"Look, Peter. Owen Davenport has nothing to do with this. None of this is his fault. If you can't give him the best treatment ... I mean, if you can't keep him as a patient because of me ..."

Peter scoffed. "What kind of unprofessional, unethical, sorry excuse for a doctor do you take me for? Of course I can do my job. Of course I'm going to give that boy the best care I can. I'm offended that you'd suggest otherwise."

And he would do an excellent job with Owen, she knew that. She was ashamed that she'd even brought it up.

"But while we're on the subject of professional ethics," Peter said, "should you really be his primary care physician? I mean, you obviously have a conflict of interest. If anybody's acting out of line here from a professional standpoint, it's you."

Bianca closed her eyes and tried to think serene thoughts. "Peter, I'm sorry I said what I did. I trust your medical judgment completely. I hope you'll offer me the same courtesy."

"Yeah, well. Don't bring your personal drama into my workplace again, Bianca. I mean it." And he hung up on her.

Now that he'd had his say, she thought he'd be all right. That was one angry, offended person she could check off her list. Now she just had Penny DeLuca to deal with.

TJ AND PENNY managed to delay the rest of the fight until after Owen's procedure. He had to stay at the surgical center for a while after the operation to make sure there were no problems. Then, TJ took him home to rest, and Penny followed—ostensibly to make sure that Owen was settled in and had everything he needed, but TJ suspected that she only came so she could yell at him.

She got her chance once Owen was lying comfortably in bed with his hand-held game console, as TJ walked her out to her car.

"You know," she said, "if this is the way you're going to handle things, it might be best if Owen comes back to live with me."

TJ had expected her to drop that particular bomb, but he hadn't expected it so soon. She'd flung it out there first thing in a daring act of post-divorce aggression that left him angry and defensive.

"If this is the ... Jesus, Penny. I'm handling things just fine. He had the test, didn't he? He's seeing the specialist. There's a problem, and I saw it, and I'm on it. What the hell else do you want?"

TJ was only now realizing how exhausted Penny looked. She took off her glasses, rubbed her eyes, then put the glasses back on. "I want you to make decisions based on what's best for Owen, not based on the fact that his doctor is a hot piece of ass."

"Don't talk about her that way." He was surprised at the vehemence in his own voice. He'd jabbed his finger toward her face for emphasis, and now he let his hand fall.

"Really," Penny said.

"Really what?" It came out more angry than he'd intended.

"The way you're defending her—standing up for her honor. You've got feelings. I thought you were just screwing her, but ..." She shrugged, looking defeated.

"I'm not screwing her," TJ said, not bothering to deny the other stuff. Why should he, when Penny was pretty much right about it?

"Ah, bullshit."

"No, really. I'm not. It hasn't gotten that far. It's ... new."

"But you like her."

"Yeah. Yeah, I really do."

At some point, TJ and Penny had stopped fighting and had started talking, as though they were friends, or at least people who didn't resent each other.

"Well." A tear slipped down Penny's cheek, and she wiped it away. "I won't pretend it doesn't hurt that you're moving on."

"You will, too," he said. "You've got a lot going on with your mom, but when you're ready, you'll do it."

"I guess." She let out a ragged breath. He wanted to hug her—just to comfort her—but he was afraid it would be misinterpreted, and he didn't want that. Instead, he stuffed his hands into his pockets and looked down at the sidewalk between his feet. A breeze ruffled through the oak trees, causing a small flock of birds to rise into the air and fly away.

"Did you mean what you said about Owen? About taking him to live with you? Because I can handle this, Penny, whatever this is. You can trust me."

Penny shrugged and shook her head. "I was angry. That's all. What's happening with Mom is awful. I don't want him to see that, especially when he ..." She didn't say the rest of it: *especially when he might be facing the same thing.* "I miss him so damned much, TJ." Her eyes were red, and she blinked hard.

"If you need more time with him ..."

"Yeah." She nodded. "Yeah, let's talk."

The fact that they *could* talk—about this or anything else—was a small miracle. TJ had seen other people's divorces and the toxic levels of anger and spite that came with them. At first, it had seemed like it might go that way between him and Penny. When the split was new, TJ had foreseen a future of fighting, court battles, and seething hostility.

But then Beverly had gotten sick, and all of that had fallen away. Penny had stopped fighting with him—probably because she could only think about her mother—and TJ had been gentle with her, not wanting to add to the stress she was under.

The result was something as prized and delicate as a rare butterfly: a mostly amicable divorce.

He said goodbye to Penny and headed back into the house to check on his son.

18

Bianca didn't see TJ much over the next couple of days. She tried not to obsess about it, knowing he was probably preoccupied with Owen. But after what had happened at the surgical center, she couldn't help thinking maybe her relationship with TJ was over before it had really started.

If he thought getting to know Bianca wasn't worth the fight with his ex, could she really blame him? In her work, she'd seen what happened to kids when their parents went through an acrimonious split. How many times had she been told not to give any information to the noncustodial parent? How many times had she been asked to call the police if the other parent so much as showed his or her face?

And that didn't even include the more routine situations: the arguments in the waiting room; the difficulties scheduling appointments around shifting visitation schedules; the disputes over what course of treatment the various parties wanted Bianca to pursue for their children.

If Bianca were in that situation, she would want to do whatever she could to shield her child from the negative effects. If that meant walking away from a relationship in its fragile early days, wouldn't she do it? Wouldn't she at least consider it?

When she added in the fact that he'd downplayed what was going on between them—practically dismissing it when he'd talked to Penny—well, that didn't make Bianca optimistic about her future with TJ.

She didn't call, and she didn't text. Her pride prevented it, as well as her sensitivity to all TJ had going on with Owen.

But that didn't mean she'd stopped thinking—or brooding.

The brooding hadn't escaped her sisters' notice, and they were starting to get annoyed.

"For God's sake, just call him," Benny said.

The four of them were sitting around a table at a restaurant in San Luis Obispo, where Benny had insisted they go a week later on Saturday night to get Bianca out of the house—somewhere other than work. Sofia had left Patrick at home watching a movie with his friend Ramon, and everyone but Bianca was in a festive mood. Cocktails had been ordered, and most of them—except for Martina, in her Birkenstocks—had hauled out their cute shoes for the occasion.

The restaurant, a trendy Japanese fusion place downtown, was packed with locals, college students, and tourists, and Benny had to raise her voice to be heard over the din.

"I mean, seriously," Benny went on. "You're adults. Just talk to the man."

"No." Bianca was slumped in her seat, staring at the brightly colored drink in front of her. "He's got a lot going on. Plus, he said it was nothing. So, what would I even talk to him about, if this whole thing is just … nothing?"

Sofia rolled her eyes. "You know he just said that to placate Penny. He'd have said anything to calm her down."

"Yeah, well … what he said was that this thing between us is insignificant. And he's right. We haven't slept together. We've only seen each other twice. We've barely kissed."

"Then why have you been moping for the past week?" Martina asked. "It wasn't nothing to you, or you wouldn't look so … so *sad*."

"She looks exactly the way she did in high school after TJ started dating Penny," Benny told Martina. "She's got that same miserable expression. Except then, she used to lock herself in her room for hours on end, crying."

"I'm not moping, and I'm not miserable," Bianca protested. She took a long drink of her fruity cocktail to demonstrate her willingness to have fun—or at least to get a little drunk. Now that she considered it, plunging into an alcoholic haze seemed like a viable plan.

"Speaking of miserable," Sofia put in, "I'm supposed to FaceTime Patrick's mother tomorrow to talk about the wedding."

"I thought you liked Patrick's mom," Martina said.

"I do," Sofia said. "I really do. It's just ... She doesn't get the thing about us having the wedding Mom planned. Or, she says she does, but she still keeps suggesting changes. Why can't we just tweak this? Or modify that?" Sofia slumped into her seat. "She wants to put her mark on the wedding, which I get. But I want it to be the way Mom imagined it. I know she imagined it for you, Bianca, not me, but ..."

Bianca, who was sitting next to Sofia, reached out and took her sister's hand. "She'd be thrilled that you're using her plan. No matter who she made it for."

Sofia swallowed hard. "I just don't want Patrick's mom changing everything. But then I feel bad about that, because of course she wants to contribute. Of course she wants to be a part of it. He's her *son*."

"Well," Martina said, "traditionally, the mother of the bride plans the wedding and the mother of the groom plans the rehearsal dinner. So, that's something she can do that won't cut into Mom's plan."

"We weren't going to have a rehearsal dinner," Sofia said.

"Oh, you have to," Benny said. "Martina's right. It's the only thing the mother of the groom gets to do. You can't take it away from her. It's your ticket out of mother-in-law jail."

Thinking about weddings made Bianca think about TJ's wedding to Penny—which made her jealous as hell. That wasn't fair, but there it was.

Benny was looking at her, noticing the incoming storm in Bianca's expression. "You know, you should flirt," she said. "After this, we should go to Ted's or someplace, and you should flirt with some guys who aren't TJ. It'll make you feel better."

"I don't want to flirt," Bianca said.

"Shocker," Sofia said dryly. "But you have to loosen up sometime. You can't be super-controlling, super-together Bianca all the time."

Was that really how they saw her? Because Bianca didn't feel super together. And most of the time, her efforts to control the things in her life fell disastrously flat. The idea that her sisters viewed her that way—and saw it as something to criticize her for—made her want to show them how wrong they were.

"Okay, I'll flirt," she said. "But not at Ted's. That place is a craphole."

THEY SETTLED on a trendy club on Higuera Street in San Luis Obispo, a place with exposed brick and heavy wood beams, somewhere that attracted the vegan, hemp-wearing crowd as well as students and tourists.

The four of them found a table near a back corner of the room, far enough away from the speaker system that they could hear each other talk, but close enough to the action that Sofia, Benny, and Martina could peruse the flirting potential for Bianca.

Bianca was going to order a club soda—she'd had a strong drink at the restaurant—but the others urged her to try the cocktail that was on special that night, something called a SLO-tini that was made with gin, pineapple juice, and a variety of other ingredients whose flavors and purposes were a mystery to Bianca.

Martina, the most health-conscious among them and, therefore, the least likely to enjoy a SLO-tini, had stopped after a single drink more than an hour ago and had agreed to drive everyone home, so there was no reason Bianca couldn't indulge.

"All right. Give me one of those SLO-tini things," Bianca told the waitress.

The club was dim and the crowd was lively. The noise level was loud enough to be festive but not so loud as to be deafening. Bianca tried to get into the spirit of things, but she couldn't seem to stop thinking about TJ.

"This is dumb," she told her sisters. "So what if I'm thinking about TJ? So what? Why does that mean I have to"—she gestured vaguely toward the crowd—"act stupid and rub my boobs against strange men?"

"Who said anything about rubbing your boobs against people?" Benny wanted to know. "I said you should flirt. Boob-rubbing is a whole other level."

"And I don't think acting stupid is required," Martina observed.

"Look," Sofia put in. "We're just saying you should have some fun, think about other things for a while. That's all. But, jeez, you're really hung up on TJ, aren't you?" She rubbed Bianca's arm in sympathy.

That was what did it. Bianca couldn't have her sisters thinking she was heartbroken again, the way she'd been in high school. She didn't want to seem pathetic now, the way she had then. If flirting with other men was what it was going to take to convince her sisters she wasn't pining over TJ, then flirting would happen.

The waitress brought the drinks, and Bianca took a fortifying gulp of her SLO-tini, which was stronger than she'd anticipated. She gasped a little as she put down the drink.

"No," she said. "I am not hung up on TJ. And I'm not sad about Peter. I'm not ... anything. I'm just here, trying to have a good time with my sisters. Is that so damned wrong?" She was aware that she sounded slightly hysterical.

"Um ... no. It's not wrong," Martina said. "But maybe slow down on the SLO-tini."

Bianca took another slug of her drink just to be defiant, then got up from her seat and went into the crowd to find someone to flirt with.

IT DIDN'T TAKE LONG.

If Bianca had stayed at her table, men would have come to them. She knew this from experience. But the men in question would have gravitated straight toward Sofia—she knew that from experience, too.

Sofia had the kind of ostentatious good looks that got men in trouble with their girlfriends when they saw her and couldn't help doing a double-take. Next to her, Bianca looked like somebody's mild-mannered English teacher.

Away from Sofia, Bianca thought she'd do pretty well—or maybe not. She reassessed what she'd worn that night and thought the English teacher thing wasn't far off. White shirt buttoned almost to the throat, cardigan sweater, jeans and boots, hair in a loose bun.

She went back to the table and looked at her sisters helplessly. "Why didn't anyone tell me I look like a librarian?"

"You look like a nice librarian," Benny said helpfully. "The kind who always helps people find obscure facts. Or used to, before the Internet."

"Lose the cardigan, and unbutton that top a little," Sofia instructed her. "And for God's sake, let your hair down. Nothing says *librarian* like a bun."

Feeling stupid, Bianca nonetheless did as she was told.

"Here, take these." Martina slipped a line of gold bangle bracelets off her wrist and handed them to Bianca, who put them on.

"And this." Sofia handed her a tube of lipstick in a raspberry color that complemented Sofia's coloring beautifully—so it likely would do the same for Bianca's. She put it on using the camera function on her phone.

"There. How do I look?"

Benny appraised her. "*Hmm.* Now you're a hot librarian."

Bianca moved out into the room scouting for interesting prospects. The crowd here was different from the usual ones in Cambria: younger and more hip, with a good sprinkling of students from the college.

The youth of the crowd in comparison to Bianca's comparative maturity discouraged her at first, until she saw a likely candidate standing at the bar. He had his back to her so she couldn't see his face, but from the rear, things looked promising. Good quality clothing, nice haircut, a body that looked trim and fit. And something about the way he held himself said he was at least in his thirties, maybe forties. She gave herself a mental pep talk and moved in.

She slid onto the barstool next to the guy and turned to him to say, "Is this seat taken?" But she only got as far as "Is this seat" before he turned to look at her, and she froze.

"Bianca?"

"Peter."

Was there any graceful way to back away? Probably not. The only polite thing to do was engage in a minimal amount of small talk before excusing herself.

"How are you?" she tried.

Peter scowled. "I suppose you're here with Owen Davenport's father. So, where is he?"

"I'm not, actually. I'm here with my sisters."

"Terrific. I picked the wrong place to come for a drink. I suppose the four of you talk about what an uptight pain in the ass I am. Don't deny it—I know you do. And, hell, maybe I am." His shoulders fell, and he stared into his drink. Now that she thought of it, she was surprised to see him holding a highball glass with a finger of amber liquid inside it—usually he drank nothing harder than wine.

"Peter? Are you okay?"

"Why wouldn't I be? I'm fine. I'm always fine."

Bianca felt a twinge of guilt, knowing she'd hurt Peter. At the time of their breakup, she'd figured he would be fine. It wasn't that she thought he was insensitive to pain—of course he wasn't—but he'd always approached their relationship with such matter-of-fact pragmatism that it had never occurred to her that he was emotionally invested.

Now, she knew she'd miscalculated.

"Peter, about us. I never meant to—"

"What do you mean, 'us'? There is no us. Not anymore." He took a healthy slug of his drink, then winced as it went down.

"I know you're upset about me ending things," she said. "But drinking isn't going to solve anything."

His eyebrows rose. "What, this?" He held up his drink. "You think I'm drinking to forget about you?" He shook his head. "No. I've had a crappy day, that's all. Got some tests back from the lab and had to tell a father that his son is dying. Puts a bad relationship into perspective, doesn't it?"

Bianca suddenly felt ice cold, and a hard knot of dread gathered in her stomach. "Oh, God. Not Owen Davenport? Please tell me he—"

"No." He shook his head again. "Not Owen Davenport. In fact, your boyfriend's kid is going to be okay."

She blinked a few times. "What?"

He shot her a look. "No harm in telling you, since you're his primary care physician. We're going to send the results to your office on Monday anyway. The kid has Wilson's disease."

"Wilson's disease?"

"Yeah. The grandmother, too, I imagine. The liver damage in the boy isn't too extensive—we'll probably be able to reverse it with dietary changes and the right meds." He shrugged. "He'll have to keep on top of it, but ... it could have been a lot worse."

"Oh, Peter. That's wonderful. Does TJ know?"

"Not yet. I left a message on his phone saying I had the results, but he hadn't called back by close of business. I'll tell him on Monday."

"It can't wait until Monday. He's terrified. So is Owen. I can tell him for you."

Peter waved a hand. "Be my guest."

Not only was Owen going to escape the painful fate his grandmother was suffering, it was likely that the news could help Penny's mother, as well.

Bianca was so relieved, so giddy with happiness, that she impulsively reached out and threw her arms around Peter. At first, he didn't return the hug. Then, tentatively, he patted her back in a little tap-tap-tap rhythm.

"Oh, God, Peter. Thank you." She pulled back from him, her eyes shimmering with tears.

"Yeah, well." She could see that he was trying to suppress a smile, but it leaked out anyway.

"You care about this guy. This Davenport guy," Peter said.

"Yes. I do."

Suddenly, something seemed to occur to him. "Then what's with the 'Is this seat taken' business? You were going to hit on me before you realized I was me."

"No, that's not—"

"That's crap. Yes, you were." He waited expectantly for an answer.

What could she say? How could she explain that she was hurt by TJ's denial that she meant anything to him? That she was insecure about what—if any—future they might have? How could she tell him that she had needed to reassure herself that she could move on if she needed to? That she'd needed a distraction so she wouldn't hear in her head, over and over, TJ telling his ex that she and he were nothing?

Peter was the last person who would want to hear anything about her man troubles—and it would be unfair tell him, in any event.

She put a hand on his forearm. "I just came over to say hello. Thank you for telling me about Owen." She gave the arm a light squeeze and then went back to her sisters.

19

Bianca went to her table, grabbed her cell phone from her purse, told her sisters she'd be right back, and went outside to call TJ. Looking at the screen, she saw that he'd tried to call her four times in the last half hour. When she hadn't answered, he'd texted her, saying the biopsy results were in but that he hadn't been able to reach Dr. DeVries before he'd left for the day. Could she call him and find out what was or was not wrong with Owen?

She tried calling TJ, but it went straight to voice mail. She tried texting, but her iPhone indicated the message had not been delivered. Was his phone's battery dead? Surely he hadn't turned it off, given the fact he was waiting to hear from her.

She headed back into the bar and to the table where her sisters were sitting, and said, "I have to go."

"What? Where?" Sofia asked.

"I have to talk to TJ. I just saw Peter, and I have Owen's diagnosis, and I tried to call, but he's not answering, so I'm just going to go over there. I know we just got here, and you have your drinks, and ... you looked like you were having fun. You can stay. I'll just ... get an Uber or something."

She was babbling, but she couldn't seem to stop herself. She was so happy to be able to deliver good news—or, comparatively good, at least—her mind was racing and she was having a hard time keeping up with it.

"Oh, jeez. Is he going to be okay?" Martina asked. Then, holding up a hand: "Wait, I take that back. I know you can't tell me. Doctor-patient confidentiality and all that. Forget I asked."

"He is," Benny said. "I can see it on her face. All right. Somebody grab the waitress so we can pay the check and get out of here."

"Really, you don't need to—"

"You're not taking an Uber. Don't be stupid. There are only about three in this whole area. You'll be waiting an hour." Benny finished what was left of the drink in her glass. "Let's hit it."

"You don't mind?" Bianca looked at the three of them, who were gathering up their coats and purses.

"Of course not. We get to tell a twelve-year-old that he's not dying. That's way more fun than drinking."

TJ MUST HAVE RECHARGED his phone, because he tried to call back while they were on their way to his place. Bianca wanted to tell him the news in person, so she texted that they she would stop by his place in twenty minutes. She deliberately chose the phrase *stop by* to make it seem more casual than it was. She didn't want him to think she was rushing over to give him traumatic news that he couldn't be trusted to hear while he was alone and without emotional support.

Sofia, Benny, and Martina waited in the car. Bianca went up the front walk, which was lighted only by the full moon and by the small porch light shining beside the front door. Her heart was pounding by the time she rang the bell.

He answered the door shirtless, wearing only a faded pair of jeans with the top button undone, and at first she forgot what she'd come here to tell him. She forgot to say hello. She almost forgot her name.

"Bianca?" he said.

"I ... uh ..." That seemed to be all she was capable of saying.

His hair was mussed, and he raked a hand through it. "Come in." He stepped aside to make room for her.

She was just over the threshold when he looked out and peered at the car. "Who's out there in the car?"

"Oh. Ah ... my sisters."

"What are they doing out there? Tell them to come in." Then he looked down at himself and seemed to notice for the first time that he wasn't fully dressed. "I'd better put on a shirt."

Yes, you'd better, Bianca thought, *or I'll never be able to string together enough words to tell you what Peter said.*

She got her sisters, he got a shirt, and they all gathered in his small living room in a way that was not entirely professional yet not quite social. There wasn't enough seating for everyone, so TJ leaned his butt against the sofa's arm.

"Okay." He scrubbed at the stubble on his face with his hand. "What's going on?"

"Where's Owen?" Bianca asked.

"He's with Penny. She took him up to her place in San Jose for the weekend."

"Okay."

"What's this about?" he prompted her again.

"I ... we ... were at a club in San Luis Obispo tonight, and I ran into Peter," Bianca began. "He told me about Owen's test results, and ... I didn't want you to have to wait until Monday. Or even tomorrow."

She saw him tense up, saw him assess everyone's expressions and body language to anticipate just what kind of news he was going to hear.

"You have a right to keep Owen's medical information private, so if you'd like my sisters to go into another room, or go back to the car, maybe ..."

"No." He shook his head. "Nah, that's okay. They can stay."

Bianca stood up, because she thought better when she was standing. "Owen has Wilson's disease. It means that his body can't process copper, and it builds up in the organs and causes damage. TJ, this is good news. With dietary changes and chelation agents, Owen should recover completely. He'll have to monitor it his entire life, but ... this is manageable, TJ. With the right care, he's going to be okay."

He stared at her, then blinked a few times. "He is?"

"Yes."

TJ's eyes reddened, and a couple of tears slipped down his face. He wiped them away and took a deep, ragged breath. "That's ... Jesus."

Then he grabbed Bianca and hugged her so tightly she could barely breathe. But that was okay; she didn't particularly feel like she needed to. She closed her eyes and gave herself over to his embrace.

"All righty, then," Benny said. "I think maybe we'll mosey on home and give you two a little privacy."

For the first time since TJ had touched her, Bianca realized that there were other people in the room. "Oh. No. We all should go. We can talk more tomorrow, TJ. I can give you some resources, some reading materials ..."

She'd gone from being lost in his arms to talking about reading materials. Bianca was beginning to get dizzy from the sudden shift.

If she stayed, it would be clear that she wasn't here only to deliver medical information. It would be clear that she was here at least partly because she wanted to be with him. Worse, they might end up sleeping together.

Usually, she wouldn't consider the danger of sex with a hot man as particularly hazardous. But this man, specifically, could do some real damage to her if he made her body sing and then decided, after the fact, that what they had together was nothing, as he'd told Penny it was.

The pain she'd felt in high school had been based on a fantasy, an illusion. If she slept with TJ now, how much more intense would her suffering be if he tossed her aside as he'd done back then?

"Are you sure you don't want to stay?" Benny hissed at Bianca. "Maybe discuss treatment options? Different therapies?"

"No." Bianca shook her head. "Not tonight. We can go over all of that tomorrow. During daylight. In a public place." She was babbling.

The four sisters headed for the door, and TJ followed them.

Bianca was the last of the women to cross the threshold, and TJ stopped her before she went down the walk toward the car.

"Bianca? Thank you." His arm was braced against the doorframe, bringing his body temptingly close to hers. All she had to do was lean in a little and he'd be holding her again....

She closed her eyes and shook her head a little to clear her thoughts. "Thank Peter. Wilson's disease isn't easy to diagnose. If he hadn't had the right instinct, this could have gone on a long time—too long—before you got any answers." Which reminded her of the other thing she had to tell him. "TJ, the disease is genetic. You have to tell Penny. Her mom ..."

"Right. Of course. But ... if that's what Beverly has, can she get better? Is it too late?"

"I don't know. I hope it's not."

He was standing so close she could breathe in the warm, clean scent of his body. She wanted to go back into the house, to be with him, to see what might happen. But her sisters were watching her. And she had to be smart.

Impulsively, she lifted up onto her toes and kissed his lips, just once. Then she rushed out to the car and got in before she could change her mind.

"Woo woo!" Benny said as soon as Bianca got into the car. "Good for you, going for the kiss. Are you sure you don't want to stay? The kid's out of town, nothing but consenting adults here, you never know what might happen...."

"Just drive." Bianca's cheeks were burning with either embarrassment or passion. It was hard to tell, even for her.

When they got home, Benny put down her purse, took off her jacket, and gave Bianca an appraising look.

"You know, it wouldn't hurt you to get laid," she said. "I suppose it hasn't been all that long, what with Peter and all, but I can't imagine it was earth-shaking with him. TJ looks like he'd be earth-shaking."

Bianca glared at her sister. "Why are you thinking about whether TJ would be earth-shaking? Keep your dirty mind off of him."

Benny grinned. "Ooh. Jealous, are we? You've got *feelings*." At the word *feelings,* she waggled her fingers in the air as though the feelings were tiny, invisible fairies flying all around them.

"Seriously," Sofia put in. "Peter was missionary position, scheduled on designated nights, no earlier than seven p.m. but no later than ten p.m. Am I right?"

Bianca's jaw went slack in surprise at how close to the truth Sofia had come. While there'd never been any kind of explicitly stated schedule, Peter had such specific preferences regarding when and how they had sex, it reminded her of how he ordered in restaurants— weekend evenings only, plain vanilla, hold the whipped cream.

She had to admit TJ looked like a guy who would go for extra whipped cream—and know exactly where to put it.

"You went off somewhere just now," Martina said. "What are you thinking about?"

"Whipped cream," Bianca said.

TJ HAD WANTED Bianca to stay—badly. He was so relieved about the news she'd brought him, so giddy with the knowledge that Owen would be okay, he wanted to celebrate. And that kiss she'd given him just before she'd left had offered some definite ideas about how, exactly, he could do it.

But it was probably best that she'd left, because he didn't want to do something stupid—and sleeping with her out of relief, without knowing exactly where they stood, might qualify.

And anyway, he had to call Penny and Owen and tell them what he'd found out.

Owen was in bed by the time he got Penny on the phone—his

illness had made him tired lately—but TJ told her everything he knew, and she promised to give Owen the news in the morning.

"Are you sure about this?" Penny's voice was intense as she pressed him for information. "TJ, are you sure?"

He rubbed the back of his neck. "Well …" Was he sure? He'd heard it from Bianca at his house, not from Dr. DeVries in the professional environment of his office. Still, Bianca was Owen's doctor. This wasn't a rumor. She wouldn't have told him if she wasn't certain. "Yeah. I'm sure. I'm going to call Dr. DeVries on Monday and make an appointment to talk about it and find out what all of it means. But Owen can get better, Penny. It's not going to be easy, I guess—he's going to need ongoing treatment—but he can get better."

Then he told her the other part: how if Owen had Wilson's disease, it was likely her mother did, too.

"God. They were so sure it was the drinking," Penny said. "They never even considered anything else. And she worked so hard to get sober."

All at once, TJ felt guilty for having been happy moments before. Yes, Owen had a good prognosis. But did Beverly? What if it was too late for her?

"I'm sorry we didn't find this out earlier," TJ said. "For your mom."

"I'll tell them," she said. "Maybe there's something her doctors can do if they know. There's got to be something."

He hoped so. He'd loved Penny once, and he wished he could give her this, even if their marriage had never been right, even if they'd hurt each other in a thousand different ways.

"Pen?" he said.

"Yeah?"

"Tell Owen … Just tell him I love him, okay?"

It was all he could really give anybody, in the end.

20

———

Bianca didn't hear from TJ for a few days after that, but she refused to call him. She'd been the one to make the last move, after all, when she'd kissed him. The ball was in his court, and if he didn't sink it into the basket, well, that was his own damned fault.

Part of her was glad he hadn't called. Dating TJ would be too dangerous, too fraught with peril. She imagined it would be like one of those thirty-dollar buffets in Las Vegas: just too much of everything to be good for anyone involved.

Her sisters, however, didn't see it that way. The nagging began the day after their trip to SLO, and by early the next week, it still hadn't abated.

"For God's sake, just text him," Sofia said at the office on Monday. "You don't have to offer him your body. Just ask how things are going. Get the ball rolling."

"His balls are his own business," Bianca said. Then: "Okay, that sounded wrong."

"You're not proposing marriage," Sofia protested. "Just ask him out for coffee or something."

"If he wanted to go for coffee, he'd have asked by now."

And that was the heart of it. She worried that he hadn't called because he simply didn't want to. Because he wasn't interested. Because he'd gotten to know her a little and had decided she was too staid, too dull—all of the same things she'd criticized in Peter.

"He really did a number on you in high school, didn't he?" Sofia propped one fist on her hip.

In retrospect, he hadn't done anything to her in high school. None of it had been his fault. He hadn't been responsible for her feelings. Bianca had done a number on herself.

The TJ of her fantasies had been a construct, not a real person. She'd made him out of imagination and longing, loneliness and need. That TJ—the one who didn't exist—was the one who'd hurt her. The real TJ hadn't done a thing.

The more she thought about it, the more she realized the chasm between the real TJ and the fantasy might be the reason she was so afraid to call him. What if the real man didn't match up to the one in her mind? What if she did get to know him better and he turned out to fall short of her expectations?

Worse, what if she fell short of his?

At work, Bianca felt Sofia scrutinizing her, and at home, Benny and Martina did the same thing. They were plotting something, she was sure. She just didn't know what it was.

AFTER TJ FOUND out about Owen's diagnosis, he spent the weekend researching Wilson's disease—what it was, and what it would mean for Owen. Then, the next week, he divided his time between working and dealing with Owen's treatment. There was an appointment with Dr. DeVries, more tests, an appointment with a nutritionist, and a meeting with another specialist—this one a hepatologist whose focus was Wilson's disease.

The hepatologist was based at Stanford—three hours away—so that meant a lot of driving. TJ had to push back some of the jobs he'd scheduled to make it all work.

At the end of each day, he was exhausted. He'd picked up his cell phone to call or text Bianca about a dozen times, but he was so raw over everything that was happening with Owen—and from having to see Penny more than he was used to—that taking an emotional risk with a woman was just too much to contemplate.

He'd call her when things slowed down.

Once a treatment plan for Owen was in place and a schedule of appointments was set, things did slow down. But by then, he'd waited too long to call Bianca. Now, any conversation with her would have to start with excuses for why it hadn't happened sooner.

He'd be starting out on the defensive, and that was never a good place to be.

If only Bianca had an electrical problem, he mused. That would make things a hell of a lot easier.

⌒

"Did you check the breaker box?" Bianca asked Benny the following Wednesday. They stood in the dark kitchen with only the moonlight shining through the window to illuminate the room.

"Of course I did. I'm not an idiot."

"Are you sure?"

"Am I sure I'm not an idiot?"

"I meant, are you sure about the breaker box? Maybe you just *thought*—"

"I'm sure I checked the breaker box. God. I know how to check a breaker box."

The power to the entire house had gone out just a few minutes before. That, in itself, wasn't surprising. Cambria was covered in trees —pines and oaks, mostly—and, unlike much of California, it still had above-ground power lines. It was a common occurrence for a tree to fall and take out the nearby wires, plunging some of the town's residents into darkness until the utility could send workers to set things right.

But a quick look out the windows showed that the neighbors on all sides still had lights burning brightly through their windows. That meant the problem was with the house, not the neighborhood. That shouldn't be happening, Bianca thought. The house had been completely rewired just a few years before when her parents had renovated the place.

"I'll go check it myself." Bianca headed for the front door so she could inspect the breaker box, in case Benny had somehow missed a problem.

"I'll do it," Sofia said. "You call PG&E to see if there's an outage."

"But there's not," Bianca protested. "Everybody's got power but us." Still, she figured it didn't hurt to check. She pulled her cell phone out of her pocket and called the utility. As she'd suspected, no outage had been reported.

"If only we knew an electrician." Martina put her index finger to her lips and raised her gaze to the ceiling in thought.

"No," Bianca said. "Not TJ. Call someone else."

"Don't be stupid," Benny said. "Do you know how hard it is to get an electrician after hours in Cambria? Or during regular hours, for that matter? Do you want to spend weeks burning oil lamps like Ma and Pa Ingalls? Call TJ. He's a friend. He has to help."

"He's not exactly a *friend*," Bianca said. In truth, she didn't know what he was. She'd gone to his house for dinner once. Then they'd been on a date. They'd kissed. He was her patient's father. And he was her high school crush. Did all of that equate to *friend*? Or more than a friend? Or less? He'd told Penny that they were nothing, so maybe that was how he saw it. He hadn't called in almost two weeks. Thinking of all of it made her head hurt.

"I don't want him to feel obligated," Bianca protested.

"*Pssht*," Benny said. "It's his job. We're going to pay him."

And that represented another level of awkwardness. The idea of paying a man she had feelings for—and who might have feelings for her—raised all sorts of issues. Yet she couldn't *not* offer to pay him. A mess—that's what it was. A mess they could avoid if they just called someone else.

"No. Not TJ," Bianca said again.

"Fine." Martina threw her hands up in surrender. "Call someone else, then."

So Bianca tried. She used the cellular data on her phone to Google local electricians, then she began calling them one by one. All of the calls went to voice mail, and she left messages about her house having been plunged into darkness.

They waited an hour for one of them to call back, but no one did.

"Okay, what now?" Sofia asked. They were all sitting in the living room with an array of scented candles lit on the coffee table. The scents of Northern Pine, Warm Vanilla, and Gentle Lavender competed in a way that made Bianca's temples throb.

"All right." She sighed, and her shoulders fell in defeat. "I'll call TJ."

TJ DIDN'T GENERALLY LOOK FORWARD to after-hours jobs, but he was looking forward to this one as he drove across town toward Happy Hill. Owen was at home watching a movie with Gary by his side. At twelve, he was old enough to stay home by himself for a couple of hours; he had TJ's cell number, of course, and he also had Mrs. Willits, the grandmotherly woman next door who was always willing —no, eager—to take Owen into her kitchen and feed him every chance she got. He'd be fine.

TJ had been trying to devise some non-awkward way to talk to Bianca again, and tonight, a solution had dropped into his lap as if by magic. Thank God for the crappy wiring in older homes. Without it, his life would have been so much less rich, in more ways than one.

He hoped the problem would be complicated, something that would require a lot of work and a healthy display of his expertise. Then he could impress her, and he could magnanimously wave off any offer of payment.

You can pay me back by taking me to dinner.

He imagined that gambit happily as he drove up to the Russo house and parked his truck. He could think of a few other ways she could show her gratitude, if she was amenable, some of them involving nudity....

He climbed the front porch steps, and the door opened before he had the chance to knock. Martina stood in the doorway, leaning her shoulder against the doorjamb, a mischievous grin on her face.

"Good, you're here," she said. "We're just sitting around in the dark. Come on in."

~

TJ's ATTEMPT TO showcase his stunning expertise on all things electrical was cut tragically short when he discovered that the main breaker was off. He flipped it back on, and presto—let there be light.

He went back into the house unsure how to tell them. He certainly didn't want to patronize Bianca—*the big, competent man has solved your silly little problem*—but there was no way around the fact that the breaker was a simple thing they should have known how to check themselves.

"Well ... looks like you're back in business." He walked back into the living room, scratching his head and trying to look modest.

"That quick? What did you do?" Bianca asked.

"Your main breaker was off. I just ... you know ... turned it back on."

Bianca, Sofia, and Benny were sitting around the coffee table, their candles still burning.

"I thought you two checked the breaker!" Bianca glared at Benny and Sofia.

"We did." Benny batted her eyelashes a few times. "I swear it was on."

"Me too. It was on." Sofia crossed her heart with her index finger.

"Huh. That's funny. Well, it's all good now, so ..."

Even as he spoke, the lights went out again, and everything went dark except for the flickering glow of the candles.

"Huh," he said.

Martina appeared in the doorway to the kitchen. "What, again?"

"Okay, I guess you do have an issue." TJ rubbed the back of his neck. "Let me see what I can do."

TJ went outside to the breaker box, a jacket wrapped around him against the evening chill, turned on his flashlight, and took a good look. The first thing he had to do was determine the location of the problem by testing each individual circuit. Once he'd isolated the problem, he could diagnose the specific issue.

He was just starting to do that when he became aware that Bianca was behind him wearing a puffy coat and peering over his shoulder anxiously.

"What's going on? We don't have some kind of big problem, do we? We don't have a short that's going to set the house on fire? Or something?" She'd gone up on her toes to see over his shoulder, and she was so close he could smell whatever girly products she used on her hair. It was a nice smell—feminine and soothing—and he wanted to lean into it and take a deep breath.

"If you have a problem, I'll find it," he told her. "And it's not likely to set the house on fire. That's what the breaker's for."

"Okay. Well."

He turned off all of the breaker switches, turned on the main breaker, then turned on power to one part of the house to see if it worked. "Could you ... uh ... ask your sisters if the lights are on in the kitchen?" He hated like hell for her to step away from him, but at least it would make it easier for him to think.

She checked, then came back and told him the kitchen lights were on. She'd clearly settled in to relax for the evening before he'd gotten there. Under the coat, she was wearing a big T-shirt and some kind of stretchy black pants that made her ass look shapely and touchable. Her hair was up in a ponytail that left stray strands of hair framing her face. He wanted to reach out and hold one between his fingers, but he restrained himself.

He should have gotten back to the breaker box by now, but instead of working, he seemed to be standing there looking at her.

"Um ... I'm sorry we bothered you so late," she said. "I didn't want to, because ... well ... you're obviously busy right now, with Owen and everything, which I'm sure is why you haven't called. Not that you had any obligation. To call, I mean. Obviously, you have an obligation to Owen. That's not what I—"

"It's no bother," he told her. "I was glad to come."

"You were?"

"Yeah." She was standing very close to him on the grass beside the house. The night had only a sliver of a moon, and he could barely see her in the pale light coming from the kitchen window. He could feel her, though. The warmth of her, even though they weren't touching. The energy of her.

TJ figured he had three choices: He could act like he was only there to do a favor for a friend, get the job finished, and go home. He could explain the reasons he hadn't called her—that first he'd been busy with Owen, and then he hadn't known what to say. Or he could bypass the conversation entirely by kissing her.

He chose option number three.

Out there in the dark, cool night, he leaned forward and let his lips touch hers, and she let out a sigh that undid him. That sigh held everything—her hopes and fears, her needs, and the tender relief she felt at his touch.

His flashlight hit the grass, and he put his arms around her, pulling her against his body and deepening the kiss until he felt it all the way in the center of his bones.

He knew he should hold back—this wasn't the time or the place for a seduction—but at the moment, he didn't give half a crap about what was appropriate. Before he knew what he was doing, he had a fistful of her hair in one hand, pressing her body to his with the other.

The thing about a great kiss was that it made everything disappear; all of the worries, anxieties, and day-to-day obligations of life seemed to evaporate into the atmosphere. And this was a great kiss.

TJ couldn't remember when he'd last had one of this caliber. He'd loved Penny, yes, but had they ever had this kind of chemistry? Maybe, once. Or maybe he'd only thought so because he'd had so little to compare it with.

He had very little experience with women and dating. There'd been Penny, and then there'd been the divorce. Now, with Bianca in his arms, he began to wonder about the possibilities and about all of the pleasures he'd missed.

When they finally broke away from each other—it might have been minutes later, or it might have been an hour—TJ became aware that they were being watched.

"Hey, you two." Benny was standing in the grass at the corner of the house, her arms crossed over her chest, a smug smile on her face.

"Oh. I ... uh ... we were just ..."

TJ couldn't tell for sure in the darkness, but he was pretty sure Bianca was blushing.

"I guess it's okay to tell you that you can stop now," Benny went on. "The work, that is. Not the kissing. I think you should go back to doing that."

"What are you talking about?" Bianca put a hand to her hair where TJ had mussed it, making a futile effort to smooth it and eliminate the evidence.

"The wiring's fine. We turned off the breaker a couple of times to get TJ out here."

TJ was having trouble making sense of it—maybe because all of the blood had flowed downward from his brain, and he'd lost his facility for critical thinking. "You turned off the breaker? On purpose?"

"You two weren't talking, and Bianca here was miserable. We all thought it was time for you two to stop screwing around and start ... you know. Screwing." She smirked.

"Oh, God," Bianca said.

TJ chuckled. Maybe dating a woman with sisters wasn't going to be half bad.

21

Bianca was mortified—not only by what her sisters had done, but also by the fact that she probably would have let TJ take her against the side of the house if Benny hadn't come outside when she did.

When had she lost all of her self-control? When had she lost her damned common sense?

She put her hand to her mouth, still feeling the heat of TJ's kiss.

"I have to go ... do a thing." Benny was grinning as she turned and went back into the house.

"I'm so sorry," Bianca told TJ. "My sisters are idiots."

"From where I'm standing, there's nothing to be sorry for," he said. "I ought to thank them."

Bianca felt heat rise to her cheeks. "I thought ..."

"You thought what?" He picked up his flashlight from the grass and hooked it onto his tool belt.

"I thought you weren't interested. And I thought ... God, I thought it was high school all over again. Me mooning over you and you not even noticing." It felt good to say it out loud.

She knew her hair must be comically mussed from where he'd

had his hands in it. Self-consciously, she took the band out, freeing her hair from its ponytail, then ran her hands through it.

"You're mooning over me?" TJ's grin pulled at her. It was that same cocky grin that had consumed her thoughts in high school.

"Yes. I'm mooning. I've been trying to act like I'm not, but, hell." Bianca let her shoulders drop. "Yes, I'm mooning."

He took a step closer to her and gently laid his palm on her cheek. "How about that? You're mooning."

"Don't make fun of me."

"I wouldn't think of it."

"It's just ... if you're *not* interested, it's better to know that now, because—" She didn't get the rest out, because he was kissing her again, and she'd forgotten what it was she'd even meant to say.

His tongue caressed hers as his thumb, rough from work, stroked her face. She wanted to resist him—it was the smart thing to do, surely; she didn't want to get hurt again—but how could she resist this? How could she refuse what he was doing to her?

When he broke the kiss, she didn't open her eyes—she was afraid if she did, it all would end, and she'd discover she'd only imagined it.

"I think your neighbors are watching us," TJ said.

Bianca's eyes flew open just in time for her to see a curtain in the neighbor's window stir. She and TJ needed to stop, but she didn't want to. Everything in her body was screaming for more.

"Oh." That was all she could seem to get out. "Oh."

"Do you want to go somewhere else?" His voice was a low rumble that glided across her skin.

"I ... yes." She hadn't meant to say yes—she knew it wasn't the responsible thing, the adult thing—and yet that's what had come out. And now that it was out there, she didn't want to take it back.

"Owen's home. So that's out. Could we maybe ..." He nodded toward the house, where Bianca's sisters were undoubtedly tittering about what they knew was happening outside.

"God, no."

"Okay. You want to neck in my truck a little bit?"

His sexy, mischievous smile was something she couldn't say no to. So she didn't.

THEY WERE both entirely too mature to have sex in a vehicle, so they didn't do that. Instead, they did some old-fashioned, fully clothed making out, something Bianca hadn't spent any real time doing since she was in her early twenties. It was damned fun, and she had to wonder why she'd given it up.

He'd pushed the driver's seat as far back as it would go, and Bianca was sitting on his lap, her arms around his neck, loving his kisses, the smell of his skin, and the rumble of his voice. The fact that it wasn't going to go any further than this—at least, not today—allowed her to let go of her anxiety and her misgivings and simply enjoy the moment.

"I should get back home," he said after a while, when they both were warm and mussed and thoroughly turned on. "Owen's going to wonder what happened to me."

"Right. Owen." Her voice was dreamy, and her head was foggy with lust.

"He's going to be with Penny this weekend. Let's go out. And then, afterward … we'll see what happens."

His hands were caressing her back, and she couldn't think with his hands on her. Was he asking her to have sex with him this weekend? She was pretty sure he was. The thought of saying no didn't even occur to her.

"We'll see what happens," she echoed.

"Yeah."

She went in for one more kiss to get her through until then. She caught his lower lip in her mouth and savored it, then nipped it lightly with her teeth. He let out a throaty groan in response. Then she climbed off of him and went out the passenger door.

By the time Bianca got back into the house, she looked like exactly what she was—a woman who'd been kissed senseless. Her sisters took one look at her and began hooting with glee.

"Did you have sex in the truck?" Benny demanded to know. "Is your bra on backward? Are you still wearing your panties?"

"No, we did not have sex in the truck," Bianca said. "I am still wearing my panties, and ... my bra is fine."

Benny's face fell. "Disappointing. Of course, you're not the sex-in-a-truck type, but TJ—"

"When are you going to see him again?" Martina asked.

"We ... this weekend. Owen will be at Penny's."

Sofia rubbed her hands together happily. "Ooh, so it's a sex date."

"No, it's ... Okay, yes. It's a sex date," Bianca admitted.

Benny stood and did a little victory dance. "Score one for a fake electrical crisis. That was Sofia's idea, by the way."

Sofia shrugged. "I'm just glad he's not a firefighter. I didn't want to have to torch the place."

Sometime while Bianca and TJ were in the truck, Patrick had arrived. He was holding a mug of tea in his hands, the paper tag from the tea bag dangling outside of the mug.

"I told Sofia not to interfere," he said. "But she thought that if it worked, you'd forget to be mad. Was she right?"

Mad? Bianca had, indeed, forgotten that she was supposed to be mad about her sisters' deception. And now that she remembered, she was too flustered by TJ and his hands and his mouth and his ... everything that she couldn't summon up any leftover anger.

"I'm thinking she was right," Martina responded when Bianca didn't.

Bianca raked her hands through her hair, which was already so badly askew it hardly mattered. "I just ... God, I don't want him to hurt me again. I know it was high school, and I know he didn't mean to, and I know it wasn't the real TJ who hurt me but a ... a fantasy I'd created in my addled teenage brain. But the heartbreak was real! It was real, and it hurt." To her horror, she felt tears coming to her eyes, and she wiped them away. "I just got out of a relationship, and I'm vulnerable, and ... and I just don't want him to hurt me again. What if he does? What if we sleep together, and it's great, and then he moves on and leaves me a broken shell of a woman?"

"What if you sleep together, and it's great, and you both live happily ever after?" Sofia asked. "I mean, why not?"

Bianca dropped into a leather club chair. "Because this is real life, that's why."

And when did I decide that real life inevitably means disappointment? When exactly did that happen? It was a question Bianca hadn't asked herself before. It seemed to her that she needed to understand the answer if she was ever going to be happy with anyone.

22

I n the couple of days leading up to her date with TJ, Bianca second-guessed herself so many times that she was driving herself crazy. More than that, she was driving her sisters crazy.

"Good God, Bianca, why can't you just enjoy it? Why can't you just relax and wallow in the anticipation of what's likely to be some really great sex?" Sofia and Bianca were at Bianca's office before opening, preparing for the day's appointments. Bianca had been pacing around, considering options for canceling the date, while Sofia sat at the reception desk getting organized for her day. Finally, Sofia had snapped. "You're not turning yourself in for a stretch at San Quentin. It's a date!"

"I know." Bianca, dressed in her professional outfit of black pants, white button-down shirt, low pumps, and white coat, was wringing her hands. She'd always thought *wringing her hands* was a silly expression that had nothing to do with reality, but here she was— literally wringing her hands. She forced herself to stop and shoved her fists into the pockets of her coat. "But what if it goes wrong? What if it's a disappointment? What if I'm not ready?"

Sofia's tone softened. "If you're not ready, then when the time comes, you'll tell him you're not ready. The point is to do something you both want to do. If you don't want to ..."

"I *do* want to," Bianca moaned. "That's the problem. I want to, so I'm not thinking straight. I'm not being rational."

"Being rational is highly overrated where men are concerned," Sofia remarked. "Sometimes, you've just got to go with your feelings."

"Says the woman who almost rejected the love of her life because of feelings," Bianca shot back.

Sofia sat back in her chair and crossed her impossibly long legs. "Look, Bianca. If you don't want to sleep with him yet, then don't. Of course, don't. But go out with him. Get to know him. Give him a chance. Then just ... see what happens."

"That's what he said. He said, 'we'll see what happens.' But I already *know* what's going to happen. I'm going to end up with my panties hanging off a lampshade and my heart broken into a million damned pieces."

"That's not fair." Sofia gave her a stern look that reminded Bianca so much of their mother that she almost cried.

"How is it not fair?"

"It's not fair because you don't know that he's going to break your heart. You're just *afraid* he will. He's paying for something he hasn't even done yet, just because you're scared."

"Sofia ..."

"You can't be practical all the time," Sofia said. "You can't be the rational one, the careful one, the smart one all the damned time! Do something stupid for once. Go get laid!"

"So you agree that it would be stupid," Bianca said.

Sofia threw up her hands in defeat. "I give up."

Bianca didn't blame her. She'd have given up, too.

"It's eight o'clock. I'm opening the doors," Sofia said.

"Thank God," Bianca muttered.

TJ WAS EAGERLY ANTICIPATING his date with Bianca, not just because he wanted to sleep with her—although he really, really did—but also because he was having a rough time, and he needed something good to look forward to.

Owen had started medication to take the excess copper out of his system, and the drugs were making him feel even crappier than he had before he'd been diagnosed. Nothing to do for it but power through, but how did you tell that to a twelve-year-old who just wanted to go to school and hang out with his friends and feel normal for a change?

TJ was worried about that, and he also was worried about the amount of work time he was losing taking Owen to doctor's appointments. Again, nothing to do for it but power through. But his checking account didn't care *why* the money was slowing down. It only knew it was.

Added to all of this was Penny. She was worried about Owen, so she'd been having him stay with her on weekends more often. They'd been meeting halfway between Cambria and San Jose to get him up there, and TJ was having to drive an hour and a half each way on Friday and Sunday afternoons.

Six hours of driving on the weekends was cutting into time he would otherwise be using to catch up on his work. He had a backlog of clients waiting for him to complete their projects, and he'd had to keep calling people to push back the dates. That was bad business. He'd prioritized anyone who had an actual electrical problem, as opposed to those who wanted to upgrade or change something that worked. And he'd been doing a hell of a lot of apologizing for the delays. Thankfully, most people had been understanding, but if he didn't get caught up, some of them would start pulling their business and going with someone else.

And then there was the fact that all of Owen's time with Penny meant that TJ had to see his ex much more often than he was comfortable with. TJ and Penny had reached the point where they could consistently be civil with each other, but that didn't mean he enjoyed the reminder of how he'd failed to keep his family together.

All of that combined meant that TJ really needed to have some fun. Sex would be great, too. He hoped that might happen on his date with Bianca, but even if it didn't, he would enjoy the hell out of the chance to have a nice night out, thinking about something other than his problems.

The last thing he was going to do, though, was let his mother know how much he was looking forward to seeing Bianca. He had enough to think about right now without maternal pressure regarding his love life.

That was why, during a visit to his parents' place on the Thursday night before his date, he downplayed the whole thing.

They'd just finished dinner—in truth, one of the top reasons he'd come in the first place was so he wouldn't have to cook—and he and his mom were sitting at the kitchen table with mugs of coffee, a plate of cookies set in front of him. Owen was in the living room watching a movie, and TJ's dad was out in his garage tinkering with his latest woodworking project.

They'd already covered the topic of Owen's health, Penny's mother, and TJ's work when Lily brought up Bianca.

"So. Did I ever mention that my friend Donna lives next door to those Russo girls?" Lily studiously avoided making eye contact with her son.

"Yeah, I think you said something about that." He wasn't sure whether she had or not, but if she had and he didn't remember, she'd lecture him on how he didn't pay attention to her. It was easier to agree.

"Well, Donna thought she saw you over there the other night." Lilly stirred her coffee and carefully set the spoon on a porcelain saucer.

"Oh, yeah?" TJ remained noncommittal, but he could see where this was going, and he steeled himself.

"*Mm hmm.*" Lily pressed her lips together until they formed a tight line. "It seems she thought the two of you were having inter-course in your truck."

TJ nearly choked on his coffee, not because of what his mother had said, but because of the way she'd said it. No son wanted to hear his mom say the word *intercourse*, not even if she was talking about the town in Pennsylvania.

"Mom!"

"Well, Troy, that's what she said. I'm not telling you how to conduct your love life, goodness knows, but I would think you could at least wait until you're behind closed doors."

"We were not having"—he could barely say it—"intercourse. We were kissing. That's all."

"I see."

"And your friend Donna should mind her own business." TJ's face was hot, and he thought he must be blushing. He'd have thought he was beyond such a thing as blushing, but apparently not. "Bianca and I are seeing each other, but we haven't slept together yet. And I don't know why I'm even telling you this."

Lily seemed unsure about how to proceed. She clearly had something on her mind, and it probably had to do with sex, because why else would she be so hesitant to talk to her own son?

"Mom, what?" TJ said.

"Well ... honey, do you really think it's smart to be going around with this woman, when you and Penny might still—"

"Mom. Penny and I are not going to get back together. I know you think we will, but ... Well, the problems went pretty deep. The marriage just didn't work."

She looked at him as though he simply didn't understand the truth of the situation—which, in her view, was that he and Penny had just hit a pothole in the road to true love. Surely they would find some way to drive around it and continue on their journey together. She'd expressed this to him more than once, and he couldn't seem to make her see the reality.

"But, Troy, are you sure there isn't some way—"

"I'm sure," he told her firmly. "We both need to move on."

"Well." She scowled. "If you really must move on, please don't do it in front of Donna's house. I have to be able to face her at the Historical Society meetings."

TJ HADN'T SLEPT with anyone since his divorce, but it was more than that. He also hadn't slept with anyone before his marriage. In his entire life there had only been Penny, and that made his upcoming date with Bianca more fraught with possibilities—both good and bad —than it otherwise would have been.

Bianca was an attractive, accomplished single woman in her thirties. Even if she'd had a fairly sedate, conservative love life, she'd probably dated—and even slept with—any number of people. It offended his sense of manhood that he was so relatively inexperienced, and that as a result, she might find him ... lacking.

Sure, he'd had sex hundreds of times—maybe thousands, who was counting?—but all of those times had been with Penny. He knew what Penny did and didn't like, what Penny's little noises meant, what Penny was trying to communicate with a look, a touch.

He didn't know if any of that information was transferable to a woman who wasn't Penny. What if Bianca's wants and needs were entirely different? What if TJ got into the game and couldn't read the signals?

"Damn it, get out of your head," he told himself the day after his visit to his mother, while he was in his truck on the way to a job. "Get out of your damned head."

If he thought too much about it, he was going to psyche himself out before Saturday night even came. He was going to head into the thing with no confidence—probably not something most women found attractive.

So, that was one thing. Then there was the fact that Bianca was a doctor, and TJ was just a tradesman. Better not to think about that one too much, especially when combined with his relative lack of sexual experience....

"Hey. You gonna get out of the car and get to work, or what?"

TJ had arrived at the job site, and the general contractor who'd hired him was standing at the open window of TJ's truck, looking at him as though TJ had lost his mind. Which wasn't too far from the truth.

How long had he been sitting here, just marinating in his thoughts?

He couldn't tell Mark that he was ruminating over his lack of prowess as a man, so instead, he said, "Yeah, yeah. Kiss my ass." It was what men did to restore male equilibrium at moments such as this.

Mark gave the roof of the truck a friendly pat. "I'm glad you're here. Looks like the previous owner tried to wire the place himself. I'm surprised the whole house hasn't blown up."

TJ DIDN'T HAVE a lot of friends—he'd been so involved with getting settled in Cambria and adjusting to life as a single father that he hadn't had time for it. But now, he kind of wished he had friends he could discuss his woman problems with. Since he didn't, he stopped by to see his dad after work.

Frank Davenport made an odd match with Lily. While she was gregarious and had a tendency to try to control her son's life, Frank mostly kept his thoughts to himself. That made him a good listener, and it also made him unlikely to share whatever TJ said to him with Lily.

Frank was out in his garage workshop when TJ drove up to the house just after five o'clock. Owen had taken the bus home, and TJ had checked on him—the kid was nicely settled in with a snack and a video game, feeling pretty good today for a change.

"Hey, Dad." TJ strolled up the driveway and into the garage, where his father was sanding a piece of driftwood he'd salvaged from Moonstone Beach. Frank made various items out of driftwood that he sold to tourists: tables, wall ornaments, garden benches. Right now, he was making what looked to be a birdhouse.

"Son," Frank said in greeting. The man liked to say whatever he had to say in as few words as possible. TJ admired it.

TJ watched while Frank worked the driftwood, smoothing the rough edges until the wood was supple, its curves sensual.

Which made TJ think of Bianca again.

"You here to see your mother?" Frank asked. It was a reasonable question; most often, TJ was here to see Lily, often because Lily herself had called him to lay on the guilt about him not visiting often enough.

"Nah. I was just passing by, and I thought I'd stop and say hi."

"Passing by?" Frank eyed the piece of wood in his hand, running his fingers over the patch he'd been sanding. "I thought you were working across town."

"I, uh ... I had an errand."

"What kind of errand?"

It was just like TJ's dad to get curious the one time TJ was lying to him. "I forgot. Listen ... I guess Mom probably told you I'm seeing Bianca Russo. You remember Bianca? From when I was in high school?"

"Yep." He grabbed his sandpaper and went at the spot on the driftwood again.

"Well ... I thought I might take her to the Sea Chest. You and Mom been there lately? How is it?" TJ had no intention of taking Bianca to the Sea Chest—it was a fine restaurant, but he had other plans. Still, he had to launch into the conversation somehow, and he wasn't about to lead with, *Hey, Dad, I've only slept with one woman in my entire life, and I'm scared shitless. Any words of advice?*

Frank's eyebrows rose, but he didn't look up from his work. "Well, it's seafood, son. I suppose one scallop's as good as another."

TJ doubted that was true, but in any case, it didn't matter. He didn't want to talk about scallops.

"Or ... I thought maybe I might make her dinner at my place."

Frank let out a grunt of acknowledgment. At only sixty-seven, the man looked nearly as weathered as the wood he worked with: bald head, deep lines on his face from hours spent in the Cambria sunshine, hands callused and rough from the work.

"It's not that I don't want to take her out," TJ went on. "It's just ...

we've seen each other a couple of times already, and it seems like it might be nice to … you know. Have some alone time. Owen will be with Penny, so …"

Scritch-scritch-scritch as Frank sanded the wood. "You got something on your mind, you might want to come out with it. Neither one of us is getting any younger."

"Right." TJ shifted from one foot to the other and leaned his butt against a metal worktable. "It's just … I married Penny pretty young, and this is the first time I'm seeing someone since the split, and … Ah, hell. I don't know what I'm even talking about."

For the first time, Frank put down the piece of wood and focused on his son. "Troy, are you asking me for advice about sex?" He scratched his bald head. "Because, I have to tell you, I don't know if I'm the man for the job."

Of course he wasn't. TJ didn't know what the hell he'd been thinking. He blew out a puff of air, embarrassed.

"Right. Look, I can see you're busy. And I've got to go home and make dinner for Owen. Tell Mom I said hi." TJ pushed off from the table and headed toward his car.

"Troy?"

TJ turned back and looked at his father. "Yeah?"

"Well … I don't want to let you down, is all." Frank ran a hand over his head, where the hair had once been.

"That's okay. Really."

"I had a little experience before your mother." Frank winced, as though the fact of that—or the act of admitting it to his son—was highly distasteful.

"Dad—"

"I figure you can't go wrong just talking to the woman," Frank went on. "You might not know what she wants, but she does."

It was a surprisingly sensitive comment coming from a man who expected his dinner on the table at six sharp and who had mostly dismissed child-raising as "women's work." TJ blinked in surprise.

"Yeah. Okay. Thanks."

"Well." Frank turned back toward his project.

"Dad?"

"*Mmm*?"

"Maybe ... don't tell Mom we had this conversation."

Frank looked at his son as though TJ had suddenly grown a hand out of the top of his head. "What would I do that for? You think I haven't learned a thing in almost forty years of marriage?" Frank scoffed and picked up the piece of wood.

Considering his father's advice, TJ thought that Frank had, indeed, learned a few things in that time. Most of them good.

23

———

On Friday night after work, TJ drove Owen halfway to San Jose to meet Penny. They made the exchange at a Starbucks in King City.

They made some small talk about Owen and school and how he'd been feeling, then they discussed the logistics of how and when he'd be coming home. Then TJ gave Owen a manly slap on the back and wished him a good weekend.

TJ thought he was going to get away from Penny without any unpleasantness, but those hopes withered and died when Penny sent Owen out to her car, saying she wanted to chat with TJ for a minute.

"Parent things," she told Owen.

Once the boy was in the car and out of earshot, Penny faced TJ, the friendly look that had been on her face for Owen's benefit now replaced by a hard scowl.

"Are you seeing that woman this weekend?" she demanded.

"Penny—"

"Are you? I deserve to know what's going on in my son's house."

TJ crossed his arms over his chest. "No, you don't—not when he isn't in it. What I do when he's with you is my own business."

"If there's someone in your life, I deserve to know. Especially if it's affecting Owen's medical care. I swear to God, TJ—"

"It's not affecting his medical care. And right now, you don't deserve to know. If, at some point, things get serious and she's going to be a part of Owen's life, I'll tell you. Until then, keep your nose out of it."

"So it's not serious?" Penny's eyes were getting red and moist, and TJ only wanted to get out of there without answering the question. Was it serious? For all practical purposes, no. Things with Bianca hadn't gone very far, and they'd never had a discussion of what they might or might not mean to each other. But even as his head was saying, *no, it's not serious*, his heart was saying, *it's serious as hell*. He didn't know which part of himself to listen to, so he didn't have an answer—even if he'd wanted to give one, which he didn't.

"How's your mom?" he asked, partly to change the subject and partly because he knew he should have asked it already and was embarrassed that he hadn't.

Penny wiped a stray tear from her cheek. "It's Wilson's. They've confirmed it."

"So that's good, right?"

Penny shrugged and looked off toward the far hills to the east. "I guess."

"But?"

"But it's too far along. She needs a transplant—she won't get better without one. If they'd figured this out earlier, if they hadn't just assumed it was her fault ..."

"Pen, I'm sorry."

"Yeah." She shrugged—a gesture of hopelessness, of futility.

"We got it early enough with Owen, though. Penny? Owen's going to be okay."

"Yeah."

He hugged her, because she needed it and because of their history. Because of years of love and mutual support, and because of the sorrow that they hadn't made it work. Then, they pushed each other away self-consciously, because they didn't want to give Owen hope for a reconciliation when there wasn't any.

"I do want you to be happy, you know." Penny hugged herself as though she were cold, even though the temperature was mild. "It's just hard."

"I know."

It was hard for him, too—being happy. But he thought he owed it to himself—and to Owen—to try.

24

***

On Saturday, Bianca shaved, waxed, moisturized, and wore a bra and panty set she'd bought for the occasion. As a matter of principle, she thought TJ should be responsible for the condoms, but as a practical woman, she tucked some into her purse anyway. She wanted to make sure she had everything covered —so to speak.

When she was dressed in a sexy but casual outfit she'd borrowed from Sofia—skinny jeans, boots, low-cut top, dangly earrings—she began to have second thoughts.

"This is stupid. This whole thing is stupid," she announced.

Martina was sitting at the kitchen island jotting notes into her laptop for her latest interior design job, and Benny was rooting around in the refrigerator for something to drink.

"She's freaking out. You owe me five dollars." Benny shot Martina a know-it-all look, her eyebrow cocked.

"No, I don't." Martina didn't look up from her computer. "I owe you five dollars if she freaks out so much she doesn't go. We're not there yet."

"You're betting on me? You made a bet?" Bianca was appalled.

"Hey, at least I actually found someone who thought you had the lady balls to go through with it," Benny said. "Sofia wouldn't take the bet."

That stopped Bianca. "She wouldn't?"

"Well, she would have, but she wanted me to give her odds." Benny shrugged. "She thought it could go either way."

Martina closed the laptop and focused on her sister. "You can do this, Bianca. I know you're freaked out because it's Troy and because you've still got all of those hormonal teenage feelings...."

"I do not have hormonal teenage feelings."

"But," Martina continued, "you're not a coward. You've never been one. And I know that if this doesn't work out, it's not going to be because you were too scared to give it a fair chance and see where it would go."

Martina's pep talk was surprisingly stirring, and it buoyed Bianca. She took a deep breath, let it out, and tried to focus.

"Okay," she said. "Okay. I'll just ... I'll go and have fun, and ... if it works, it works, and if it doesn't, I'll be fine. He's just a guy. He's not some ... some mythical man-god with the power to enchant me and keep me locked in his love dungeon until the end of time." Which, when she thought of it, sounded pretty appealing.

"There you go," Martina said encouragingly.

"Okay, that's not fair." Benny pointed one finger at Martina. "There was nothing in the bet that said you could make a big, stirring speech."

"There was also nothing that said I couldn't."

Bianca checked the clock and saw she was running a few minutes late. She grabbed her purse and went out the door, leaving her sisters still arguing about whether Martina's speech had voided their wager.

THEY WOULD BE HAVING dinner at TJ's place with the implied intention that, if all went well and both parties were agreeable, the night would end in sex.

That, alone, would have been enough to make Bianca nervous.

But the fact that she had wanted him for so long—almost two decades—made the situation nearly unbearable.

Thank God he offered her a glass of wine as soon as she got there. She accepted it, then waited until his back was turned and downed half of the glass while Gary, his ancient dog, watched her with his head tilted to the side.

TJ looked ... well. He looked like her teenage fantasy grown to perfect, peak adulthood. Dark, wavy hair still damp from the shower. Tall, strong body in jeans that fit him as though they'd been custom made. Shirt open at the throat, giving her a tease of the lean, muscled physique underneath. Good God. The idea that the man she'd spent so many years longing for might finally be hers ...

"Bianca? Are you all right?" He was looking at her with curiosity and not a little concern. Had she been staring?

"Yes. Fine. I'm ... yes. Just ... thinking about something going on at work." She couldn't admit she was nervous. Her womanly pride prohibited it.

"Oh. Nothing too serious, I hope."

"It's ... things should resolve themselves soon. Very soon."

He smiled at her, really seeing her, and the fine lines at the corners of his eyes deepened. When was the last time any man had smiled at her like that? Her knees nearly gave out with her desire for him.

She needed to pull herself together, so she focused on things other than his eyes, his smile, and whatever unknowable, wonderful, frightening things he might do to her if she let him.

He was cooking, so she turned her attention to that. They talked about the food, how it smelled, and whether she could help. They talked about Owen, how he was feeling, and how Penny was dealing with his diagnosis. They talked about TJ's day, his work, and how he'd felt about coming home to Cambria. They talked about Gary, and Bianca scratched the dog behind his ears while TJ told the story of his adoption.

They ate—a pasta dish with chicken and asparagus—and Bianca barely tasted it. She drank more wine, hoping it would relax her.

The wine didn't ease her nerves, but it did make her tipsy. The overall result was that she was both nervous and afraid that her defenses had been lowered to a point where she would not be able to make a rational decision.

The whole thing brought her back to the point she'd made earlier in the evening with her sisters. This was stupid.

She excused herself to use the bathroom, pulled her cell phone out of her purse, and texted Martina.

Call me in five minutes with an emergency.

The response came back almost immediately: *What? No.*

Martina, please.

Did something go wrong? Is he being an ass?

Bianca considered the question. *No. He's perfect. And I can't handle it, Martina. I can't. Just call me.*

If it had been Benny, she wouldn't have called. She'd have refused in a stubborn attempt at matchmaking. But it was Martina, and Bianca knew she could count on her. She knew her sister wouldn't let her down.

Bianca checked herself in the mirror, washed her hands, and went back out into the living room, where TJ was waiting for her.

He'd already cleared the table and stacked the dishes in the kitchen, and he was sitting on the sofa, his long legs stretched out in front of him.

"Do you want some more wine?" He'd put the bottle and their glasses on the coffee table, and he lifted the bottle, ready to pour.

"No, thanks. I think I've had a little too much already."

"Okay." He put the bottle down. "Do you want to come and sit down? I could put on a movie if you want. Or we could just talk. Or ... we could go out. I didn't really plan anything, so ..."

He was fidgeting with the wineglasses, repositioning them on the table. Then he rubbed at his chin with his hand.

For the first time since she'd arrived, she realized that he was nervous, too. How had she not noticed that? All at once, it seemed to her that she'd built him up in her mind so much—Troy, her impossibly perfect teenage crush—that she'd failed to realize he was human.

It changed the dynamic, and for the first time that evening, her shoulders lowered from where they'd been up around her ears.

"Put on a movie," she told him and sat down beside him while Gary curled up on the rug in front of the fireplace.

HALF AN HOUR LATER, Bianca had ignored Martina's text and she and TJ were making out on the sofa like sixteen-year-olds on prom night.

Bianca was on her back on the sofa with TJ on top of her, his hands on her body, his mouth devouring hers. The movie—a romantic comedy—droned on, unheeded.

She'd imagined this for so long—so many years. Now that it was happening, she savored it, savored him. She grabbed fistfuls of his shirt in her hands, and he rose up a little to unbutton it and throw it aside.

"Is this okay?" His voice was ragged. "Bianca, if you're not ready …"

She'd thought she wasn't ready when the night began. She'd thought that if her dream became reality, she might break apart, never to be whole again. But now that he was here with her, now that she could taste him and feel the warmth of his body, the pounding of his heart under her hand, she felt no hesitation. Only desire.

"Take me to your bedroom," she said.

He got up off of the sofa, held out his hand to her, and led her to his room, closing the door behind them so Gary couldn't watch what they were about to do.

TJ HAD KNOWN Bianca as a shy, awkward girl in high school. He'd known her as a crisp, competent professional in her role as Owen's doctor. When he'd thought of how this would be—how they would be together if this moment ever came—he'd imagined that she would be self-contained, reserved. Maybe even prim.

Instead, she was standing in front of him, looking at him with such raw need that it took his breath away.

He'd had it in mind to take things slowly, carefully. To gauge her comfort and willingness each step of the way, to be considerate of her needs. He wanted to be a gentleman.

But as she unbuttoned her blouse and slipped it off of her shoulders, those doe eyes locked on his, he began to reevaluate his expectations. She wasn't some delicate flower who needed his protection. She was a sexy, sensual woman who knew what she wanted.

What she wanted was him—and the fact of that made him nearly crazy with desire for her.

He held himself in check—barely—until she was down to nothing but a bra and panties, lacy slips of fabric that teased about the delights underneath. Then she said his name on a ragged breath —just his name—and his restraint broke.

HE PULLED her into his arms, his mouth taking hers, with a ferocity that made her gasp. He lifted her up, his hands cupping her ass, and she wrapped her legs around him as he moved her to the bed and lowered her onto it.

He stood beside the bed just long enough to undress the rest of the way, then covered her body with his. His hand slipped inside the waistband of her panties and found her wet, warm core, his fingers caressing her.

The sensation almost made her weep with pleasure.

It wasn't a slow build. There was none of the gradual, rising tension, no long, gentle increase of anticipation. Instead, her body spasmed just moments after his fingers entered her. She cried out and bucked her hips, clinging to him, her eyes shut tight, every part of her consumed by him.

Orgasms weren't a novelty to her. She'd had them regularly with

Peter. But things with Peter had been ... routine. Serviceable. Safe. And it hadn't been out of the question for her to fake it just to avoid an uncomfortable conversation afterward.

But this wasn't safe. It wasn't predictable. It was a force of nature beyond her control.

TJ HADN'T WANTED to rush things. He'd wanted to take his time, savoring all of it—taking off her clothes, basking in the sight of her, touching and claiming her body. But it had been a long time since he'd been with a woman, and even longer since he'd enjoyed it. The idea of taking his time was a nice one, but he didn't know if he could manage it.

He pulled down the cup of her bra and took her breast in his mouth, teasing the erect nipple with his tongue. She threw her head back and sighed, and the sound of it—knowing that she loved what he was doing—made so much pleasure surge through him that it almost ended things there.

Penny—he didn't want to think of Penny right now, but there she was—had mostly endured his attentions the last few years. Knowing that Bianca was enjoying this, enjoying him, sent a rush of pure electricity through him.

And, God, Bianca was beautiful. Her smooth skin with its subtle Mediterranean tones, her dark, thick hair, her eyes, deep brown and expressive. He felt immeasurably grateful to be here with her, to be allowed this intimacy.

He reached behind her and unclasped the bra, then pulled it off of her. When she went for the waistband of her panties, he stopped her. "Wait. Let me." He hooked his fingers into the elastic and drew the garment down slowly, slowly.

When she was nude, he pressed his tongue between her thighs, tasting her. She gasped and grabbed his shoulders, clutching at him. Penny had never liked this—had never let him do it—and he reveled in the freedom of being able to taste and explore.

"TJ ... oh." Bianca breathed his name as she grabbed fistfuls of his hair.

He could feel her rising, rising, then she spasmed with pleasure again. And with that, he couldn't wait anymore. Couldn't resist anymore.

"I brought condoms," Bianca said.

He grinned. "You brought condoms?"

"Well ... I'm a doctor, so ..."

He loved that she'd brought condoms, but they wouldn't be needing hers. He reached into his bedside drawer and brought out a little square packet. She took it from him, opened it, and rolled the condom onto him, caressing and stroking him as she did.

"Ah ... I'm not going to make it if you keep doing that." He groaned, his eyes closed tight.

"All done." She pulled him down to her, and at last, he slid into her silky, warm depths.

Once that happened, all thoughts of Penny were gone. There was no past and no future, only what he had right now. And this was enough. He didn't need more if he could have this.

She made noises as he thrust into her—groans and purrs and sounds that might have been words—and it turned him on so much that he felt it like a hot vibration down his spine.

He reached between their bodies and caressed her nub with his thumb as he moved inside her, and she cried out and shuddered. When his own orgasm hit, it slammed into him like lightning, like a sudden, savage storm. He could neither speak nor think for minutes afterward as he lay heavily on top of her, gasping.

"TJ?"

"*Uhnnn.*"

"Could you ..." She pushed at his shoulder a little, and only then did he realize that he was probably cutting off her breath with his weight.

He rolled off of her and onto his back, feeling obliterated. Was this what he'd been missing all these years? Had this been out there all the time, waiting for him? He felt doors opening, suns rising, new worlds being born.

She purred his name and tucked her body against his side, laying her head on his chest.

THERE WAS time to talk afterward, when they were standing in the kitchen with glasses of water, him wearing only a pair of jeans, her in panties and one of his T-shirts.

"So." He leaned his butt against the counter, a glass of ice water in his hand. Gary sat on the floor nearby, watching TJ faithfully. "Did you … I mean … I really had a good time, and I hope …" He wasn't accustomed to feeling painfully awkward, and yet, here he was, stammering and unable to complete a thought.

"Are you asking if I enjoyed myself?" Bianca asked.

"Well … yeah."

"I enjoyed myself three times." She held up three fingers.

"Right." He grinned, pleased with himself. "That's good."

"I mean," she went on, "have all of the other women you've been with enjoyed themselves three times in one night? Maybe it's a regular thing for you, but for me—"

"There haven't been any other women," he blurted out. "Besides Penny, I mean."

She froze, eyes wide, mouth slightly agape. "What?"

He shrugged. "We got married young, and then after the divorce … I didn't really date anybody until you."

"I'm the first person since Penny."

"Well … yeah."

"And there was nobody before Penny."

"No."

She gulped some water while she took that in. "This is a big deal, then," she finally concluded.

"It is. For me, anyway. If it's not for you …"

"It is. It is a big deal for me. It ... really is."

They sat with that for a minute, each of them trying to gauge how big a deal it was for the other and what that might mean.

25

The next morning, Bianca was at home, sitting on the sofa with a mug of coffee while Sofia got ready to go kayaking and Martina worked in the kitchen. Sofia was packing her wetsuit into a gym bag along with a towel and travel-sized shampoo and conditioner bottles when Bianca finally broke her silence about what had happened the night before.

"You know how, last week, Benny was talking about how all men are man-whores who will jump on top of any woman who will lie still long enough?"

"Yeah?" Sofia stopped what she was doing to look at Bianca.

"Oh, don't tell me TJ's a man-whore. That's why you're not talking about the date. Oh, no." Martina, who was standing at the kitchen island preparing a tray of homemade granola, tilted her head in sympathy.

Benny wasn't home—she was out on a boat doing some kind of research on kelp and had left before dawn—but if she were here, she'd have been interested to know whether her hypothesis about man-whores had been proven correct.

"No," Bianca said. "He's not a man-whore. In fact"—she put down her mug and ran her hands through her hair—"he's only slept with Penny."

Sofia's jaw went slack. "What, you mean in his whole life? Only Penny?"

"Well, and me now."

The other two hooted in triumph.

"You did it!" Sofia pumped a fist in victory. "I knew it! At least, I thought so. But when you were so quiet earlier this morning, I thought ... Oh, no. Was it bad? Was it terrible? Is he so inexperienced that he couldn't find your clitoris? Oh, jeez ..."

"It wasn't bad." In fact, it was so *not*-bad that Bianca found herself growing misty-eyed at the memory of it and how deeply it had moved her. "It was good. It was very good." Her voice was squeaky with emotion.

"Oh, boy." Martina wiped her hands on a towel and went to the sofa. "The granola can wait. Bianca ... what happened?"

"We did it, and it was great. I mean, God, it was so ... And he ..." Bianca gestured ineffectually with her hands.

"Bianca, take a breath." Sofia sat next to her. "Just tell us."

" 'The angels wept.' That's a cliché about great sex, right? Except I think they actually might have. There might have been actual angels, and they might have wept. And then, and then, he told me he hadn't slept with anyone except Penny before me. And now ..."

Sofia put a hand on Bianca's shoulder. "And now?"

"And now," Bianca went on, "he's free! He's not married anymore. He can do whatever he wants. He can date people, and have sex, and find out what he's been missing."

"So?" Martina asked.

"So, what if what happened between us was just ... just him finding out what he was missing? What if I'm just an experiment? Just ... exploration? What if he's thinking, 'Well, that was great. I wonder if all of the non-Penny sex is like this!' And then he decides to go and find out?"

"Oh." Sofia frowned as she considered that. It didn't escape Bianca's notice that neither of her sisters was telling her that she was wrong and that her scenario was out of the question.

"That could happen," Martina conceded.

"See?" Bianca exclaimed.

"Or," Martina continued, "he might be thinking, 'That was great. I think I'll pursue a meaningful relationship with Bianca so I can have more of it.' "

Bianca moaned and plunked her head down onto her knees.

"Wait a minute." Sofia pointed a finger at her. "If it was so great, why are you here and not there? Why didn't you spend the night? Owen's not home, so why aren't the two of you over at his place making moony eyes over pancakes?"

"Because." Bianca's voice was muffled as she said the word into her flannel pajama pants.

"I can't hear you, Bianca," Martina said.

Bianca lifted her head. "He didn't ask me to stay."

"Did he ask you *not* to stay?" Sofia said.

"No. He just ... We had sex, and it was so ... and I was so ... and I didn't know whether to stay or not, because he hadn't sent me any signals, and the last thing you want to do is sleep over when the guy is silently wishing you would go the hell home."

"That's true," Sofia agreed.

"So I decided it was better to go home and have him wishing I'd stayed than to stay and have him wishing I'd left."

"I can't fault the logic," Martina observed. "On the other hand, if you'd just asked him what he wanted, then you might be having morning sex right now."

"I love morning sex," Sofia said. "I'm going to have a lot of morning sex after Patrick moves in."

"When is that happening, by the way?" Martina asked.

"Soon. He can't get out of his lease, but he's found someone to sublet the place, so it's all systems go. Are you guys sure you don't mind? His place is small, but we can find a bigger rental if we have to. Still, the mortgage on this place is paid, so ..."

"Of course we don't mind," Martina said.

"Can we get back to me, please?" Bianca made a time-out gesture with her hands.

"Right. You're worried he was just using you to get back in the game, so to speak, so you cheated yourself out of morning sex," Sofia summarized.

Martina squeezed Bianca's forearm, her own arm jingling with silver bracelets. Her hair was in a thick braid down her back, and she was wearing a tank top and a pair of loose, flowing linen pants. And that was another argument against morning sex: Bianca had never, on her best morning, looked as flawlessly elegant as Martina did now.

"Bianca," she said, "you're overthinking this. Can we guarantee you TJ isn't just using you for experience? No. Can we guarantee he won't want to move on and play the field? No. Can we promise you won't get hurt? Of course not."

"You're really not helping," Bianca said.

"But," Martina went on, as though Bianca hadn't spoken, "things with TJ definitely won't work out if you're so scared and defensive you don't give him a chance. Love is risk. It always has been. But you still have to try."

It was a stirring speech, and Bianca found herself feeling a little bit better—except for the regret that she'd cheated herself out of morning sex.

"Yeah. I guess you're right," she said.

"Of course I am," Martina said.

"You know," Sofia put in as she slung the strap of her gym bag over her shoulder, "the kind of guy who gets to his late thirties having only slept with one woman isn't the kind who's going to suddenly start screwing around just for sport. For what it's worth."

"I think it's sweet," Martina said.

Bianca did, too. It was one of the many things that made her ache for him, and she didn't want to ache. She'd had enough aching where TJ Davenport was concerned.

And yet, here she was, aching.

Damn it.

TJ MADE his morning coffee while calculating how long, exactly, he had to wait before calling Bianca.

If he called her this early, he might wake her up, which might annoy her, and rule one of wooing women, he figured, was to try not to annoy them.

On the other hand, if he waited too long, *that* might annoy her, and in addition, he might miss a chance to see her today.

And he really wanted to see her today.

It was Sunday, and he didn't have to get Owen from Penny until this evening. That meant he had a stretch of time in the morning and afternoon that lay wide open, just waiting for him to fill it with something.

He wanted that something to be Bianca.

He whistled as he measured coffee grounds into the filter. By God, he was whistling. He hadn't even been aware that he knew how to whistle. There was no end to the new things a man might learn about himself.

And one thing he'd learned was that he hadn't felt good in a very long time. In his marriage to Penny, he hadn't been living—just existing. And then, during and after the divorce, all he could do was get by, taking care of Owen, working, paying the bills, looking forward to that distant time when he might not feel like he was struggling just to hold his shit together.

He hadn't felt good in a very long time, but right now, he was feeling good. He felt alive and optimistic in a way that was wholly foreign to him. He wanted to keep feeling that way—and for that, he needed to see Bianca.

He poured his coffee and took his mug out onto the front porch, where he sat on a white wooden swing that looked like something straight out of the *Andy Griffith Show*. Damn, it was a beautiful day. Of course, he probably would have thought it was a beautiful day even if it had been hailing.

But it wasn't. The sun was shining, the sky was a clear, bright blue, birds were singing in the oak trees in his front yard, and a squirrel was happily running across the grass.

He was still thinking about the squirrel and the birds and especially Bianca when his cell phone rang in his back pocket.

He pulled it out and saw the number: his mother.

"Hey, Mom." His voice sounded unreasonably chirpy even to him.

"Hi, sweetheart." Despite any issues TJ might have had with his mother, hearing the pleasure and warmth in her voice when she greeted him always made him feel safe and loved, as though he were still five years old, being tucked into bed after a story and a snack.

"What's up?" he asked.

"Troy, I was wondering whether you could come over for lunch today. Your aunt Paula is visiting, and she'd love to see you."

Lily always referred to her sister that way when talking to TJ —"your aunt Paula"—as though he might not remember exactly who she was if not given a reminder.

"Oh."

"Are you busy? Because she's only here for the afternoon, and I thought—"

"Ah, no. No, I'm not busy."

The truth was, he'd have loved to see Paula under other circumstances, but he was hoping to get together with Bianca today. The news of his aunt's visit would have been happy for him if it hadn't spelled doom for his plans to be with his girlfriend. Because he was already thinking of her that way—as his girlfriend—even though they had no arrangement of that sort. He couldn't seem to help thinking of her that way.

"Oh, good," Lily said. "We were planning to eat here at one, if that works for you. It's too bad Owen won't be here, but I was hoping ..."

She was still talking, but he'd zoned out. He couldn't focus on what his mother was saying because he was preoccupied with all of the things he now wouldn't be doing with Bianca this afternoon.

"Look." He interrupted his mother, who was going on about the lunch menu and Paula's travel plans. "I'm not sure I'm going to make it."

"But you said you're not busy."

"Well ..." He scratched his head. "I'm not. But I'm hoping I will be."

"What does that mean?" Her voice was flat. She clearly was not pleased with him.

He thought of making up a story, but decided on the truth instead. "I was just about to call Bianca and ask her if she wants to do something today."

"So you don't have plans, then."

TJ saw what he had done, and he scolded himself for his stupidity. Why had he admitted he didn't have plans? What would it have hurt to have told his mother one little white lie?

"Well ... no. I guess I don't. But ... Hey. I have an idea. Why don't I bring her along? You always make more food than we need." If Lily didn't have enough leftovers to feed a family of four, she figured she hadn't done her job adequately. TJ could eat enough to prepare for hibernation and Lily would still have adequate supplies to send him home with a plate for the next day.

"You want to bring her? So, you and this woman are serious, then?"

TJ should have been tipped off to trouble by the way his mother had said *this woman*. But, for whatever reason, he'd missed the signal. All he knew was that he wanted to see Bianca, and at the same time, he knew he couldn't get out of going to his mother's.

It made sense to combine the two things, didn't it?

"I'll call her and ask her if she wants to come," he said.

"Fine." Something in Lily's voice said that it wasn't really fine, and if TJ had been less of an oblivious fool, he would have noticed it.

26

"You want me to meet your mother?" Bianca sounded both surprised and full of dread, which was not how TJ wanted her to feel.

"Well ... I'm sure you've already met her. You live in Cambria, and she lives in Cambria, and it's a small town, so I figure you must have run into each other. And anyway, I don't mean *meet her*, meet her. Not in a *come home to meet my parents* kind of way. This is more of a *I want to see you, and I have to see my mother, so why not do both* kind of deal."

TJ squeezed his eyes shut, contemplating just how big of an awkward mess he was making of this conversation. He looked at the cell phone in his hand as though it might offer him some guidance, but it was silent on the subject. He put it back to his ear.

"You know, forget I asked," he said. "It's awkward, I get it. Owen will be with Penny again next weekend, so maybe then we can—"

"Yes, I'll come to your mother's house," Bianca said.

TJ was so surprised that he worried he hadn't heard her correctly. "You ... wait. What?"

"What time would you like to pick me up?"

TJ was just enough of an idiot to think it was a good thing that she'd said yes, and he grinned. "How about noon?"

"You slept together once and he's already taking you to see his mom? That must have been some really great sex." Martina had heard Bianca's end of the conversation and hadn't been able to resist commenting on it.

"I'm not *seeing his mom*. His mom will be there and I'll be there. That's all." Bianca knew that sounded almost as dumb as what TJ had managed to stammer out, but she went with it.

"You're going to his mother's house. The day after you slept together for the first time. Unless he's planning to pretend you're his Pilates instructor, this is big."

Was it? Part of Bianca wanted to believe that was true, but another part of her was horrified by the thought. As strong as her feelings for TJ had been over the years, and as much as she wanted things to work out with him, it was impossible to miss the giant red flag flapping in the distance.

Meeting his mother this soon could mean he was desperate to get his life back after the divorce and was suffering from a severe case of rebound. She didn't want to be his rebound woman, because that kind of thing was doomed to fail.

On the other hand, if it really was what he'd said—he wanted to see her, and he had to see his mom, so he was conveniently combining two things—then it could be that there wasn't a problem.

Another thing to consider: Bianca believed you could learn a lot about a man by the way he treated his mother, so this was a prime opportunity for her to gather some key facts about TJ before she got in too deep.

"It's just fact-finding," she tried.

"Fact-finding," Martina repeated.

"Yes. If we're going to be seeing each other, why wouldn't I want to know about his mother? And his father? And the home he grew up in? Those are all ..." She scrambled for a coherent argument. "They're key factors in predicting the odds of relationship success," she concluded.

"I suppose," Martina said, considering it.

"Well ... I can't say no," Bianca told her sister. "Because saying that I don't want to see his mother would be making a statement. A statement that all of this is just fun. That we're just playing around. And I'm not playing."

"I know you're not." Martina looked at Bianca with sympathy. "That's what worries me."

BIANCA DRESSED CONSERVATIVELY for the lunch with TJ's mother. It wasn't her professional look—too formal—but it wasn't what she'd normally wear on a Sunday at home, either. She aimed for the sweet spot in between: something that said she was serious but relaxed. Attractive but not going out of her way to advertise it.

Walking that tightrope was already exhausting, and she hadn't even gotten to his parents' place.

By the time TJ picked her up, she'd run the pro and con scenarios of going through with this a thousand times. It wasn't too late—she could still plead illness or insanity. When she opened the door to him, she was more tense than she would have been if she'd been preparing for a job interview.

"You look nice." He put a hand on her shoulder and gave her a quick kiss.

"Do I?" she blurted out. "If the two extremes are 'stripper on her day off' and 'nun,' then I want to hit something right in the middle. Something like 'attractive receptionist.' But I don't know if this is 'attractive receptionist,' TJ. It's been a long time since I've met a man's mother. Peter's mother is dead. Oh, God."

Bianca hadn't meant to spew out all of her insecurities to him. They hadn't been seeing each other long enough for her to be sure he wouldn't flee in terror. But somehow, it had all come out anyway. She wished she could turn back time by two minutes and staple her lips shut.

"You look great," he said. "Although, maybe a little freaked out."

IT WASN'T until Bianca's rant at the door that TJ realized he'd miscalculated the situation. He'd thought bringing Bianca along today was a matter of multitasking—he'd wanted to see her and see his mother at the same time. But now he could see that Bianca was reading more into it. She wasn't just meeting his mother, she was Meeting His Mother. That wasn't how he'd intended it, but there was no way to walk it back now. There was no acceptable way to say that he wasn't serious enough about her at this point to add those capital letters.

Especially when part of him was exactly that serious.

He tried to downplay the situation in a way that wouldn't offend her or make her decide she didn't want to sleep with him anymore. Because that really would be TJ's worst-case scenario.

"Look. I hope you don't think ... This isn't ... My mom wanted me to come over because my aunt is visiting, but I really wanted to see you, so I thought ..."

Damn it. He was bungling this badly, making his prospects for future sex dim with each passing second.

"This isn't what? What isn't it?" Bianca looked as confused as he sounded.

"There's just no pressure, that's all." That seemed like a safe enough thing to say. "I don't want you to feel uncomfortable or nervous. It's just a casual lunch." He reached out and took her hand in his.

But now that he realized his misstep, he wondered if what he was saying was true. He thought of it as casual, as no big deal. But clearly, Bianca didn't. Did his mother? Had she also misread the situation? Did she think Bianca was Meeting His Mother?

As he led Bianca out to his truck, he felt a sense of impending doom. Maybe something would happen to derail this thing before he got to his mother's place.

A flat tire wouldn't have been unwelcome.

THE DAVENPORT HOUSE, situated amid a stand of pines and oaks in the Lodge Hill neighborhood, was a 1920s bungalow that had been renovated in the 1970s and had barely been touched since. The front porch needed a paint job, but the flower garden lining the front walk had been tended with care, with daffodils and calla lilies springing robustly from the earth.

"Well, this is it," TJ said as they both got out of his truck. "This is where I grew up." He pointed to an oak tree in the front yard. "See that tree? I used to have a tire swing hanging from that branch. My dad cut it down after I fell out of it and got a concussion." He grinned at the memory. "Shall we?" He extended his arm to her, and she took it.

BIANCA KNEW THE HOUSE—SHE'D ridden past it on her bike more than once during the height of the crush years—but she'd never been inside. Now, her desire to see the place where TJ had come to manhood outweighed her nerves about what today might mean.

The front porch had that distinctive creak that older homes had when you walked on the wooden floorboards, and something about it made Bianca think of grandparents and summer afternoons and homemade cookies.

She was beginning to feel better about the whole thing—until TJ led her inside and his mother came to greet them.

Of course, Bianca had met Lily Davenport. You couldn't live in a small town for any length of time without meeting virtually everyone. But they hadn't said more than polite greetings to one another, and they certainly hadn't gotten to know each other. And never before had Bianca been presented to her as her son's date.

TJ hugged his mother, then Lily extended her hand stiffly for Bianca to shake.

"Bianca," she said. "How lovely." The way her lips were pressed together, causing fine lines to fan out from the edges of her mouth, said she thought it was anything but lovely.

"Mrs. Davenport." Bianca shook the offered hand. "You have a lovely home."

"*Mmm.* Not as lovely as yours, though, is it? I recall your house being featured in the design magazines some years back after your parents had it done up. All of that fancy design is a little too hoity-toity for me, but to each his own."

So, that was how it was going to be. Lily had landed the first blow before Bianca had even gotten past the foyer.

"Mom," TJ said. "Bianca's house isn't hoity-toity."

"I suppose you've gotten a good look at it," Lily remarked. "Including Bianca's bedroom, I imagine."

With that, Lily turned and headed into the kitchen, leaving Bianca and TJ to follow her.

"I'm sorry," TJ told Bianca, resting his hand at the small of her back. "I don't know what this is about."

"It's about the fact that you got a divorce," Bianca guessed, hissing the words under her breath so Lily wouldn't hear. "And the fact that I'm not Penny."

"Ah, man."

"Are you coming, or do you expect me to serve you lunch in the foyer?" Lily called to them in a frosty tone.

27

Lunch was crab salad with crusty bread and mixed greens with balsamic vinaigrette. They sat at the dining room table, TJ and Bianca on one side and Lily and Paula on the other.

It seemed to Bianca that two sisters could hardly have been more different from each other. Where Lily was tall and thin, Paula was shorter and a bit plump. Where Lily's hair had gone gray and was pulled back into a tidy bun, Paula's was dyed a vibrant red. And while Lily's manner was frosty, Paula's was warm and friendly.

Bianca was grateful that at least someone seemed glad to see her.

"Oh, I'm sure you don't remember me, Bianca, but I saw you in your high school play back when Troy was a senior. *Arsenic and Old Lace*. My nephew couldn't act, but I came out from Arizona to see him anyway." She smiled at TJ fondly.

"He was Mortimer Brewster," Bianca recalled. TJ must have gotten the lead based on attractiveness and charisma, because Paula was right—his lack of talent had been glaringly apparent. Bianca had played a bit part: she'd been cast as one of the police officers, usually a male role, to address a critical shortage of boys who had auditioned for the production.

Bianca had only participated in the play to get close to TJ, though she wasn't about to admit that now.

TJ looked at Bianca in surprise. "You were in that play?"

So, it was true, then. She really had been invisible to him.

"Yes," she answered tightly. "I was. It was a small part, but I was there. Every day. For months of rehearsals."

Lily and Paula silently watched the exchange, until Paula said brightly, "Well. Would anyone like dessert?"

BIANCA WAS MAD—ANYONE could see that. What TJ didn't know was why.

He knew it had something to do with the school play, but what? He really didn't remember her being in it, so surely he hadn't been rude to her or otherwise acted like a fool at the time.

Had he?

Or maybe it didn't have anything to do with that. Maybe she was upset because of his mother's cool attitude toward her. TJ liked that scenario best, because it meant whatever was bothering Bianca wasn't his fault.

They made it through the rest of the meal with polite but stilted conversation. Apple cobbler and coffee, then Bianca offered to help Lily clear the table, but Lily refused, saying, "I think I'm capable of cleaning up after a meal without help, thank you."

TJ got Bianca settled on the living room sofa talking to Paula—who seemed to like Bianca and therefore was unlikely to make trouble—then went into the kitchen to talk to his mother.

He entered the room carrying a used plate in each hand, giving him a handy excuse for being there. When she saw him, her eyes widened in mock surprise.

"Why, Troy, this is a date to put down on my calendar. The day my son helped clear the table without being asked."

"What do you mean? I help." But now that he thought about it, he didn't. He usually sat watching some kind of game with his father while his mother did all the work. Today, his father was at a Rotary Club lunch, so that wasn't an option. "Well," he amended, "maybe I don't help. But I should."

She looked at him suspiciously but smiled in acknowledgment of this unexpected event. "All right, then. Put this leftover crab salad in Tupperware, would you?"

TJ started rooting around in a cabinet for a container and its corresponding lid. While he did that, he took the opportunity to say what he'd really come into the room to say.

"Mom ... you're not being very nice to Bianca."

"Oh?" Lily stacked plates into the dishwasher without looking at him.

"Don't act like you don't know what I'm talking about. You've been giving her a hard time ever since she got here."

"Well, I suppose it was partly the inconvenience of having an uninvited guest." She hit the word *uninvited* with an extra bit of snark.

"Since when are you put out when I bring a friend over? You've always loved having an extra person at the table." Lily usually liked to feed as many people as possible as often as possible. All throughout his teen years, she'd been offended when he *hadn't* invited his friends. Now it was too much work to set an extra place at the table?

"Mom," he said. "Just stop it, and be nice to her."

Lily was holding a dishcloth in her hands, and she wrung it and hung it neatly on a rack next to the sink, not looking at him. When she finally faced him, her expression was rigid and stern.

"I just don't understand you, that's all. You told me you wanted to work things out with Penny. How do you expect to do that if you're dating other women?"

TJ stared at his mother. "I said that a year ago. Before the divorce."

"Yes, well. I don't see why you have to give up just because you signed a piece of paper. People get remarried. People reconcile."

He sighed, suddenly exhausted. He rubbed his forehead and squeezed his eyes shut. "Penny and I are not going to reconcile."

"Well, you're certainly not if you keep running around with this

Bianca person." Lily hissed out the words in a tight whisper so the women in the other room wouldn't hear.

"We're not 'running around.' We're dating. Getting to know each other. It's what people do."

"And for you to be getting serious about someone so soon ... what about Owen? What about stability for your son? Oh, Troy ..."

"We're not getting serious." It didn't feel right saying the words—it didn't feel true—but it seemed to TJ like the easiest way to calm his mother and derail her ire. If he played down what was happening between him and Bianca, maybe Lily would stop feeling like she had to chase Bianca away. Because that was obviously what she was trying to do. And TJ was afraid if she kept it up, it might work.

"Really." Lily crossed her arms over her chest, clearly not believing him.

"Really. We're just having fun. I haven't had fun in a long time. I'm overdue."

Lily's expression softened, and she let her arms fall from their defensive position. "I suppose."

And then he said the thing he was going to end up regretting more than anything he'd ever said besides, maybe, *I do.*

"This thing with Bianca is nothing." He shrugged. "We're just playing around."

And that was when he looked up and saw Bianca standing in the doorway, staring at him.

BIANCA HAD COME into the kitchen to refill Paula's glass of iced tea. She had heard TJ and Lily murmuring to each other, but she hadn't known what they were saying.

That last thing, though, had been as clear as an alpine lake: TJ telling his mother that their relationship was nothing—that they were just "playing around."

It was the second time he'd said something like that, and Bianca didn't need to hear it a third.

"Paula would like a refill of iced tea." She handed TJ the glass. "Could you do it, please? I have an emergency. A patient. I have to go. Lily, thank you for a lovely lunch."

Years of keeping her voice neutral while discussing children's health problems allowed her to hold onto her composure.

"At least let me drive you," TJ said. "You don't have your car."

"Oh. That's all right. I can walk home from here and get my own car. I'll be fine."

But that was stupid, she realized. Lily's house was a couple of miles from hers, with steep hills; it wouldn't be an easy walk, and Bianca was claiming she had an emergency to attend to. There was no credible way she could refuse to let TJ drive her home to get her car.

"It's no problem," he told her. "Mom, I'll be back in a minute." He kissed his mother on the cheek. "Okay," he said to Bianca. "Let's go."

Bianca didn't want to be that woman who ranted and screamed at a man who'd said something to offend her. If this wasn't going to work out—if he really thought she was nothing—then yelling at him wasn't going to change his mind.

The only thing to do was stay calm and stick with the emergency story.

"Are you okay?" he asked as he began to drive her toward home.

"Yes."

"Are you sure? Because it doesn't seem like it. Look. That thing you overheard—"

"Forget it. It's fine," she said. "I'm worried about a patient, that's all."

He seemed to accept that, because who wouldn't? Her job was rife with stress and worry and potential catastrophe, and doctor-patient confidentiality prevented her from talking about it—which made it the perfect excuse.

Implying that she had a dying patient made her feel like shit, though, even more than she already did.

When they got to her house, she couldn't wait to get out of the car and flee inside.

"Okay. I'm just going to ... get my car and go to the hospital. To meet my patient. Thank you for the ride." She reached for the door handle.

"Is there anything else I can do?" he asked.

"No. Thank you. You've done enough. With the ride, I mean." She got out of the car and hurried up the walk without another word to him.

TJ WAS PRETTY sure Bianca didn't have an emergency with a patient—he was pretty sure she'd fled because she was pissed about what she'd heard him say.

But he could hardly accuse her of lying, could he? What if she did have a patient? What if there really was a dying kid, and he made her waste precious time while he accused her of making it up?

No, he had to let her go and save the discussion for later. If she would even agree to talk to him later.

He felt terrible about the whole thing, but instead of focusing those terrible feelings where they belonged—on his own stupidity—he directed his anger at his mother.

Surely, she deserved at least some of the blame.

"What the hell, Mom?" He'd barely closed the door before he started in.

"Troy, I don't like your tone of voice." She was sitting on the sofa with Paula, each of them with a tall glass of iced tea, and both of the women were looking at him in alarm.

"Well, I don't like the way you treated Bianca. And I've told you before, stop calling me Troy. I go by TJ. If you had any respect for my wishes, you'd have gotten that by now."

"Well." Paula patted her hands to her thighs jauntily. "I have ... a phone call to make. Upstairs. I'll just go."

She started to stand up, but TJ stopped her. "Stay. Please. You saw everything; I need a neutral third party here."

"Well." She sat back down.

"A neutral third party for what?" Lily made a show of looking baffled. "I simply don't understand what you're so upset about, Troy. TJ."

TJ rubbed his eyes with his fingers and prayed for patience. "I'm upset, Mom, because you were rude to Bianca. And then she left angry."

"She didn't seem angry to me," Lily said, wide-eyed.

"Yeah, well, she was. And I'm not surprised. You made her feel about as welcome as a bad case of malaria."

"Really. Well, if she *was* angry," Lily said, "then I imagine it might be because she heard you say you were just 'playing around' with her. That was the phrase you used, wasn't it? 'Playing around'?"

"Oh, dear." Paula's eyebrows drew together. "You didn't say that, did you?"

TJ didn't like the way this was going. He'd been set to put the blame squarely on his mother, but Paula and his mom seemed to have other ideas.

"Wait a minute," he said. "I didn't—"

"You said it wasn't serious. That it was nothing. If that's the case, I don't know why you're so upset," Lily shot back.

"Oh, TJ," Paula moaned. "After all those years of marriage, I would think you'd know more about women."

"I know about women." Though he was beginning to think that what he didn't know could fill a multi-volume encyclopedia.

"You'd better go and apologize to her," Paula said.

"I don't see why," Lily remarked. "He was only telling the truth about how he feels. Hardly something he should have to apologize for."

"Unless it wasn't the truth," Paula said. "Is it the truth, TJ?"

"Ah, hell ... I don't know." He knew he liked her. A lot. He knew that sleeping with her had been the most positive thing that had happened to him in months—maybe years. He knew that he wanted to see more of her. And he knew that the idea of her being upset with him made him feel like shit.

Did that mean he was serious about her? What did *serious* even mean?

"If you're not serious about her," Paula said, "you should get that way before she dumps you and finds someone else. I mean it. That girl is a catch."

Lily made a rude sound with her mouth. "I hardly think she's as special as all that. And if he wants Penny back—"

"Penny has moved on," Paula said. "And so should he."

28

———

Bianca didn't have an emergency—other than the fact that her own stupidity had reached critical levels. How could she have let TJ Davenport hurt her again? How could she have repeated the most traumatic event of her entire four years at Coast Union High School?

Still, she was prepared to stick with the emergency pretense as she went inside, grabbed her keys, and went to her car. If any of her sisters had been home, she'd have told them what she'd told TJ—she had a patient she needed to attend to. She didn't want to answer their questions right now, not until she'd had time to think things over. And they would have questions if they saw she'd come home early.

None of them were home, though, so that made things simple. She grabbed the keys, went to the car, got in, and drove away before TJ had even left the premises. Good. The way she'd rushed off, he'd likely believe the lie she'd told him.

She drove in the direction of the hospital in San Luis Obispo—partly to support the lie, and partly because she didn't know where else to go. All she knew was that she needed to be away from TJ and away from her sisters until she had a better handle on her emotions.

"God, I'm stupid. I'm such an idiot. I'm so freaking stupid!" Bianca smacked her hand against the steering wheel as she drove down the coast on Highway 1. She'd let him get to her. She'd slept with him, and then she'd let herself be swayed by some ridiculous fantasy of love and romance and sexual fulfillment.

It was the hormones—that's what it was. Stupid damned hormones that flooded her senses with mooney-eyed lust. They'd made her weak. They'd made her feel things she shouldn't feel and want things she couldn't have.

She should have followed her head and not her heart. She should have listened to her brain, and not her ... other body parts.

Bianca didn't know where she was going, but while she internally stewed and ranted, she seemed to be driving south on autopilot.

Well, she'd said she was going to the hospital, so that was where she'd go. She didn't like to lie, so she wouldn't be a liar. She did have a patient at Sierra Vista, after all—it was nothing critical, but that didn't mean she couldn't stop in and see how her young charge was doing.

Once she had a destination, she felt a little better. If she could just go into doctor mode, she would be able to shove her feelings down enough to cope with the fresh, raw wound that was tearing at her. She'd always felt more comfortable as Dr. Russo than she had just being herself. That was probably worth examining, but not now. Now, she just needed the armor of her white coat.

She got to the hospital, parked in the physicians' parking lot, grabbed the coat and hospital ID she kept in the trunk of her car, and suited up.

Candace McLain was in the pediatric unit recovering from dehydration as a result of salmonella poisoning. Bianca didn't normally monitor her patients who were hospitalized—the pediatricians on staff did that—but what would it hurt to pop in?

When she poked her head into Candace's room, the thirteen-year-old was sitting up in bed reading a John Green book. Her mother, a cute, energetic brunette in her thirties, was sitting in the visitor's chair tapping something into her laptop.

The woman smiled brightly when she saw Bianca. "Dr. Russo! I didn't expect to see you today. Candace is feeling better. Aren't you, sweetie?"

Candace lowered her book. "Yeah. I really am. Can I go home? Please?"

Bianca had reviewed the girl's chart before coming in. "You're out of danger, but your electrolytes aren't what I'd like to see. It wouldn't hurt to stay a little longer." Bianca used her gentle, motherly voice, trying not to sound like she was scolding the girl. After all, Bianca could imagine how much it sucked to be stuck in a hospital bed when all you really wanted was to be hanging out with your friends.

"I hate it here." Candace's blue eyes shimmered with tears. "It's boring. And the food's bad. And the kid next door keeps crying really loud."

"She does." Gina, Candace's mother, wrinkled her nose and nodded. "Poor thing. I think she's in a lot of pain."

Bianca wondered if it had been a mistake to come—on top of feeling shitty about everything that had happened with TJ, now she felt guilty that Candace couldn't go home.

"I don't think it's a good idea to go home today. I'm glad you're feeling better, but we should play it safe." Bianca gave the girl a reassuring smile.

Candace scowled and picked up the book.

Bianca left the room, and Gina followed her and stopped her in the hall. "Dr. Russo?"

Bianca turned to look at her.

"I just want to tell you how much I appreciate you checking on Candace. With doctors, it's easy to feel ... overlooked. That isn't to say ..."

Bianca reached out, squeezed Gina's hand, and released it. "I know what you mean."

It hurt to feel that you were not being seen—especially when you were a teenager. Bianca knew that as well as anyone.

He didn't even know I was in the play.

That might have hurt even more than TJ saying he was just

playing with her. She'd been there all along, loving him, and he hadn't even seen her.

AFTER BIANCA HAD CHECKED on Candace, she had no further excuse to hang around the hospital. She could honestly say that after she'd rushed off, she'd come to look in on a patient.

Now, she didn't know what to do with herself. She didn't want to go home, in case TJ or one of her sisters might be there. And she didn't want to be quiet and still, because that would allow the feelings to come rushing in and drown her.

She went to the hospital's neonatal unit to look at the newborns, thinking that might make her feel better, but it made her feel worse. The tiny, squirming infants represented all that Bianca longed for but didn't have.

She'd go to her office—that's what she would do. There was always paperwork to catch up on, always phone calls to return or supplies to order.

She was on her way out the front door when she heard a voice behind her.

"Bianca?"

She turned to see Peter standing by the vending machines in the lobby with a dollar in his hand.

"Oh. Peter."

Talking to him was the last thing she wanted to do. She didn't need him adding to her emotional burden by acting judgmental and hurt. Only he didn't seem hurt, and he didn't seem angry.

"I didn't think I'd see you here today," he said mildly.

"Just ... checking on a patient."

"Me too—I've got one recovering from a colostomy and another going in for a tumor resection. Stepped out here to get a granola bar, but the damned machine won't take my money."

To demonstrate, he slid the dollar into the slot on the machine, only to have it spit back out at him.

"We could go across the street and have coffee," Bianca suggested. She wasn't sure why she'd said it. Maybe because Peter seemed almost friendly today, and she needed someone to be friendly to her. Maybe because she needed to talk to someone about anything other than TJ. Or maybe because, if she really needed to listen to her brain in making sensible choices for herself, she could do worse than Peter DeVries.

"All right," he said. "I've got a little time."

AT THE CAFÉ across the street from the hospital, Peter ordered a gluten-free, high-fiber muffin, and Bianca had a cup of herbal tea. Her instinct was to get a chocolate croissant and stuff it into her mouth until she was so loaded on sugar and carbs she couldn't feel her face anymore, but she reminded herself that she was being sensible.

She was being smart.

"So, how are things going with that Davenport guy?" Peter asked when they were settled at a table.

Damn it. How had she thought he wouldn't ask?

"Wait a minute." She got up, went back to the counter, and got a chocolate croissant. If she was going to talk about this, she was going to be under the influence of sugar when she did it.

ONE CROISSANT, a cup of herbal tea, and a frothy coffee drink later, Bianca had told Peter the essentials of what had happened: how she'd thought things were going well with TJ, how TJ had dismissed their relationship to his mother, and how Lily had been rude and dismissive from the moment Bianca had crossed her threshold.

"I'm stupid," she said at last, when she'd revealed all of the relevant details. "And I shouldn't even be telling you any of this. We broke up. I broke up with you. I can't expect you to ... to listen and comfort me about my disasters with other men."

"That's true," Peter said. "Not the part about you being stupid. But the part about expecting me to comfort you. You hurt me, Bianca."

"I'm sorry. I just didn't think ... It didn't seem like we were compatible."

"I don't know why not." Peter looked down at the table, where the gluten-free crumbs from his muffin were scattered. "You want, what? Marriage? Children? I want those things, too. It seems to me we're more compatible than you realize."

What he was saying made sense. Maybe Peter hadn't been a lot of fun, but how much fun was she having now? How much fun was it to be told you were nothing but a distraction, a pleasant way to kill some time?

Fun was overrated.

"If I hurt you, I'm sorry." Bianca didn't want anyone to feel the way she was feeling now, didn't want any part of inflicting that kind of hurt on another person.

"You know ... we could try again." He swept the crumbs into his napkin and folded it carefully with the mess safely tucked inside. "If you want to. I know there are things about me you found ... less than inspiring." His face colored a little. "But I could work on them. We could ... try new things."

The way he was avoiding her gaze and the shy uncertainty in his voice made her think that when he said they could *try new things*, he meant in bed. Thinking about sex made her think about TJ, and that wasn't where she wanted her head to be.

She didn't want to have sex with Peter, even if they did try new things. She only wanted to be with TJ. But she didn't want to be with TJ if she was only a bit of fun for him, only a lark or a way for him to transition from his divorce. She didn't want to be a pleasant diversion. She wanted to *mean* something. And she'd meant something to Peter. If she hadn't, he wouldn't be talking about marriage and children. He wouldn't be talking about her future and about second chances.

His eyebrows rose. "Will you think about giving it another go?"

"I'll think about it. And, Peter?" She reached out and took his hand. "Thank you. For listening to me, I mean. You didn't have to do that, not after I ended things. You didn't need to sit there and listen to me talk about another man."

He shrugged. "If it means we can try again, it's worth it. I really do care about you, Bianca."

A little voice in the back of her mind pointed out that he'd said he cared about her, not that he loved her. She wasn't sure that caring—without real love—was enough to build a marriage and a family on. On the other hand, there was a lot to be said for how sensible Peter was, how reliable. How willing he was to give her the things she wanted.

The problem was, what she wanted was TJ Davenport, and there was no way Peter could give her that.

29

TJ knew he had to fix things with Bianca, but he didn't know exactly how. He really had said the thing she'd heard him say, and that was going to be damned hard to explain.

Still, he had to try. He could just tell her the truth: He'd been trying to make his mother back off, and playing down their relationship had seemed like an expedient way to do it. He didn't think that what they had together was any of his mother's business, so he'd seen no obligation to be truthful about it.

If that didn't work, he'd have to do something desperate and go with Plan B: telling her he thought he was falling in love with her.

It was the truth, after all, but he didn't want to admit it if he didn't have to. They hadn't been seeing each other very long, and such an admission would make him look like an idiot. Who fell in love with someone after just a few dates? He'd like to keep that piece of information to himself for a while if he could. But if telling her was the only way to fix things, then he would tell her.

He could figure out what to do about his mother later.

He tried calling Bianca that evening, but it went straight to voice mail. He'd tried texting her, but she didn't respond.

When she still wasn't taking his calls or answering his messages the next day, he decided to show up at her house. It was damned hard to ignore someone when they were standing on your doorstep looking at you.

After work, he gave Owen his dinner, got him settled doing his homework, then told him he'd be back in a half hour to an hour at the latest. Then he drove to Bianca's house, parked his truck, and walked to the front door feeling nervous and a little bit unsteady. Initially, he'd hoped she wasn't pissed, but she clearly was. He had to make things right with her, whatever it took.

Sofia let him in. She told him Bianca had popped over to a neighbor's house for a few minutes but would be back any moment. Did he want to wait?

He did.

He got settled on the sofa, sitting nervously on the edge of the cushion and fidgeting, his right knee bouncing up and down, while Sofia went into her room and did whatever she was doing in there.

TJ tried mentally rehearsing what he wanted to say, but that just made him more nervous. Instead, he began picking up random items from the coffee table, examining them, then putting them back down.

One of the items was a thick binder packed full of papers, Post-it notes in various colors peeking out from the edges. His first thought was that it was Benny's and it had something to do with her marine biology research. But then he saw that he was wrong; the binder was full of pictures of wedding dresses and cakes, pamphlets for DJs and caterers. Okay, so it was Sofia's. He knew her wedding was coming up, though he wasn't sure of the date.

Huh. Nice dress. A little poofy, though.

He was happily leafing through the binder, giving his silent mental judgment on the choices Sofia had made, when he saw something that shocked him so much his brain short-circuited, sending back error messages when he tried to make sense of it.

Because the name of the groom in the binder wasn't Patrick Connelly, as he'd expected. Instead, it was Troy Davenport.

TJ dropped the binder as though it were on fire.

What should he do? Should he wait for Bianca and ask her why the hell she'd been planning their wedding without his knowledge or consent? Or should he just run like hell, change his name, and move to a different town without leaving a forwarding address?

He opted for the latter option—at least, the part about running like hell. Moving and changing his name was a daunting prospect, but getting his ass out of this house as quickly as possible seemed nonnegotiable.

Sofia came back into the room just as TJ had his hand on the doorknob.

"Aren't you going to wait for Bianca? She should be home any minute."

"Ah, no. I've got a ... I have to ... There's a ... a thing I have to do."

"Oh." Sofia frowned. "Do you want me to tell her you were here?"

"No!"

She looked at him funny, and he realized he'd shouted the word. "I mean ... that's all right. You don't have to. I'll just ... call her later."

He went out the front door, got into his truck, and burned rubber on his way down the street and out of the neighborhood.

"He did? That's weird." Of course Sofia had told Bianca about TJ's visit, even though he'd said not to. That was what sisters did. Now, Bianca was trying to figure out what he might have wanted and why he'd left without talking to her. "Did he say what it was about?"

"No. He just said he wanted to talk to you. Then he hurried out of here like his house was on fire."

Bianca didn't particularly want to talk to TJ—not after everything that had happened—but she figured it was inevitable. At some point he would ask to see her again, and she'd have to tell him no. The sooner they got it over with, in her mind, the better.

Still, she wouldn't mind hearing his apology—one she richly deserved. Surely that was why he'd come, but why had he left without the groveling she was entitled to?

Then she saw Sofia's binder sitting on the coffee table, and her jaw fell in horror. "Oh, my God. Was that sitting there when he was here?"

Sofia looked at the binder, puzzled. "I guess so. Why?" Then, after a moment, her eyes went wide and she slapped her hand over her mouth. "Oh! Oh, shit!"

"Did he see it?" Bianca demanded. "Did he?"

"I don't know!" Sofia sounded near tears. "I don't ... I don't know! But he could have. He was sitting on the sofa, and I was in the bedroom, and ... Oh, God. He ran out of here like there were zombies on his ass. He saw it. He must have. Oh, shit. I'm sorry, Bianca. I'm so sorry."

Bianca let out a harsh laugh and sank onto the sofa.

"I'll call him," Sofia offered. "I'll explain. I can fix this. Don't worry. I can make this go away."

"No." Bianca's voice sounded resigned.

"What do you mean, no? Why not?"

What was the point of having Sofia explain things, of chasing after TJ and trying to soothe his nerves? He thought what they had together was insignificant, anyway.

It was almost too perfect. Him seeing the binder and misinterpreting its meaning was simply saving Bianca the time, effort, and emotional anguish of breaking things off with him.

"Just don't," Bianca said to her sister. "Don't talk to him, don't try to smooth things over. Just ... don't."

And it wasn't like he'd completely misread things, had he? Bianca really had planned a wedding between herself and him. She really had nursed an exquisitely painful and intense crush. What did it matter that all of it had happened when she was sixteen? Either way, it was humiliating. Either way, it was likely to make him flee like a rabbit from a circling hawk.

This thing with TJ had been a fantasy from the beginning—it wasn't reality. It wasn't practical, and it wasn't responsible.

Maybe the misunderstanding had been the perfect way out.

TJ WAS STILL SHAKEN at work the next day. Eduardo, the new guy at his latest job site, was helping him reroute the wiring in the master bathroom to accommodate a heated towel rack. As Eduardo cut a strategic hole in the drywall where the rack would be, TJ couldn't help talking a little about what was on his mind.

"You married?" he asked Eduardo.

"Nah, man. You?"

"No." They sat with that information for a moment. "Let's say, hypothetically, you'd just started dating someone. And you went to her house and accidentally found out she'd planned a wedding for the two of you. Without, you know, being engaged, or even telling you about it. That's weird, right?"

Eduardo stopped what he was doing, drywall saw in his hand, and looked at TJ. "That's worse than weird. That's freaking crazy, man. That chick's a bunny-boiler. You better start sleeping with pepper spray under your pillow." Eduardo let out a barking laugh and went back to making the hole in the drywall.

TJ was torn between wanting to defend Bianca—who certainly was not about to murder any household pets—and agreeing with Eduardo.

He wasn't sure what to believe. His instinct told him she wasn't like that—she wasn't some kind of clingy nightmare out of a cheesy horror flick. She was ... well. She was lovely. She was everything he'd thought he wanted in a woman since time and experience had taught him that he didn't want Penny. She was warm and beautiful, kind and intelligent, and, God, when he'd had her in bed ...

"You okay?" Eduardo looked at TJ with his head cocked to one side.

"Yeah. I guess."

"Just figuring out how to lock up your pets?" he asked, and brayed out a laugh.

"Something like that."

He knew he couldn't keep seeing her—not now, not knowing what was in that binder. But that didn't mean it would be easy to stop thinking about her.

BIANCA WENT about her days as though nothing had happened. At least, she tried to. She saw patients, did paperwork, took her clothes to the cleaners, met with her accountant, and kept up on her end of the household chores.

She made dinner when it was her night, and she got her teeth cleaned on schedule.

But she did all of it in a fog of pain, anger, and resentment as she tried not to think about TJ.

"Are you sure you're all right?" Sofia asked her, not for the first time, as Bianca was making sauce for pasta on her night to cook.

"Yes, I'm all right."

"Because if you're not …"

"I wish you'd stop asking." Bianca kept her eyes on the cutting board as she diced tomatoes, onions, and garlic.

"If you want to talk, you know I'm here, right?" Sofia tried. "We all are."

Bianca knew that. It was impossible not to know that, since all of her sisters kept attempting to start a conversation about TJ and about Bianca's heartbreak.

She didn't want to talk about it. Why should she? If she talked about it, she would feel all of the feelings she'd been trying so hard to suppress, and that just wasn't acceptable. If she felt the feelings, then they would all come spilling out, filling up the world around her and drowning her.

The feelings had to stay dammed up, walled in, under control.

Because it wasn't just sadness inside her, struggling to claw its way out. There was a fair amount of anger, too.

Why shouldn't she have what she wanted for once? Why shouldn't she have a man who made her knees weak and her heart sing? Why should this, like every other romantic venture in her life, end in disappointment?

But it had, and here she was. Again. Without a soulmate, without marriage, without the children she so desperately wanted.

TJ had run without even asking her for an explanation, without even waiting to hear her side. He'd dismissed her to his mother, then he'd vanished at his first glimpse of that damned binder.

He didn't deserve her, she thought. If he did, he'd have waited to hear what she had to say. He'd have talked to her about what he did and did not want from a relationship. And he sure as shit would not have told his mother that what they had was nothing.

Bianca hated that TJ had hurt her so much—and for the second time. In neither case had he done it maliciously. He'd simply failed to see her. He'd failed to take full account of her feelings, and of her worth.

No more.

Since she'd refused to talk about it to her sisters, they made erroneous assumptions one Friday night after work when Bianca emerged from her room dressed for a night out.

"Oh, thank God." Martina let her shoulders slump in a showy display of relief. "I'm so glad you and TJ worked things out. It's about time."

"I'm not going out with TJ," Bianca said.

"Oh." Benny cocked her head to one side, considering it. "You going to some charity thing, then? Children's hospital auction or something?"

Bianca considered being evasive, but what was the point?

"I'm going out with Peter," she told them.

She'd called Peter a few days ago, when her loneliness and sadness had been too much for her and she'd opted to combat them with some kind of action. He'd repeated his offer about trying again, and Bianca had thought, why not? Why not Peter? It wasn't as though she had another, more suitable man vying for her affections. Peter *was* the more suitable man, after all, and he was the only one who seemed to care.

"Wait. Peter?" Martina looked alarmed.

"Does Sofia know about this?" Benny demanded to know.

Sofia, who was at Patrick's place that night, did not know. If she had known, she'd have been trying to kick Bianca's ass this very moment.

"It's none of Sofia's business," Bianca said. "Or yours, for that matter."

"Maybe she's trying to make TJ jealous," Benny said to Martina. "Which could work, actually. But only if he sees them together." She turned to Bianca. "Where will you be? You want me to figure something out to get TJ over there? I'm sure there's some way we could manage it."

"I'm not making anybody jealous. For God's sake. I'm just going out with Peter, that's all." Bianca felt close to tears, but she didn't want her sisters to know that. She needed to stop acting on emotion and start making smart choices. Choices that made sense.

"Oh, Bianca." The pity in Martina's voice made Bianca want to throw something. Preferably at her sister.

"Stop it. Both of you. I won't be late. I'll be back by eleven, eleven thirty at the latest." A sensible time for a sensible date with a sensible man.

"Way to live it up," Benny said sarcastically.

30

That night, TJ heated up a frozen pizza and opened a bagged salad for himself and Owen. Gary was sitting on the kitchen floor patiently waiting for some morsel of food to fall.

"What happened to Dr. Russo?" Owen asked. He was sitting on a stool at the kitchen bar, watching TJ prepare the food.

"What do you mean?" TJ stopped, salad bag in hand, to look at his son. "You got referred to a specialist. I thought you knew you weren't going to be seeing as much of her."

"I didn't mean that, Dad. Duh. I meant, what happened to you going out with her?"

TJ stopped, speechless. He'd mostly seen Bianca while Owen was at Penny's. How did he even know about it?

"Who told you I was dating Dr. Russo?" he asked. "I mean, yes, she came for dinner that one time, but that was hardly a date. It was … you know. Dinner."

"Grandma called Mom, and I heard them talking about it. I heard Mom's side, anyway. She was saying stuff like, 'Calm down, Lily.' I think Grandma was pissed."

"Oh." TJ wasn't surprised that his mother had been angry about him seeing Bianca. He already knew that. But he was surprised that Penny and his mother still talked after the divorce. "Does that happen often? Grandma calling your mom, I mean?"

"Sometimes." Owen shrugged. "I think Grandma wants you and Mom to get back together."

TJ put down the bag of salad and focused on his son. "Is that what you want, too?"

Owen let out a derisive puff of air and rolled his eyes. "Oh, jeez, no. I mean, I wish I didn't have to go back and forth, and I miss my old school. But listening to you and Mom fight every day wasn't exactly my idea of a great time."

"I guess not." TJ felt a little bit ashamed of himself, knowing he'd put his son through that.

"You're nicer now," Owen said.

That came as a surprise to TJ. "I'm nicer? What do you mean?"

Owen shrugged again. "You and Mom used to yell at each other, and then afterward, you'd be all tense and uptight." Owen lifted his shoulders up toward his ears to demonstrate. "Like this. And every time you talked to me, it was like you were trying to act happy, but you weren't really happy."

"Yeah." TJ couldn't argue, when the kid was right. "So ... it doesn't bother you that I was dating Dr. Russo? Bianca?"

"No. She's nice." The shrug again. "And she's a doctor, which is really cool. Plus, if Mom's dating somebody, why shouldn't you?"

This last bit made TJ freeze, his mouth slightly open in shock. "Your mom is dating someone?"

"For the last couple of weeks, yeah. She thinks I don't know. Just like you thought I didn't know. You guys must think I'm stupid or something."

At the moment, TJ was the one feeling stupid. All this time, he'd thought Penny was toiling away taking care of her mom, living the celibate life of a selfless caregiver. The thought that she was actually dating someone, probably having sex instead of spending all of her time with her mom, made him feel ...

Good.

It made him feel good.

He hadn't realized how much guilt he'd felt about Penny caring for her dying mother alone—or about him dating Bianca, for that matter—until Owen had raised the possibility that Penny might not be entirely miserable, after all. If she was seeing someone, maybe someone who made her happier than TJ had, then wasn't it possible he could let go of the guilt? Wasn't it possible he could get serious about seeking his own happiness?

He still cared about Penny, and he wanted her to be happy. She hadn't been happy with him. Why shouldn't she be happy with someone else?

"This guy your mom's seeing," TJ said. "Have you met him?"

"Sure. He's Grandma's home health care guy. Comes over and takes her blood pressure and gives her medicine and stuff like that."

"Huh." TJ considered that. "Is he nice?"

"Yeah. I guess." Owen picked up his phone and scrolled through his text messages while they talked—something TJ could never seem to get used to. "Grandma likes him a lot. He tells dumb jokes and makes her laugh, which is nice, because it kind of gets her mind off being sick."

"Huh," TJ said again.

What Owen had said didn't change things with Bianca. Anyone who would make elaborate plans for a wedding to someone she'd just started dating had issues—issues TJ wanted to avoid as though they were a pile of exposed plutonium. But if Penny had moved on, and if Owen was really okay with TJ dating ... then surely TJ could think about moving his life forward instead of just standing in one place.

It was something to think about.

BEING WITH PETER WAS ... fine.

He'd taken her to a good restaurant, a new place down in Morro Bay with sleek furniture, subtle lighting, and cuisine described as "modern California fusion," whatever that meant.

The place was pleasant and the wine was good, and Peter was on his best behavior, having examined the menu online and decided what he wanted ahead of time.

The mood between them was a little tense, maybe, but that was to be expected. It was, after all, their first time going out since Bianca had dumped him. The guy was handling himself remarkably well under the circumstances.

"I'm glad we're doing this." Peter reached out and took Bianca's hand on the tabletop. He rubbed her knuckles with his thumb. "I'm glad you decided to give us another chance."

The touch of Peter's hand—the fact that it was his hand and not TJ's—suddenly made Bianca want to cry. But thinking about TJ wasn't going to get her anywhere. It wasn't going to get her the things she wanted.

"I'm just glad it's not too late," she said, her voice unsteady.

"Never." He grinned, squeezed her hand, and opened the wine menu. "Now, what do you say we spring for a bottle of the Ridge Vineyards white? It's organic."

TJ WAS TRYING NOT to think about Bianca. He was trying so hard that he barely went out anymore because of the danger he might see her. He dropped Owen off at school every morning, went to work, and then went home, where Owen was waiting for him, having taken the bus home from school.

He went to the Cookie Crock for groceries and did the necessary errands around town, but he tried to do it during times when Bianca would normally be at work. He only had to take such measures for a while, he figured. Eventually, he would stop thinking about her, and then he could go about his business normally.

He didn't know when that would be, but he hoped it would be soon, because the very idea of her was torturing him.

She hadn't called or texted him—that was one thing.

He didn't want her to call or text. Of course he didn't. After seeing the binder, he'd done what any sensible person would do—he'd fled like he'd had an angry pit bull on his ass. And nothing about that had changed. If she *did* call or text, he would have to put her off for his own health and safety.

Still, it bothered him that she hadn't. Somehow, he'd thought she would get over what she'd heard him say at his mother's house and would reach out to him. He'd mentally rehearsed what he would do when that happened.

The fact that she hadn't done that was puzzling. Did it mean she didn't want him? Did it mean that she didn't have feelings for him?

None of that mattered, he reminded himself, because he was moving on. He'd heeded the red-flag warning of the binder, and he was turning his mind and his attentions toward other things.

So why did it hurt so much?

Some time after the binder incident, when he was having a pretty good day thinking about things other than Bianca, his mother called and shot his composure to hell.

"What's going on with you and that Bianca Russo?" she asked.

The phrase—"that Bianca Russo"—suggested his mother still didn't approve of any relationship he might have had with Bianca. Somehow, knowing he and his mother were on the same side for once did nothing to make him feel better.

"Nothing's going on," he said truthfully. "Why?"

"I just thought you should know she's been stepping out on you."

Stepping out? It sounded like something one might do in a 1940s musical.

"What do you mean?"

Lily sighed theatrically. "Your father and I went to dinner at that new place in Morro Bay—the one next to the art gallery? The prices are far too high, if you ask me, and it wasn't as though the food was so good it made it worth it. I told your father—"

"Mom." TJ squeezed his eyes shut and prayed for patience.

"I'm just saying—"

"*Mom.* What about Bianca?" He could feel the beginnings of a headache forming behind his eyes.

"Oh. Yes. Well, she was there with some man. Holding hands with him, drinking wine, sharing a dessert. It was all very cozy. I was sure you didn't know about it, and I don't want you getting yourself all tied up in a knot over a woman who's seeing someone else behind your back."

"I don't ... That's not ... What guy? What did he look like?" TJ was trying not to care, but he wasn't managing it.

"Oh, I don't know. Early forties, I would guess. Medium brown hair. Glasses. He looked like a shoe salesman."

Peter.

TJ felt as though he'd been stabbed in the chest, but he tried not to let on to his mother. "We're not seeing each other anymore, so she can have dinner with whomever she wants."

"Oh." Lily sounded surprised. "You're not? Well ... what happened?"

"I don't want to talk about it." That part, at least, wasn't deception.

"But you're ... I mean ... Is it ... Was this your choice?" She was clearly trying to find out if he was okay, but she was dancing around it. It must have been hard to balance her glee that Bianca and TJ had split with her concern for her son's possible broken heart.

"It was mutual." Because it had been, hadn't it? He'd decided to stop seeing her, yes. But she hadn't called or texted, and she was the one already dating someone else. They'd both bailed, but apparently TJ was the only one in a funk about it, feeling like shit.

"Oh. Well, sweetheart, it's for the best. Now you can start thinking about how to patch things up with Penny, because I really think—"

"Mom. For the last time. Penny and I are not getting back together."

"But how do you know, honey? The two of you—"

"She's seeing someone. And you know what? I'm glad. She deserves to be happy. I didn't make her happy, so I'm glad she found someone who could. And you should be, too." The rightness of what he'd just said swelled up inside him and made him know, one hundred percent, the divorce had been the right thing and that they were both better off. He'd known it before, but he hadn't felt it. Now he did.

"Oh," Lily said.

"She deserves better than a failing marriage where everybody's pissed off all the time. We both do," he said.

But he couldn't help thinking that what he really wanted was Bianca. He didn't necessarily deserve her, but he wanted her.

The binder, he reminded himself. If he pursued Bianca after that, it would be like walking into a clearly labeled minefield. He'd only have himself to blame if he got blown to hell.

31

Sofia had been nagging Bianca about TJ and the binder since the moment he'd seen the thing and stormed off. Now, weeks later, she was still doing it.

"This is really stupid." Sofia and Bianca were at Bianca's office before opening, getting ready for the day. "Obviously, if he hasn't called you it's because he was freaked out by seeing his name in there. He probably thinks it's recent and you're some kind of wigged-out, crazy—"

"I get it," Bianca assured her.

"If you just tell him you did it when you were sixteen, he can't possibly hold it against you. Everybody's crazy when they're sixteen. It's expected."

"I suppose." Bianca looked at a patient's chart to avoid looking at her sister.

"So why haven't you told him yet?" Sofia demanded in an exasperated voice.

"This is none of your business, Sofia." Bianca sighed and put down the chart.

"Like hell it's none of my business. A, I'm the one who left out the binder that day, so it's my fault. B, I'm the one who didn't explain things to him the day it happened, like I should have. And C, I have to live with you and your misery."

"I'm not miserable," Bianca lied.

"Well, now you're just making crap up," Sofia accused.

"Look." Bianca took a seat at the reception desk next to where Sofia was sitting. "It's just … It's easier this way."

"Easier than what? Than having your kidney removed through your nose?"

"Easier than …God. Than falling in love with him again and then hearing him tell his mother that he and I are … are nothing!" She threw her hands into the air in despair.

Sofia's eyes widened. "He said that? To his mother?"

"Yes. He said that."

"And you're in love with him again?"

Bianca considered lying again, but what would be the point? "Yes! Yes. God help me, yes. I'm in love with him again. And I can't be, because it's too hard. Because it hurts too much when he … when he dismisses me the way he did in high school. He hasn't changed, Sofia. Nothing has changed. We're older now and we can drive ourselves and we have more money, but everything else is the same."

"Well … your fashion sense is better. Remember those lace-up jeans and that tattoo choker you used to wear? Ugh." Sofia half-grinned.

"I do remember. And you know what? None of that stuff was me, Sofia. I wore those things to try to get TJ to notice me. And he never did."

Sofia's eyes filled with sympathy, and she reached out to put a hand on Bianca's arm. "If he said that to his mother, that really does suck, and I'm sorry. But dating Peter again? That's not going to solve anything. You don't love him."

"I can learn to love him."

"You shouldn't have to."

It was time to open the doors, so Sofia stood and retrieved the office keys from her desk drawer. Before she went to unlock the door, she stopped and looked at her sister. "If TJ doesn't value you, he's an idiot. But that doesn't mean you should just give up and settle for someone you don't really have feelings for. And for what it's worth? It's kind of a sucky thing to do to Peter, making him think he's got a chance. He's not a bad guy. He doesn't deserve it."

Bianca knew Sofia was right about so much of it. But Peter was offering her everything she wanted. Wasn't it worth giving it a shot? Wasn't it worth accepting those things and trying to be happy?

WHEN TJ GOT a text from Bianca's sister, he braced himself for something unpleasant. What that unpleasant thing might be remained a mystery. Was Sofia planning to deliver some kind of message from Bianca? Was she planning to kick his ass? She might be a girl, but she was an athlete, and there was a fair chance she could do it. It was certainly something to keep in mind.

Because he didn't know what to expect, he almost declined when she said she wanted to meet him for coffee. What good could possibly come of it? Instead, against his better judgment, he found himself agreeing. It was just curiosity, he told himself. It had nothing to do with the fact that he couldn't quite seem to let go of the idea of Bianca.

They met on a Tuesday morning at Jitters, a coffee house on Main Street in Cambria.

"I'm supposed to be at work," Sofia told him as they sat down at a small table toward the back. "But I told Bianca I had errands to do. I wanted to do this while she was working so she wouldn't walk in and see us."

"Look, Sofia ... you're a very beautiful woman and all, but ..."

Sofia's eyebrows shot up. "I'm not *interested* in you, you ass."

He considered defending himself, but he probably *was* acting like an ass, so he let it go. He took a sip of his latte to hide his embarrassment. "Okay. So ... why are we here?"

Sofia had an iced, blended coffee drink with a cloud of whipped cream on top—surprising, given her attention to fitness. She took a sip and then licked a bit of whipped cream off of her upper lip.

"We're here," she said, "because I believe there's been a misunderstanding, and Bianca's too pigheaded to clear it up. So I thought I'd do it for her."

TJ felt his defenses go up. "If this is about what I said at my mother's house ..."

"It's not. Although, now that you mention it, if you really meant what you said—that you're just playing with Bianca—then let me know now, and we'll skip the rest of it, because there would be no point."

"No." His throat felt thick suddenly, and he cleared it. "No, I didn't mean it."

"Fine." Sofia nodded. "You should tell her that. And you should apologize for being enough of an idiot to say it."

"Now, wait a minute...."

"But that's not what I came here to say," Sofia told him. She took a deep breath, then continued. "The notebook you saw—the one with the wedding plans in it—is not what you think."

"It's not?" He looked at her, eyebrows high. "You mean it's not Bianca's plan for a big, elaborate wedding? To me?"

Sofia opened her mouth, then closed it again.

"Okay, it is what you think. But she did it when she was sixteen, TJ. When she had a crazy teenage crush on you and you wouldn't give her the time of day. It was a way to channel her emotions. She did it for fun, because you were never going to pay attention to her, and she needed to put those feelings somewhere. She never expected it to be real. It was a fantasy. An exercise."

Sixteen?

"But ... if she did that more than twenty years ago, why was it out on your coffee table? Why ..."

Sofia's face got that dewy, pink look women got when they were about to cry. Which TJ absolutely did not want her to do.

"Let me back up," she said. She looked at her drink, which she held in both hands, instead of at him. "Our parents died a few years ago. Her from cancer, him in a car accident a short time later. We were destroyed. All of us. Because of the grief, and the pain, and the … the *feelings*, I had a hard time with the idea of marrying Patrick. I needed to feel like my mother was there, like she could be a part of it. Bianca made that fantasy wedding plan with our mother. They did it together, as a kind of bonding thing. So when things got serious with Patrick, and I was sad that my mom wasn't there to help me plan a wedding …"

Now TJ was catching on. "You decided to use the plans she'd already made," he finished for her.

"Yes. Exactly." A fat tear slid down Sofia's cheek, and she wiped it away. She took a deep, ragged breath, then steadied herself. "So, that's why the binder was out. Because I'm planning my wedding. Bianca is not trying to rush things between you. She is not some crazy stalker who's planning to wear your skin like a man suit."

TJ was starting to wonder if maybe he'd been stupid for jumping to conclusions. It wouldn't have been the first time.

"But … if she knew that's what I thought, why didn't she say something? Why didn't she tell me what you just told me?"

"Why should she, when what the two of you have is *nothing*?" Sofia looked at him pointedly. "Why should she fix it, when you were just *playing around* with her, just having a good time?"

"Oh, God." TJ rubbed his face with his hands, then ran a hand through his hair. "I shouldn't have said that."

"You think?"

He groaned. "The truth is … I care about her. A lot. But my mother wants me to get back together with Penny, and she was giving me a hard time, so … so I pretended that I was just … I don't know. Just getting my feet wet with Bianca. Just getting back in the game."

Sofia cocked her head and considered him. "Well, are you?"

Because he'd never put the question to himself exactly that way, he didn't know what to say.

"Listen." Sofia leaned toward him, her elbows propped on the table. "If you need some time to play the field after your divorce, I don't think anybody's going to hold that against you. I get it. It's a normal thing to want to do. But Bianca's not the woman to do it with, because she has real feelings for you."

When he didn't say anything, she gathered up her purse and her drink and stood up. "I've got to get to work, or Bianca's going to start asking questions. You might not want to tell her we had this conversation."

"Right." TJ nodded.

"I mean, you can if you want to. If she asks me about it, I'll just say that somebody had to be the adult in this situation. But, all things considered, I'd rather not have to."

"Yeah. I get it."

She walked out humming a little tune, full of the satisfaction of a woman who'd just handed a man his ass.

IT DID MAKE a difference to TJ that Bianca had made the wedding plans when she was sixteen, and it did make him feel better about their potential future. But he still had to figure out whether he was ready to have a relationship—with anyone.

Whether he was or wasn't, he still owed her a proper apology about the things he'd said to his mother. TJ hadn't been raised to say unkind, untrue things that hurt people's feelings, and he certainly hadn't been raised to avoid apologizing afterward.

And all things considered, he'd be better off setting things right before things with that Peter guy went any further.

He waited until that evening, when Bianca would be home from work. He decided to drop by her house without calling first, in case she decided not to take his call.

He parked his truck, trotted up the front walk, and knocked on the door—which was answered by a scowling Sofia.

"You might already be too late," she said. "She's with Peter."

For some reason, he hadn't considered that possibility. "What?"

"She's seeing her ex again. Instead of you. Because you hurt her feelings." Sofia spelled it out for him as though he were a particularly inattentive kindergartner.

"Ah, man." TJ had come over here uncertain about where he wanted things with Bianca to go—if anywhere. But hearing that she was, this moment, with her ex-boyfriend made him feel as though he'd been punched in the throat.

"I wouldn't tell you where they were, even if I knew," Sofia went on.

"Well, of course. I didn't—"

"If I knew they were having dinner at Neptune, for instance," she continued, "I wouldn't tell you that, even if I knew you could probably go there and break up the date somehow."

"Oh." TJ blinked a few times. "You think I should—"

"I absolutely do not think you should go to Neptune and break up Bianca's date with Peter," Sofia said. "Even though they don't belong together, and if they do end up getting married or something, it'll mean a lifetime of misery for both of them. So, don't do that. Even though, if they had a hypothetical reservation at six thirty, they'd just be sitting down to dinner about now."

"Okay. I won't do any of that," TJ said, playing along.

After he'd said goodnight to Sofia and she'd closed the door, he got back into his truck and hauled ass over to Neptune.

32
____

Owen was at TJ's parents' house that evening, which meant TJ had all of the time and freedom he needed to make an ass of himself.

Because he didn't particularly relish the *ass* part, he considered his strategy before going into the restaurant, as he sat in his truck in the parking lot.

He could go in there for dinner and just happen to see her, then drop by her table to say hello.

He could try to catch her eye without Peter seeing him, then maybe have a private word with her.

Or, he could feign some kind of emergency to get her away from her date.

The last one seemed the most likely to get results, though he hated to use his son's medical condition to forward his own love life. Still, Owen wanted TJ to keep seeing Bianca, so maybe the kid wouldn't mind.

Still not completely clear on his plan, he decided to just charge in there before he lost his nerve.

Bianca and Peter were sitting at a table by the window, with a view of Main Street. TJ spotted them a moment after he pushed past the hostess, claiming he was there to meet someone.

He moved with more confidence than he felt—then doubted his decision as soon as he found himself standing at Bianca's table, looking down at her.

"TJ." Bianca sounded surprised to see him—and not the happy kind of surprised.

"Oh. Hello." Peter peered up at him through his dark-rimmed glasses.

"I ... ah ..." The idea of claiming some kind of Owen-related emergency evaporated when he realized that Peter was Owen's doctor, too. "I was just going to ... have dinner," he said, settling on one of his other scenarios.

"How nice for you." Bianca's voice was frosty.

"The bisque is particularly good," Peter said. "Ah ... would you like to join us?"

Damn it. The guy was so courteous that he was actually offering to let TJ—a guy who'd slept with Peter's date—horn in on their evening. TJ almost felt guilty about what he was about to do.

Not guilty enough not to do it, though.

"Thanks, I think I will." He pulled out a chair and sat down at the table between the two of them.

"What are you doing?" Bianca said tightly.

"I'm here, and you're here, so ..." TJ indicated the table, the restaurant, Cambria, the state and country beyond. "We might as well be here together."

"Peter and I are on a date," Bianca said. "Maybe you didn't realize, but ..."

"Bianca and I were just discussing our living arrangements," Peter said. "She's planning to move in with me."

Ah, so Peter wasn't being courteous after all. He'd invited TJ to sit down so he could stake his claim at his leisure. It was game on, then.

"Really," TJ said. "Congratulations."

Bianca appeared flustered. "That's ... I don't ..."

"I guess we're celebrating, then," TJ went on. "We should order a bottle of Champagne."

"Champagne makes me break out in hives," Peter said.

"Two bottles, then," TJ said mildly, a predatory grin on his face.

"Excuse me. I have to use the ladies' room." Bianca got up from the table and hurried toward the back of the restaurant, her heels click-clicking on the hardwood floor.

When she was gone, Peter took the napkin out of his lap, folded it carefully, and placed it on the table beside his plate. "What's this about?"

"What do you mean?" TJ looked at Peter innocently. "I was here to have dinner, and—"

"That's crap, and we both know it."

The fact that the guy couldn't even bring himself to say the word *bullshit* probably said something about him, though TJ wasn't sure what.

"Okay, then why am I here?" TJ asked.

"You're here because you're jealous," Peter concluded. "You slept with her and made her think there was something there, that it might go somewhere, then when you talked about her to your mother, you acted like she was less than the dirt on your shoe. Then you stopped calling, stopped texting—stopped everything. And now that she's moved on, now that she's seeing someone who actually wants a future with her"—Peter spread his arms in an expansive gesture —"here you are."

TJ couldn't argue with anything Peter had said. It was all true, and he felt ashamed of himself because of it. All he could do was answer truth with more truth.

"She wasn't happy with you before or she wouldn't have ended it. So, what are you doing now?"

"I'm dating her," Peter said, "and you're not. Not anymore."

Peter had always seemed like such a mild-mannered guy when TJ had been to his office for Owen. But now the man's face had colored with anger and outrage.

"You know, I'm rethinking dinner," TJ said mildly, standing up. "I hate bisque."

BIANCA'S DATE with Peter had been going well enough—it was amiable, if dull—until TJ showed up.

Now, she didn't know what to think. Had he been there by coincidence, as he'd said? Or had he come there to break up the date? If it was the latter, what did that mean?

She'd fled to the ladies' room to have a chance to think.

While she was in the bathroom staring into the mirror over the sink, she pulled her cell phone out of her pocket and called home. Benny answered on the second ring.

"Is the date sucking?" she asked. "Do you need me to call you in five minutes with an emergency? I've got some chipped toenail polish; I think that qualifies. It looks really bad."

"TJ's here. I don't need you to manufacture an emergency. I've already got one."

"You need Sofia," Benny said. "Hang on."

In a second, Sofia came on the line. "He's there already? Jeez, he must have run every red light on the way over."

"Sofia. What are you talking about?"

Sofia sighed as though Bianca was trying her patience. "I'm talking about the fact that I sent him over there. You can thank me later."

"But—"

"He came here looking for you. Finally. He should have done it weeks ago. But better late than never. I told him you were out with Peter, and where. If he's going to make his move, I wanted to be sure he did it before Peter did something stupid, like proposing."

"Oh, God."

"Did he already propose? Oh, shit. Jeez. I hope you didn't say yes, Bianca ..."

"He didn't propose. The two of them are out there at the table ...

talking. I think they plan to eat together." She said the word *eat* as though Peter and TJ were planning to eat each other.

"Oh. Well, I didn't expect that."

"What am I supposed to do?" Bianca wailed.

While she was talking, a woman in a low-cut black dress came into the bathroom, gave Bianca a look of sympathy, and went into a stall.

"All right, Plan A, the thing Benny said before. I'll call you in five minutes with an emergency," Sofia offered.

"Do that," Bianca said. "In five minutes. Not seven, not six, or I'll give you a real emergency to worry about."

TJ WAS WAITING for her when she came out of the bathroom.

He was leaning against the wall of the hallway outside the ladies' room with his arms crossed over his chest and one foot propped against the wall as though he were simply relaxing there, killing a pleasant fifteen minutes between courses.

"What are you doing here?" Bianca asked as she came out of the bathroom.

"Waiting for you."

"No, I mean ... what are you doing here at the restaurant in the first place? Because you didn't come here for dinner."

He leveled a blue-eyed gaze at her that almost made her knees weak. "I came here to talk to you." He took two steps toward her until they were standing so close she could smell his warm skin.

"I don't have time to talk," Bianca said. "Peter's waiting for me." She turned away from him and started toward the dining room.

"Bianca, wait."

She told herself not to turn around, not to listen to what he had to say. Because what good would it do? It wouldn't change anything. It wouldn't make TJ feel things for her he didn't feel.

But he'd always held power over her, from the first day she'd seen him in Mrs. Parker's English class in eleventh grade. So she stopped, and she turned, and she looked up into those gorgeous eyes.

"What? What do you want?"

"I want to apologize." A waitress was trying to get down the hallway past them, so they stepped aside to let her through. TJ lowered his voice, and the intimacy of it made Bianca feel hot and soft inside.

"That thing I said to my mother—it was unforgivable," TJ went on. "It was cruel, it was thoughtless ... and it was a lie. I only said what I did to get her off my back. She still thinks Penny and I have a chance, and she's ..." He shook his head and raked a hand through his hair. "It was just easier to let her think things between us weren't going anywhere. So, I'm sorry. If I hurt you, I'm so sorry."

It was what she'd wanted to hear, and now that she'd heard it, she felt herself weakening. "And then there was the binder. Which you misunderstood," she said.

"Yes."

"TJ ... that was mortifying. It was mortifying that you saw it, and even more so that it exists in the first place. But I was sixteen...."

"I know. Sofia told me."

"She did?" She blinked at him in surprise.

"Yes."

"Well ... I'm not that person anymore," Bianca said, unsure whether it was the truth. "I'm not that crazy, over-the-moon teenager trying to cope with the feelings of having her first crush. I'm an adult now, and I have to make adult decisions for myself."

But looking at him now, in the dimly lit hallway, with him standing so close to her, she felt exactly like that girl, that irrational, love-crazy girl. But she had to be smarter than that. She had to be.

"Bianca." He reached out and laid his hand on her cheek, and her eyes closed. Then he drew her to him for a kiss, a kiss so slow and deep and thorough, she forgot she was in a public place until she heard a waitress's voice say, "Excuse me? This is a restaurant, not a by-the-hour motel."

AFTER THE KISS, after they were interrupted, Bianca went back to Peter's table. TJ couldn't believe she went back.

What was the point of cornering a woman near a restaurant ladies' room and kissing her senseless if she was still going to have dinner with another man?

He stood in the hallway after she left, his hands on his hips. "Well, shit," he muttered. If the kiss hadn't worked to break up Bianca's date with Peter, then he didn't have a Plan B.

He knew he should just go home, have a beer, and try not to think about whether that asshole's hands would be touching Bianca later that night. The idea of that made him crazy, irrational. He wanted to go back into the dining room, pick Peter up by the scruff of the neck, and toss him through a plate glass window and out onto Main Street.

But he couldn't do that, could he? Aside from the inevitable jail time that would result, there was the fact that Peter had been right. Peter was ready to give Bianca the things she wanted, and TJ wasn't. Peter was a doctor, and TJ wasn't. TJ had treated Bianca like crap, and Peter hadn't.

What if Peter really was better for her?

What if TJ was just wasting her time?

TJ went into the men's room, splashed cold water on his face, then dried it with a paper towel from the dispenser. Then he gathered whatever was left of his dignity and walked out of the restaurant.

33

When Bianca got the fake emergency call from Sofia, she used it, even though TJ was gone and the uncomfortable situation she'd been in had passed.

She couldn't just sit there with Peter, pretending everything was okay, after the kiss. Because now, the kiss was all she could think about.

She played up the emergency, claimed alarm at some fictional situation with a patient, and let Peter drive her home.

She said goodbye to him at his car, went inside, watched through the peephole until he left, and sagged against the front door, feeling spent.

"Home already?" Benny smirked. "Even on a date with two men at once, you can't manage to stay out past eight?"

"You're hilarious." Bianca's eyes were getting hot and wet. A tear fell, and she swiped at it, sniffling.

"Oh, jeez. Come on. Sit down. Tell all." Benny patted the spot beside her on the sofa.

Normally, Bianca would have resisted. She'd have wanted to keep her personal business to herself, and she'd have excused herself to go to her room, pleading fatigue or some mysterious tropical illness.

But she didn't have it in her tonight, so instead, she flopped down on the sofa and put her hands to her face.

"Oh, God. He apologized, and then he kissed me, and … I thought I had a plan! I thought I knew what I was going to do, but now …"

"Wait. Which one of them apologized and kissed you?" Benny asked.

"TJ. TJ did. I had convinced myself that Peter was a better choice, Peter was the smart way to go. But now … the kiss …"

While Bianca was wailing and complaining about her love life, Martina came into the room and perched on the edge of a club chair near the sofa.

"Oh, no. What happened?" she asked.

Benny filled her in, and then said pointedly, "She thought Peter was the smart choice. But then TJ kissed the pants off her at Neptune. Metaphorically, I mean. She kept her pants on. I'm assuming."

"Bianca." Martina got up, moved to the coffee table, and sat on it so she could face Bianca knee-to-knee. "I know you want to make good choices. I know you're used to doing what your brain tells you instead of following your instincts. But … Peter isn't the smart choice. Not if you're letting another man kiss you at Neptune."

Bianca let her head flop onto the back of the sofa, and she stared at the ceiling. "I didn't let him. He just did it."

"But you liked it."

"I … yes. Oh, God, yes."

"The way that kiss made you feel?" Martina put a hand on Bianca's knee. "That's the way you're supposed to feel when you're in love with someone. And Peter doesn't make you feel that way. And he never will."

Bianca wanted so much to argue with Martina's point, but she couldn't. Not without lying to both her sister and herself.

"There's more to a relationship than *feelings*," Bianca said. "There's compatibility. And shared goals. And mature, responsible—"

Benny made a rude raspberry noise with her mouth, cutting Bianca off. "What a steaming pile of bullshit. You sound like you're planning a financial portfolio instead of choosing a man."

"She's right." Martina nodded sagely.

But how could Bianca trust her feelings, when her feelings told her she was in love with TJ, and that clearly was impossible? Whatever she was feeling for him, it couldn't be love. She couldn't love him when they'd been seeing each other for such a brief time. She couldn't love him when so little between them seemed, on paper, like it should work. And she couldn't, simply couldn't, still be in love with him after all these years.

Could she?

~

WHATEVER TJ's feelings about Peter after that night at Neptune, he had to suck it up for the sake of Owen's health. Peter was still Owen's doctor, and Owen still had a good deal of medical care ahead of him before his condition would be fully under control.

In fact, Owen had a follow-up appointment that week, and while TJ would rather have eaten broken glass than face Dr. DeVries, he had no choice but to man up and take care of his son.

The idea that Bianca might have gone home with Peter that night, though ... the vision of it that kept running, unbidden, through TJ's brain ... It was all he could do to remind himself that he was here for his son and therefore couldn't run over the man with his car.

"Mr. Davenport. Owen," Peter greeted them with a bland smile as they sat in an examining room, Owen on the exam table and TJ in a hard-backed plastic chair. "How have you been feeling?" Peter asked the boy.

They went over that—the side effects Owen had been suffering from his medication, the latest blood test results, the adjustments Peter would be making to the dosages, and what they should look out for—and then Peter offered TJ a dead-fish handshake and made to head out of the room.

"Dr. DeVries?" TJ said, stopping him. "I wonder if I might have a word? Owen, could you go wait for me in the lobby? I'll just be a minute."

When Owen was gone, Peter turned to TJ, holding Owen's chart against his chest. "What is this about? I have other patients."

"I'm sure you do." TJ hadn't been sure what he'd wanted to say to Peter, only that he had to say something in acknowledgment of all that had happened at Neptune. He wasn't sure what he wanted with Bianca, whether he was ready for another relationship so soon after Penny, and what that would look like if he did. Bianca wanted a future, and Peter was willing to give her that, so TJ knew he should make some sort of manly speech about stepping aside. He knew it was the right thing to do—the sensible thing.

But he couldn't stop thinking about Bianca and the way she felt in his arms. Her smell, the feel of her skin, the purr in her voice when she talked to him after a kiss or after their one night of delicious love-making. And he knew he didn't want to give up those things for anyone—especially not for Peter DeVries.

"We're not done," TJ said, when he finally found the words. "Bianca and I aren't done. I don't know where it's going to go, or what I can offer her, but ... we've just gotten started, and I'm not going to walk away."

Peter regarded TJ with narrowed eyes. "Is that right?"

"It is. I respect you as a doctor, and I appreciate all you're doing for my son. But I believe Bianca wants to be with me, so ... I have to pursue that."

Peter listened, then nodded mildly. "Interesting. If she wants to be with you, though, I wonder why she spent the night with me after you left us? Seems ... inconsistent."

TJ was still staring at him, speechless and slack-jawed, as Peter walked out of the room.

TJ HAD KISSED HER, then he'd left. And now Bianca didn't know where things stood, what his intentions were, or what she was going to do about them, whatever they might be.

He'd seemed like he wanted her, and yes, his apology had been good to hear. But a kiss wasn't a conversation. It wasn't a plan. It wasn't a promise.

After a couple of days of stewing over it, she decided that someone had to figure out what the hell was going on between herself and TJ, and that person might as well be her. She was running out of excuses for why she couldn't see Peter, and something had to be done.

By the time she texted TJ three days after the incident at Neptune, she had gotten herself into such a lather that she was already yelling.

WHAT THE HELL WAS THAT ABOUT?

Her iPhone told her almost immediately that the text had been read, and she waited impatiently as three little dots appeared on her screen, showing her that he was composing his answer.

You looked like you needed to be kissed, that's all. Don't tell me that uptight asshole you were with has any idea how to do it, because I won't believe you.

Bianca stared at the text, opened her mouth as if to respond to the walls of her office, then closed it. She typed out several texts—some of which were reasonable and calm, and some of which were riddled with random obscenities—then deleted them. Then she told herself to calm down, took a few cleansing breaths, and settled on a response.

When a person interrupts another person's date and then kisses her, it's confusing. Was that supposed to mean something? Or were you just passing by looking for someone to kiss?

He didn't respond for a few minutes, then when he did, his answer made Bianca cock her head in question like a cocker spaniel hearing the distant opening of a box of treats.

Does it matter? You slept with Peter again anyway, so I guess I wasted my time.

The conversation was becoming too confusing, and too personal, for text messages. Bianca tapped in his contact info and hit CALL.

"What makes you think I slept with Peter again?" she asked as soon as he picked up the phone.

"Why does it matter why I think that? You did, and I assume

you're going to do it again, so ... You've made your choice, and that's fine. The better man won."

Bianca closed her eyes and shook her head, trying to clear her thoughts. "I didn't sleep with Peter. I mean, yes, I did in the past, when we were together, but not since you and I ..." She shifted her stance, moving her weight from one foot to the other. "I don't know what business it is of yours, anyway, since you apparently don't really want to be with me. You just want to kiss me in restaurant hallways."

"Just one restaurant hallway," he corrected her. "And what do you mean, you didn't sleep with Peter?"

"I went home!" She was nearly yelling now. "After you left, I made an excuse, and I went home! So I don't know what the hell you're talking about!"

"You went home?" She could almost see the surprise on his face.

"Yes. Not that it's any of your—"

"I know, I know. It's not. But ... really? You went home?"

"I went home. Alone."

"But Peter said ..."

Suddenly, it was starting to make sense. "When did you talk to Peter?"

"When I took Owen in for his follow-up. We had a ... a man-to-man talk, I guess you could call it. Or, man to weasel."

Bianca didn't know what to address first—the fact that the two men in her life had apparently discussed her and her love life behind her back, or that Peter had lied about her. She started with the latter.

"Peter said we slept together? That night, after you left the restaurant?"

"Yeah, he did. And are you moving in with him? Shit. Bianca ..."

So, Peter had talked trash about her, claiming she'd done things she hadn't, and TJ had believed it without even talking to her and had written her off because of it.

"Bianca?" he prompted her.

"I've about had it with both of you. Maybe you and Peter should go out. You seem to have a lot to say to each other." Then she hung up the phone.

34

Bianca couldn't confront Peter right away because he was working, and so was she. She had a full day of appointments, and today was Monday, so she knew he'd be in the outpatient procedure center all day doing colonoscopies.

That was fitting, considering the fact he was a complete asshole.

She waited until after work, then drove to his place and was waiting for him outside his apartment door when he arrived home.

"Bianca. This is a pleasant surprise. Did I forget we had a date?" He had his suit jacket over his arm, and he looked tired.

"No, you didn't. I came over because I need to talk to you."

"About?"

"About why you lied to TJ about us sleeping together."

Peter rubbed his forehead, his eyes squeezed shut. "Do we have to do this right now? I've had a really long day."

"No. No. We don't have to do this now. We don't have to do this ever. We're done."

Peter put his briefcase down next to his feet and let his shoulders slump. "He's what you want? An electrician? You want to be some ... some blue-collar man's wife and have his lower-middle-class babies?"

Actually, the thought was immensely appealing—if TJ weren't a complete jerk. Which he was.

"You lied about having sex with me, like some teenager in a high school locker room," Bianca said archly. "Just because you're a doctor doesn't mean you have class."

She turned and walked back to her car with him still calling her name.

~

TJ HAD MISHANDLED this whole thing from the beginning. That much was clear. The problem was that he'd had so little experience with women who weren't Penny. That had to be it. Otherwise, he'd have to admit he was just a jackass, and that thought wasn't one he wanted to embrace.

He wished he had someone he could talk to about it, but he didn't. His mother was out, obviously. He'd had friends in San Jose, of course, but it was funny how friends seemed to fall away when you got a divorce. It was almost as though he'd divorced his entire former life, and not just his wife.

He needed to go over things—his own mistakes, and where to go from here—with another guy. After considering all of his options, he had what he thought was a brilliant idea. He would talk to Patrick, Sofia's fiancé. He'd met the guy a few times, and he seemed like a good person. Plus, he knew Bianca as well as any man TJ could think of, except Peter.

He called Patrick at his office at the university—the only number TJ could find for him—and Patrick agreed to meet him for beers at Ted's one night after work.

The place was only moderately busy, as expected on a weekday night. A couple of guys were playing pool, and two more sat at the bar. A couple who looked to be in their sixties and weathered by life shared a round table toward the back of the room.

The lights were dim and the place smelled like spilled beer and sweat. TJ and Patrick took seats at the bar, and TJ bought two mugs of cold beer.

"It was ... interesting to hear from you." Patrick adjusted his glasses, which made him look like the English professor he was. "Unexpected."

"Yeah, well." TJ took a deep swig of his beer to gird himself for the conversation to come. "I just thought ... You know Bianca, so ..."

"*Mmm.*" Patrick adjusted his butt on the barstool. "I want to help, but I can't break the code of honor. I'm about to be part of their family, you know."

"Right." TJ nodded. "I get that. But it wouldn't be breaking the code just to listen a little, would it?"

"I guess not." Patrick nodded amiably.

So TJ told him all that had happened: how Bianca had been the first woman he'd dated since Penny; how it had been going well until TJ had lied to his mother about Bianca's importance; the thing with the binder; the incident at Neptune; and then the conversations with first Peter and then Bianca.

"I screwed up," he concluded, rubbing at the stubble on his face with his hand. "I shouldn't have said that to my mom. And I apologized, but ... I can't seem to get things back on track."

Patrick half-turned his body on the barstool to face TJ. "Let's look at what we know." He started ticking points off on his fingers. "She was in love with you in high school, but you broke her heart when you didn't notice her." TJ started to object, but Patrick put up a hand to quiet him. "Then, you reconnected and really hit it off. You invited her home to meet your mother—a step with great significance and a good deal of symbolism—but then you told your mother it didn't mean anything. When you saw evidence of how much you mean to her—the binder—you pretty much cut off all communication with her. Then, you kissed her at Neptune and vanished again." Having ticked off all of the relevant points, he gave TJ a pointed look. "It's not breaking the code of honor to lay out everything you already know."

"I guess not."

"If I were analyzing this as the plot of a literary work," Patrick continued, "I'd notice themes of betrayal, emotional unavailability, and repeated unrequited love."

Was that how it looked to Bianca? Like she'd given him nothing but love, and he just kept backing away?

"When you put it that way, I look like an ass."

"And Bianca looks like a lovely, vulnerable woman who keeps putting herself out there and not getting much in return."

"Well ... shit." TJ felt uncomfortable with the direction this talk was taking. "It's just ... I'm getting back in the game for the first time since Penny...."

"There's your problem," Patrick said casually. "To Bianca, it's not a game."

TJ HAD SUSPECTED that he was bungling things with Bianca, and his conversation with Patrick confirmed it. Still, he wasn't sure what to do about it. When it came down to it, he wasn't sure what he wanted.

When he'd told Peter that he and Bianca weren't finished, that had felt right. It had felt like the truth. He knew he wanted her in his life, but he wasn't sure what form he wanted that to take—or how to get there.

She'd never answered his question about whether she was going to move in with Peter, but after their conversation, when she'd told him that she and Peter hadn't slept together lately, he assumed the answer was no. If he'd read that wrong, then the whole thing was moot anyway.

He and Bianca would have been so great together. But it all seemed like a mess of missteps, misinformation, and poor timing. If only he'd played it differently. If only she weren't still seeing that ass DeVries ...

Because it was all so confused in his mind, and because it was easier not to take action, TJ spent the rest of the week and part of the weekend bonding with his son on one of the rare Saturdays when Owen was with him and not with Penny.

The kid was still feeling like crap from his medication, so they took it easy, going out for ice cream (no chocolate or nut topping because of his low-copper diet) and playing video games on TJ's big-screen TV.

In between games, when TJ got up to refill the bowl of popcorn they'd been sharing, he casually brought up the topic of Bianca.

"So ... I talked to Bianca last week. Dr. Russo."

Owen looked up from where he was seated on the sofa. "Really? I kind of thought that wasn't happening."

"You did? Why?"

Owen shrugged. "Because you've been moping around, and because you've got nothing better to do on a weekend than play video games. You don't even like video games."

"But I like you, and *you* like video games."

"I guess." Owen shrugged again.

"It's just ... hard. With women, I mean."

Owen let out a *pfffft* sound and rolled his eyes.

TJ, starting to become irked, brought the bowl back to the sofa and sat down. "What's that supposed to mean?"

Owen reached into the bowl and took out a handful of popcorn. "Last year when I was too scared to ask Kaitlyn Blanchard to the sixth grade dance, you called me a wuss."

Had he said that? It sounded like him. He slumped into the sofa cushions. "Well, maybe *I'm* the wuss."

"Maybe."

To change the subject, TJ asked, "How's your grandmother doing?"

"They're trying to get her a liver transplant. Mom's at the hospital this weekend working on it."

"What? Your mom's working on it? How?"

"I dunno. But that's what she said."

TJ hadn't asked about his mother-in-law—former mother-in-law —enough. He hadn't supported Penny enough. He vowed to do better. In the meantime, who needed a love life? He had his son, he had popcorn, he had work he enjoyed.

That seemed like it should be enough, didn't it?

35

The lease on the guesthouse Patrick rented in the Leimert neighborhood was finally up, and that meant he and Sofia would, at last, be living together. Their wedding day was still months away, but neither of them was old-fashioned enough to think they had to wait that long before setting up house together.

The question had been where to do it.

Bianca had suffered through endless dithering by both of them about where they wanted to live. His place was too small. She loved the house she shared with her sisters, but she did, in fact, share it with her sisters. Should Patrick move into Sofia's room despite the lack of privacy? Should they rent another house together, someplace bigger than Patrick's tiny one-bedroom but still small enough to be affordable? Buying was out of the question on Patrick's salary, given the sky-high property values and Sofia's meager income.

Finally, about a month ago, Bianca had had enough.

"I'll buy you a house myself if it means you'll shut up about it!" Bianca had exclaimed during yet another discussion.

"Really?" Sofia's eyebrows had shot upward. "What kind of house? Because we'll need a spare bedroom for the—"

"I'm not buying you a house." Bianca had been making dinner—

manicotti with homemade marinara and a salad—and she'd been holding a chef's knife in her hand. She pointed the tip of the blade in the general direction of her sister.

"Oh."

In the end, Bianca, Benny, and Martina had talked Sofia and Patrick into living with them. The Russo house was big enough, especially considering the fact that Sofia's room was the largest. And it would allow Sofia and Patrick to save money for their own place, since the house was paid for and there was no mortgage payment or monthly rent.

So, Patrick had sublet his place and the two of them had packed his things in preparation for the move.

A lot of his things had gone into storage, of course; he'd had a house, albeit a tiny one, and now he would be sharing a single room with common-area privileges. Still, the things he'd decided he couldn't live without amounted to a daunting number of boxes and one very large suitcase.

They made the move on a Sunday after breakfast. The day was clear and bright, with a tang of the ocean in the air and a light breeze coming in off the water. A flock of birds in an oak tree outside the Russo house screeched their inscrutable messages to one another and to the world.

Bianca helped—they all did, except for Benny, who was out on the ocean doing research on the dolphin population—and as she hauled boxes out of Patrick's U-Haul trailer and carried them toward the house, she tried to be happy for her sister and Patrick.

She tried, but it was hard. Because all she could think about was how happy they were, how they were embarking on the next part of their lives together, full of love and hope and optimism for the future, and here Bianca was, alone.

It seemed that despite her attributes—she was an accomplished professional, kind to animals and children, and not unpleasant to look at—she would always be destined for loneliness.

It's my own damned fault. I could have been with Peter.

Most women would consider Peter a catch. But TJ had ruined

Bianca. She only wanted him, and now, looking back on it, she realized she'd always only wanted him. It had always been him.

She couldn't make him want her, though. She couldn't make him
feel about her the way she felt about him. And she couldn't make
herself be satisfied with Peter because he lacked one essential quality
—he wasn't TJ.

Bianca sighed and told herself to focus on the things she did have:
a satisfying career, her sisters, a community she loved. Then she went
to Patrick's U-Haul for another box.

TJ WASN'T STALKING BIANCA. Of course not. Only assholes and
pathetic losers did that sort of thing, and he liked to think he was
neither.

He'd just been thinking about her, that's all. And he'd had the
idea that he might drive over to her house, see her car, and get up his
nerve to go to the door and knock.

So far, he'd done three drive-bys and had zero results to show for
it. The first time, her car wasn't there. The second and third times, it
was there, but he hadn't known what he would say to her if she came
to the door, so he'd kept right on driving.

This time, he was determined to get out of the damned car and
talk to her. And if that went well, maybe he'd kiss her. They could
work the rest out later.

But what he saw when he rounded the corner toward her house
shook him up so badly it was a wonder he didn't crash his truck into a
power pole.

She was moving out. There was a stack of cardboard boxes in the
driveway to prove it.

She hadn't said she was moving in with Peter, but she hadn't said
she wasn't, either. She'd avoided the question when he'd asked.

He got the hell out of there, not wanting her to see him. He didn't
want to be that guy who came to a woman's house pleading for her
attention just to find out she'd chosen someone else.

He drove home shaking, his hands gripping the wheel so hard they hurt.

He'd fucked up. He'd dithered around, unable to make a decision, unable to take any kind of real action, until it was too late. And what for? What had he been waiting for? Some kind of sign from beyond? Some kind of divine message from God telling him Bianca was the one?

He was an idiot.

When he was in high school, his idiocy had hurt Bianca. And now, he was only hurting himself.

"Fuck. Fuck."

Before he even knew what he was doing, he drove to his parents' house, parked on the street, and took the porch stairs two at a time.

He burst into the house as though he were there to announce that the place was on fire and everyone had to evacuate.

"Mom!"

She wasn't in the front room, so he hunted around, looking for her.

He found her out back, on her knees next to a flower bed, gardening gloves on her hands and a wide-brimmed hat shading her from the sun.

"TJ." She looked up and squinted into the sunlight behind his head. "What's got you all worked up? Is everything okay? Is Owen all right?"

His heart was beating fast, and he said what was on his mind before he had a chance to stop himself. "I'm in love with Bianca. I love her, Mom. I was already in love with her before, when I brought her here and told you I wasn't. Which was stupid. Telling you that, I mean. Not bringing her."

He was aware he was babbling, so he stopped to take a breath.

"But Penny ..." his mother said.

"Penny's moved on, and I need to do that, too. I don't love Penny anymore. I care about her, but ... I'm not in love with her. I'm in love with Bianca."

Lily got up off the ground, took off her gloves, and brushed a bit of stray soil off her clothes. Then she looked at her son. "I don't know what you want me to say, Troy."

He ran a hand through his hair, leaving it stuck up haphazardly in places. "I want you to say you'll be nice to her. That you won't try to chase her away. I want you to say you support me. That you want me to be happy."

Her eyes grew moist, and she blinked a couple of times. "I do want you to be happy. You know I do."

"She makes me happy, Mom. She's who I want. And I need you to be okay with that."

Her face went through a range of emotions—pain and sorrow were there, but so was love. "How does Owen feel about all this?" she asked.

"He thinks I'm stupid for waiting this long to go after her." Now that he considered it, TJ thought his son might be smarter than he was.

"All right. Then, I'll try."

TJ felt a surge of hope. "You will?"

"Yes."

"You'll be nice to her? You'll try to get to know her without judgment, and without ... I don't know. Without wishing she were Penny?"

"I said I'll try, son. I'm not a saint, but I'll do my best."

TJ pulled his mother into a tight bear hug, then abruptly released her and headed back toward his car.

"Where are you going?"

"I have to stop Bianca from moving in with Owen's doctor."

TJ STILL DIDN'T HAVE a plan or a strategy as he got into his truck and drove away from his parents' house. His first thought was to go straight to the Russo place, but then he second-guessed himself and headed home instead.

He parked the truck, got out, and hurried into the house, where he found Owen sitting on the sofa watching TV.

"Owen." TJ stood in the doorway, mussed and breathing hard as though he'd run from the truck. Which he had.

"Huh?" The boy looked up from the screen. "Dad. What's going on? Am I in trouble?"

"No, no. Just ... Are you sure about Bianca?"

"What about her?"

"Are you sure it's okay with you if I ... if we're ... you know. A couple. Because I think I might love her." Listening to himself, he realized he was still dithering, and that had to stop. "I don't think it, I know it. I love her."

Owen rolled his eyes. "I already told you I like her. What are you waiting for?"

It was an excellent question. What the hell *was* he waiting for?

"All right." TJ bounced on his feet a little in nervous excitement. "I'm gonna tell her. Right now. I'm gonna go over there and tell her."

Owen sat up straight from where he'd been slumping on the sofa. "Cool. Can I come?"

36

———

By midmorning, all of Patrick's things had been moved into the house, and he was unpacking in Sofia's room amid a flurry of boxes, packing materials, books, and random belongings including, but not limited to, toiletries, T-shirts, framed family photos, personal electronics, and clean underwear.

"Where are you going to put everything?" Bianca asked doubtfully as she stood in the doorway, her shoulder leaning against the jamb. "The books alone ..."

"About that." Sofia looked up from where she was rooting around in a box. "I was wondering if Patrick could have some space in the hall closet ... maybe just a shelf. And then there's the garage...."

"Sure." Bianca nodded. "I'll move some things around, do some consolidation. I'm sure we can find some room."

"Thank you." Patrick paused in his work, holding a handful of balled socks. "Not just for that, but for letting me move in."

"You say that now," Bianca told him. "Just wait until you've had to share a house with Benny for a few months. You won't be so grateful then."

"Hey! I heard that," Benny called from somewhere else in the house.

Bianca was vaguely aware of the sound of someone knocking on the door. Probably Mrs. Markowitz from next door, complaining about the U-Haul parked on the street. Mrs. Markowitz was always complaining about something.

"Tell Mrs. Markowitz the U-Haul will be gone in an hour," Bianca called to whomever was answering the door.

A few moments later, Martina came down the hallway to Sofia's room.

"It's not Mrs. Markowitz," she said. "TJ and his son are here to see you."

Bianca froze. When she'd gathered herself, she said, "About what?"

"I don't know." Martina crossed her arms over her chest, her bangle bracelets jangling. "But he seems pretty worked up."

Her first thought was that Owen must be sick. Why else would TJ have brought him? And why else would he be worked up? The boy had taken a turn for the worse, and it was a weekend, so her office was closed....

She hurried into the living room, already worried.

"What's going on? Is he okay?" She went straight to Owen and began a quick physical examination, looking at his coloring and the whites of his eyes.

"I'm fine," Owen said.

"He's fine," TJ agreed.

He did seem okay. His color still wasn't normal, exactly, but it had improved since his treatment began. And he didn't look sick. He looked ... excited. He was bouncing on the toes of his sneakers and smiling.

"Okay, then ... what's going on?"

TJ looked like a man who had something on his mind that was about to burst out of him. He also looked anxious and a little upset ... and damned adorable, standing there in faded jeans and a worn T-shirt, his thick hair mussed and his chin showing a shadow of stubble.

"It's ... I think ..." TJ looked at Owen uncertainly.

"Dad, jeez. Tell her." The kid rolled his eyes.

"I don't want you to move in with Peter," he blurted out.

Bianca tried to stop him, but he interrupted her. "TJ, I'm not—"

"I know I haven't handled things between us very well," he went on. "I know I've screwed some things up. And now, you're moving on. With Peter. But, Bianca, I don't want you to move on. I don't want you to move in with him. I want you to be with me. Because I love you, Bianca. I couldn't say that before, because I wasn't ready. But I'm ready now. I love you. Please don't do this. Peter isn't right for you. I am. Or, at least, I can be. I know I can. Please let me try."

Bianca felt stunned, and her heart was pounding. "TJ ..."

"Wait." He held up a hand to stop her. "I know I'm just a blue-collar guy and Peter's a doctor. I know that. And I know you could do a lot better than a guy like me. But—"

"Peter and I broke up," she said.

"What?" TJ's eyes widened as he realized that she'd said.

"We broke up."

"But the boxes ..."

"Patrick is moving in. With Sofia."

"Oh." TJ rubbed at the stubble on his chin, and Bianca could see the tension leaving his face and his body. "That's great. That's ... that's freaking fantastic." He gave her a lopsided smile that made her insides melt.

"What about the part where he said he loves you?" Owen put in.

"I do," TJ said. "And I told my mother that, too. I love you."

Bianca had been doing her best to hold her feelings in check, to act with her mind and not with her heart. But looking at him, at the hopeful, vulnerable look on his face, something in her broke, and she threw herself into his arms.

"I love you, too."

He kissed her, and she gave herself to him, her lips, her body, her heart. She wrapped her arms around him and savored him, and never wanted to let him go.

"Ah, jeez," Owen said.

Bianca broke the kiss and laughed. Still in TJ's arms, she looked at

Owen. "Are you all right with this? With me and your dad being together?"

"Yeah, but maybe you could do this"—he gestured vaguely toward the way the two of them were holding each other—"some other time."

They would do this some other time, Bianca thought—many, many other times, God willing.

Only then did Bianca become aware of the faces poking out from doorways and around corners. Benny, Martina, Sofia, and Patrick all were watching while trying not to be seen.

"You can come out now," she told them.

"It's about time," Benny groused.

Bianca thought she was exactly right.

THEY WENT OUT TOGETHER—ALL three of them—for lunch at the Main Street Grill, because it was Owen's favorite restaurant. They ate burgers and fries, and Bianca and TJ held hands under the table.

Afterward, they took Gary for a walk, then they went to a movie Owen had been wanting to see. Bianca could barely follow the story because she was so aware of TJ's body next to hers, his hand in hers atop her thigh.

When the movie finished, TJ suggested that maybe Owen might want to visit his grandparents for the evening—an idea Owen went along with easily, either because, even at twelve, he knew about the needs of an adult couple in love or because his grandmother spoiled him, it was impossible to know.

In any case, Owen was dropped off with TJ's parents before dinnertime, and Bianca and TJ were back at his place, blessedly alone, as the sun was setting on the horizon. TJ took her into his arms before she'd even put down her purse.

"Owen is a wonderful kid," she said, her voice barely above a whisper.

"He is."

"Are you sure it's okay with him if—"

"It is."

"I think ..."

"You think too much. We both do." TJ pressed a kiss to her lips. "Maybe we should try feeling for a change."

TJ took the strap of her purse and eased the bag down her arm, letting the purse fall to the floor. Then he put his hand on the side of her face and kissed her, and all rational thought, all analyses of how and why, left her. She only knew this, she only knew him. The feel of his arm around her, his mouth on hers, the taste of his tongue, the smell of him.

She'd waited so long for this. Since she was a sixteen-year-old girl uncertain of herself, certain only of her feelings for a boy who'd never noticed her.

He was noticing her now.

His mouth moved down to her jaw and then to the hollow of her throat, and she threw her head back, reveling in the sensations. A moan escaped her throat.

"Can I ...?" He moved his fingers to the buttons of her blouse.

"Yes."

With every inch of flesh that was exposed to him as he undid one button after another, she felt more desperate to have him, not just now, but always. She whimpered at the maddening tease of it. "Please," she said. "Right now. Please."

He scooped her into his arms and carried her to the bedroom.

TJ HADN'T IMAGINED, even in his best-case scenario, that his declaration of love to Bianca would go this well.

Because this, surely, was more than he deserved. This was a better and greater bounty than any man deserved.

He finished undressing her and then himself in the dimming light of his bedroom, and when they were skin-to-skin on his bed, pressed together, he almost wept with relief.

He'd been an idiot before, but he was finally setting things right.

"You're beautiful," he murmured into her skin as he nuzzled her neck. "In every way. You're gorgeous."

"Don't talk." She was squirming against him with desire, with need. "No more talking."

He eased himself into her, and after that he was too busy to talk. There were other, better ways to let her know what he was feeling.

LATER, as they lay in bed together with only the moonlight in the window to light them, they were both warm and happily exhausted, completely sated.

"I've got a kid," he said, holding her in his arms, tracing one finger along her bare shoulder. "A kid with a medical problem. Are you sure you're ready for that?"

"*Hmm.* If only I knew something about children with medical problems," she said.

"You know what I mean. It's one thing to deal with that kind of thing professionally, but it's another when it's your own ..."

"Family?" she suggested.

"Yeah. When it's your own family."

"I'm ready. I've always wanted kids."

"Yeah?"

She rolled over so she was lying on top of him, her body covering his. "Yeah. As a matter of fact, how do you feel about babies?"

For a moment, TJ was dumbstruck. Babies? Plural? But after a moment, he was surprised to discover that what he was feeling wasn't fear ... it was excitement.

"I feel fine about babies," he said. And he looked forward to the time when they both would be ready to get serious about them. Because it wasn't a matter of if. It was a matter of when.

37

About a month later, TJ, Owen, and Bianca sat in the surgical waiting room at a hospital in San Francisco, waiting for word on Penny and her mother.

Once Beverly's doctors had diagnosed her with Wilson's disease, they were optimistic that a transplant, along with dietary changes and medication, might cure her.

That had still left the matter of finding a donor—until Penny was found to be a match. Because the liver had the ability to regenerate itself, Penny would be able to donate a portion of her liver to her mother, and the organ would grow inside both of them, giving Beverly another chance at life.

For Owen to have Wilson's disease, both Penny and TJ had to be carriers. But because Penny's liver was healthy, that didn't eliminate her as a donor.

None of this would have been possible without Peter DeVries, TJ had to acknowledge. The guy was a pompous ass, but if he had a hand in saving Penny's mother, TJ guessed he could give him the credit he was due.

TJ was here at the hospital because Penny and Beverly were still his family and always would be, through Owen. Also because Owen wanted to be here for his mom and his grandmother. And Bianca was here because, now that she'd had a part in diagnosing Beverly—if only through her connection to Peter—she wanted to see things through.

Various other DeLuca family members and friends were here: Penny's sister, Regina; Regina's five-year-old daughter; Beverly's brother, Hal; and a woman Beverly knew from her book club who went by the name Peaches—that couldn't have been her real name, but nobody was asking questions.

Penny's family members were cool but polite to TJ, which was about the best he could hope for in the aftermath of a divorce, especially when he'd shown up here with another woman.

"You look well, TJ," Regina said to him when he came into the room, which was decorated with posters about maintaining good health. A TV played soundlessly where it was mounted to the wall in a high corner, and a coffee setup stood on a side table at one end of the room, waiting to caffeinate the anxious loved ones of patients.

"You too, Regina."

It probably said something—and not something good—that the best thing they could think to say to one another was that neither of them looked sick. But it was better than screaming insults, TJ guessed.

"And who's this?" Regina looked coolly at Bianca.

Before Bianca could answer, TJ stepped in. "This is Bianca Russo, the doctor Owen saw who helped us get Beverly's diagnosis. Her correct diagnosis," he added.

All at once, Regina's face changed from frosty appraisal to warmth and gratitude. "Oh! Dr. Russo. Thank you for helping my mother. I'll never be able to repay you, but ..." She reached out and pulled Bianca into a tight hug.

"Oh. Well ... I didn't do that much." Bianca's voice was muffled by Regina's embrace. "It was Dr. DeVries who diagnosed Owen. I just made the referral."

"Bianca's here in a personal capacity, too," TJ said, before any assumptions could be made that might lead to awkwardness. "She and I are together."

"Oh." By now, Regina had released Bianca, and the two women were standing at arm's length. Regina's face went through another transformation, from admiration to surprise, then to guarded acceptance. "Well." Regina turned toward Owen, either in a genuine greeting or because he provided a handy way to change the subject. "Owen, it's good to see you, honey. Your mom's going to be just fine. Come sit with me."

TJ made the necessary introductions to the others in the room, and it went fine; Regina was the one with the biggest stake in disliking TJ, and if she had decided to let that go, then nobody else wanted to stick with it, either. They all made polite conversation, and Bianca chatted a little with Regina's kid, a bouncy blond with a pale complexion and pigtails that whipped around when she moved.

The mood was tense but hopeful. They all knew today's events might lead to Beverly's recovery, but they also knew things sometimes went wrong. Sometimes, they went very wrong.

About a half hour into the wait, a tall, serious-looking guy in a polo shirt and khakis came into the room, looking anxious. The guy had thinning hair, a trim build, and a face that women probably would have considered handsome if he'd had more hair.

"What's happening? Has there been any news yet?" the guy asked, focusing on Regina.

"Not yet," Regina told him.

"I couldn't get here earlier, I couldn't get out of my shift. My boss—"

"It's all right." Regina patted his arm. "You're here now."

"Who's that?" Bianca whispered to TJ.

"I've never seen him before," TJ responded.

The guy looked around the room, and he grew still when his gaze landed on TJ. He seemed to weigh something in his mind, then came over to TJ and held out his hand. "Bruce Gray. You must be TJ."

TJ stood and shook hands with him. "I guess I must be."

"Penny and I ... I don't know if she told you, but we're ..."

"Ah."

"Anyway. It was nice of you to bring Owen."

Owen looked up at the sound of his name, and Bruce sent him a wave. Owen wiggled his fingers back at the guy. "Hey."

"I wanted to be here, too," TJ said. "Penny and I were married for a long time, so ..."

TJ introduced Bruce to Bianca, and it could have been painfully awkward, but it wasn't. It was okay. The guy seemed all right—he seemed genuinely concerned about Penny, and that counted for a lot.

When Bruce went over to greet Owen, the two had a rapport; TJ could see that from all the way over here. That threatened him a little, but it also made him feel he'd been freed from a confinement that had lasted way too long. Penny wasn't alone, and neither was he. It was possible that both of them might come out of this thing okay. Both of them might find a way to make themselves whole.

TJ HAD Owen full-time for the next two months while Penny and Beverly each recovered from their surgeries. The transplant had gone well, and the two of them looked a little better every time TJ took Owen to visit them.

He was a little worried about what would happen when Penny was fully recovered and would no longer have to care for a much-improved Beverly. Of course she'd want to see more of Owen. Would she want him to live with her again? Would TJ become one of those sorry bastards who only saw his son every other weekend?

"You worry too much," Bianca told him when they were lounging in bed on a Saturday morning at TJ's house, Gary sleeping heavily on the bed at their feet. "Penny saved her mother's life, and everyone's happy. Just enjoy the happiness for a while."

"That Bruce guy ... he and Penny are engaged now. Did I tell you that?" he grumbled.

"Yes, you did." Bianca snuggled her head against his shoulder, her open hand on his chest so she could feel his heartbeat.

"He's gonna be Owen's stepfather. Owen's going to have a stepfather."

"Owen likes him," Bianca reminded him.

"Yeah, yeah."

"But that doesn't mean you're going to lose your place, TJ. You're Owen's dad. Nothing is going to change that."

"You're damned right it isn't," he said.

Bianca, who was naked except for the sheet pulled up over her chest, rolled onto her side, her head propped up against her hand as she looked at him. "Speaking of you being a dad ..." She gave him a mischievous grin.

He didn't get it at first. He thought she was speaking generally, about the topic of fatherhood as a concept. Then she rolled over, reached into a bedside drawer, and brought out some kind of plastic stick that she offered to him.

The stick had a little oval window in which the word PREGNANT was displayed.

"Is that ... Is this ..." He was stammering like an idiot.

"Owen's going to be a big brother," Bianca said. "And you're going to be a dad again."

"But ... when ...?"

Bianca sat up in bed, the sheet wrapped around her breasts. "You remember that night after the concert in San Luis Obispo? The condom box was empty, and you said ... I remember exactly.... You said, 'Screw it, let's roll the dice.' "

"We rolled the dice," he said in wonder.

"We did."

"And it came up 'baby.'"

"It did."

He didn't say or do anything else for a moment. He just lay there, unable to process what she'd said. Her face went from excited to worried to alarmed.

"TJ ... you're not upset, are you? Because this is good news. At least, it is for me. If you're worried about Wilson's disease, only one of us is a carrier, so the baby will be fine."

He still didn't say anything.

"If you're not ready," she went on, "we can talk about it. We can—"

He grabbed her in his arms and let out a whoop of excitement. He wanted this—he wanted all of it. Bianca, the baby, Owen ... everything. They kissed, and in that kiss was the promise of a future TJ had all but given up on when his marriage had collapsed. In that kiss he felt all of the hope and anticipation of a life that was so much more than he'd expected or deserved.

"You think your sister would be okay with it if we announce our engagement at her wedding?" he asked.

"Our engagement?"

"Well, yeah." TJ pressed a kiss to Bianca's lips. "You don't think I'm going to leave the mother of my child without a husband, do you?"

Tears shimmered in Bianca's eyes. "Oh, TJ."

"Is that a yes?"

She nodded and laughed through her tears.

BIANCA WISHED her mother could be here to see this. She'd helped Bianca plan her wedding to TJ so many years ago, and now it was actually going to happen. TJ had been Bianca's first crush, and now he was the only man she would ever need.

She was a sister and a lover, and now she was going to be a mother, a stepmother, a wife.

He was offering her everything she'd ever wanted from him, and she couldn't wait to take it.

ACKNOWLEDGMENTS

First Crush required more research than my previous novels, and I would like to thank the medical professionals who generously came to my aid to help me with the details of Bianca's career and of Owen's medical condition. Nurses Melissa Kliss and Jane Temple read my first drafts and provided valuable feedback, and Dr. Neri Cohen pointed out several gaps in my medical knowledge to help make this a better book. My additional warm thanks go to Linda Dagen.

I'd also like to thank electrician Shan Joseph for explaining that TJ would not go into a crawlspace to diagnose a dead outlet, and my editor, Grace Wynter, for helping to smooth my prose. I couldn't have done it without all of you.